THE OWL SANG
THREE TIMES

THE OWL SANG THREE TIMES

Vera Kelsey

COACHWHIP PUBLICATIONS
Greenville, Ohio

The Owl Sang Three Times, by Vera Kelsey
© 2023 Coachwhip Publications edition

First published 1941
Audrey Vera Kelsey, 1892-1961
CoachwhipBooks.com

ISBN 1-61646-556-5
ISBN-13 978-1-61646-556-8

1

Death in the Gates

The first sound of an owl's call brought Jane back from the light uneasy sleep she had won after hours of tossing. Without opening her eyes she tried to recapture it, only to find that she was listening as alertly, as tensely as before. The house did that to her, she thought; this old one-storied Brazilian house with its broad, encircling veranda and always-open, barred windows seemed to be eternally listening, waiting. Yet strain her ears as she would, there was nothing—nothing—

Again the call came, prolonged and forlorn. And again.

As the third one died away silence, like a soundproof curtain, closed round her. Jane felt smothered with it, weighted, unable to move. And yet an owl's call was no strange thing. She had heard it often in the Wisconsin woods. And on several of the thirteen nights that had passed since her arrival in Rio de Janeiro she had heard an owl call softly from the mango trees sheltering the back gate, two long notes, plaintively urgent.

But this time there had been three. And—she opened her eyes suddenly to the darkness—they had not come from the mango trees.

She felt for the cord of the bed lamp above her head, then dropped her hand. Better not turn on a light. She might only rouse Vivian, and she had learned very quickly, after becoming the guest of her sister and brother-in-law, not to rouse Vivian. Better perhaps if she had never come to this beautiful city and this house with its strained silences; with Jack, whom she was to have married five years ago, tense as a new spring, and Vivian, who had married Jack, oddly unapproachable and hostile, her gaiety brittle as—

Jane's eyes, roaming the darkness, fixed on a small point of light. The glow hung in the black square of her French doors, wide open to the veranda and the soft April night.

It was motionless, and as she stared a mass darker than the darkness took form and substance about it. Someone stood there, listening too. She could feel the intensity of his—or her—listening.

The servants were all in their quarters beyond the gardens; none of them would dare approach the house at this hour. Then it could only be Vivian or Jack. She released her pent-up breath carefully. Jack, of course. That point of light was the dial of his wrist watch.

But why was he up and out at this hour? Why listening so intently from her doorway? No one could have entered the grounds. A ficus hedge, twelve feet high and two feet thick, its small leaves and sturdy branches clipped to the smoothness of a wall and as impenetrable, ran round them. With only two entrances, both screened inside locked gates by arrangements of trees and shrubs, it was impossible for anyone to see into either house or grounds, much less enter them.

As she drew herself to a sitting position the muffled boom of combers breaking on Copacabana's matchless beach, just beyond the hedge and the Avenida Atlantica, intensified the silence. In the heart of Rio's fashionable foreign colony, the house had the quiet and isolation of a hut in the jungle. Jack's one desire had been to secure privacy, and in this, Jane thought, suddenly shivering, he had been singularly successful.

Still that point of light remained motionless, the body to which it was attached silent. Her feeling of relief fled swiftly. She waited a moment, then, leaning forward, whispered, "Jack?"

The point of light vanished. After another moment a whisper came back to her. "Yes. Come here."

Slipping into sandals and robe, she hurried to him. His hand closed like a vise on her arm; she could feel his whole body, towering above her, tight with tension too. "What woke you?"

"The owl. What's the matter?"

His hand, his body, relaxed. "Don't ask questions now," he said quickly. "And don't be afraid. There isn't the slightest danger."

He was silent, as if expecting some answer from her.

"You—you mean you want me to do something?"

"Yes." Without warning he thrust a flashlight into her hand. "Go down the back steps, then round the other side of the house to the front gates. If you see nothing there, come back and go to bed. If you do see something—anything—run back, calling my name. Is that clear?"

"Yes, but—"

"Later. We mustn't wake Vivian—yet." His hand, releasing her, gave her a slight push. Then he was gone, speeding silently and surely up the veranda without colliding with any of the gay lounge chairs and tables spread about. "He must have done that often," Jane thought irrelevantly.

A moment later, by sense rather than sound, she knew that he had entered the French doors to his and Vivian's rooms, that she was alone. Mystified and apprehensive, she turned and slipped down the veranda and round to the back steps.

As her feet struck the graveled path and she followed it about the house the darkness appeared paler, or else she was becoming accustomed to it. She could see the strikingly contrasted masses of fir and tamarind and flamboyant trees rising above the hedge against the night sky and below it whitish blobs that by day were flowers on hibiscus and rose bushes.

The creak of gravel under her thin sandals sounded loudly in her ears, and she stepped off onto the cool grass. At the front of the house she cut across the lawn to the first of the flowering shrubs that helped conceal the grounds from the gates. Here the combers crashed more loudly and sullenly on her ears, but otherwise there was no sound or movement anywhere.

Until then she had walked as if in sleep, drugged by the urgency of Jack's whispers; but now, when she must leave the lawns to follow the broad, curved sweep of the driveway to the gates, reluctance seized her. What could Jack have expected her to see or hear? Why hadn't he come himself?

The first creak of her sandals on the gravel echoed her thoughts like a thin scream, startling her to haste and to turn to the reassurance of the flashlight. But its bright round eye revealed nothing on the curve save the white spread of sand, nothing round that curve either. And the tall, stately ironwork of the gates was a lovely pattern against the night, lovelier when the light rested on a huge old-fashioned padlock and she saw that they were securely fastened.

At the gates, Jack had said, and she sighed with relief as she swept the light downward. There was nothing here and she could go back—

She stopped, the flash trembling in her hand. Its beam had fallen on something just outside the gates, crumpled in the shelter of one of the tall granite columns crowned with porcelain pineapples from ancient Portugal. With widening eyes she stared at the thing that lay so still there, then moved forward slowly and, stooping, focused the light upon it.

A man lay there, a man she had never seen before.

A nondescript Brazilian in nondescript clothes, he lay on his back, his left arm doubled under him, his right flung out against the gates. The right wrist, resting on the bottom bar, supported a hand just above the gravel inside. And the hand was tightly grasped about a little branch tipped with slender dark green leaves.

Run back, Jack had instructed, calling his name! But she could not run, even move, could not utter a sound. She could only crouch and stare at the man and at the thought that Jack had sent her out here to find—death.

The light on the man's face grew brilliant, picking up a purplish bruise on one cheek. As she looked up, startled, the gates rattled and a sharp voice spoke. A khaki-clad policeman stood there, and now as she gazed at him he swept the light of his flash upward to her face and, raising his left hand to his lips, sent a shrill whistle through the fading night.

Stiffly she rose, her eyes fixed on his while she sought for some word in Portuguese.

"No," she achieved finally. *"Momento."*

Then she was running toward the house, calling Jack's name, calling it frantically. Behind her the shrilling whistle and the rattling of the gates mingled continuously with the crash of rolling surf.

Darkness was thinning rapidly now. She could see Jack coming up the veranda toward her, knotting his black robe about him as he ran, his black hair rumpled, his face a pale, strained blur. And behind him came Vivian, clicking in high-heeled mules. One of them slipped off, and she paused to kick the other from her.

In that moment Jack had time to reach Jane, to murmur, "Careful. Say nothing." Aloud he demanded, "What's the matter? What are you doing out here?"

Jane stared, then pointed wordlessly to the gates where the noise was increasing. There seemed to be two voices there now, or three, demanding entrance. Jack ran on past her.

Her sister had stopped on the bottom of the three steps to the veranda. Even with her fair hair awry, her dark eyes enormous in a white, pinched face, her beauty and appeal struck through Jane's fright.

"It—it's all right, Vivian," she tried to say calmly. "Jack's there now. And the police."

"Police!"

"There's a man—dead. At the gates."

Vivian's face seemed to grow even smaller and her eyes darker and larger. Visibly she shuddered. "Who?"

"I don't know. Jack will be here—"

Jack was there, running up behind them, saying as he approached, "Wait here, Jane, while I get the key. You'll have to go back to the gates with me."

"You mustn't run like that!" Vivian cried. "You—"

"Damn my heart!" He grasped her arm, turned her toward the house. "Darling, are you mad to stand out here like that?"

"But who is it?" she demanded, resisting him.

"No one we know," he told her lightly.

She mounted the steps with him then but at the top turned to send a long glance back to Jane. Though light was dim, Jane felt in it again that odd hostility.

2

"Jack's Incessantly on Fire . . ."

The sun was high above the hedge when, police and ambu-
lance gone and the neighborhood excitement calmed, Jane,
outwardly calm herself, entered the breakfast room. Jack
sat there alone, eating golden mamão as if this were any
other Saturday to be devoted to leisure and recreation. A
half-eaten melon and crumple napkin testified that Vivian
had been there too, would be there briefly again and again,
for her mornings were usually a series of telephone calls.

Her crisp, clipped words drifted down the corridor
from the telephone niche across from the library. ". . .
frightfully annoying . . . no one we know, of course . . .
victim of hit-and-run driver, the police say. . . ."

Relieved and surprised, Jane paused in the doorway,
taking reassurance from the sunshine flooding in through
the French doors and decorative patterns of the window
bars to play over flowers, crystal and silver and height-
en the color in the gay informal draperies and breakfast
linen. The police, their prolonged, searching stares, their
examination of the street, the hedge, the beach that had
made her think their investigation had not ended when
they removed the body, became remote and pointless here.

Jack's flashing smile reassured her further. "Enter the
late Jane George of Hudson, Wisconsin," he greeted her
gaily and sprang up to place her chair. "You will excuse

our beginning breakfast without you," he went on for the benefit of Inah, a pretty mulatto maid who had followed Jane in with her melon. "Having nothing in the world to do all day, we were in a hurry to—"

But as Inah departed he stooped to Jane's ear. "Don't mention last night before Vivian and don't even think of what happened while servants are about. They're mystic as the devil. Maria, especially, she can walk right into your mind and look around."

"Do sit down, Jack," Vivian said from the doorway. "You look too utterly roguish whispering to Jane in an empty room." She dropped a kiss on the top of Jane's head and slipped into her chair in one graceful movement, not unaware of the pleasure both her husband and sister were experiencing in the picture she made or that all the decor of the breakfast room fell into place at once as background for her luminous beauty.

"That was Varta calling," she told Jack. "The servants' grapevine has been working overtime as usual, and she was all agog for details. Seemed to think I was holding out on her for some reason. I think she was really disappointed to hear the man wasn't murdered."

"Angelo should have taken up criminal law when he married her," Jack said idly. "The woman's mad for excitement—"

"She was really calling for Angelo," Vivian broke in. "You're to remember to take out that lucky golf sweater of his you walked off with last Saturday. And to be on time. They want to tee off at eleven."

"We're playing no golf today. Send it out to the club by Arnaldo."

To Jane's astonishment Vivian was determined that they should go on with their regular Saturday schedule of golf and luncheon at the club, dinner somewhere with friends in the evening. When Jane begged off she nodded, but with Jack she was adamant.

"Just because some hit-and-run driver kills a man at our gates we can't change all our plans," she protested. "We don't even know who he is. You've got to have some exercise after the week you've had, Jack. I'm not going to have you sick again."

Jack flung down his napkin and rose.

"Where are you going?" Vivian's voice was suddenly taut.

"To call Garcia. He's going to get that report here to-day or—" From the door he turned back to ask, "Can you help me this morning, Jane? In about half an hour?"

Jane nodded, then turned to her sister, and for a moment their eyes probed one another's in silence.

In general appearance they were much alike—tall, slender, fair. But Vivian's hair shaded to gold and Jane's to brown with glints of red here and there. Both had large brown eyes behind thick lashes, short straight noses, beautifully modeled lips. Resemblance stopped there.

Jane's sturdy chin, that could set stubbornly on occasion, spoiled the perfect oval of her face; her mouth was a bit too wide to be truly proportioned. Vivian's was an authentic beauty. Combined with a vivacity and chic all her own, it gave her the effect of an exotic bird. Even in the simple yellow linen dress with a scarlet gadget that matched her lips she was luminous and younger, apparently, for all her thirty-five years, than Jane with twenty-three.

Vivian broke the silence, her voice troubled. "What a fool I was to remind him of the office!"

"I know," Jane said in quick understanding. "I won't let him work long, Vivian. And I'll tell him this morning that I won't work with him any more." She hesitated, then plunged. "Darling, when Doctor Ames says Jack's heart is so bad, why don't you take him back to the States for a rest?"

"I'd row him up if he would leave Rio. But with this horrible war in Europe cutting off Brazilian markets and making a mess of things generally, he's more determined than ever not to go. I—I'd like to have him retire—go back to the States to live."

"Jack! Stop work entirely? I can't imagine him doing that unless— Why, I thought Doctor Ames said a year's rest is all he needs."

"Perhaps it is," Vivian agreed slowly. "Perhaps I'm just thinking of myself." She shrugged. "It's impossible, of course. Jack can't pull out of Houghton and Hardwicke until there is someone ready to take his place. There's no one in Brazil who could do it—except Phil, and he has his own interests."

"But surely, if the war is cutting off exports, this is just the time for him to get away. Noel Hardwicke looks capable of carrying on for both of them. Anyway, why should Jack risk his health, his life perhaps, for Houghton and Hardwicke?" Jane spoke hurriedly, avoiding her sister's invitation to talk about Phil Monroe.

When Vivian, older, more beautiful and experienced, had taken Jack from her she had accepted it as inevitable and continued to love them both. Now, however, it was difficult to watch Vivian constantly turning to Phil—

"It's taken Jack and Noel twenty years to build H and H," Vivian was saying impatiently. "For either of them to leave permanently is out of the question. Jack's really a genius at seeing opportunities in Brazil for industries and developments. And it's his job, too, to find the capital for them, here or in the States or Europe. Noel's just as good at organizing and supervising the companies they form. But Noel lacks Jack's flair for showmanship or whatever it is that makes men invest money through him in Brazil, and Jack hasn't Noel's patience for handling people and detail."

This was an unusually long speech for Vivian to make at any time, and now, bored, she moved to rise.

"I'm afraid I don't know exactly what H and H is or does," Jane persisted. "You never mentioned Jack's work in your few letters home, and Jack seldom speaks of it."

"Perhaps he assumes that since he has given you shares in nearly all the H and H companies you have taken the trouble to learn something about them."

Vivian's voice was so light and casual that a moment passed before color crept into Jane's cheeks. She took up her glass of water, set it down firmly untouched before she turned to face her sister's bright, intent gaze. At the unconcealed curiosity she saw there she laughed clearly, almost happily.

"The old herring trick!" she exclaimed. "You wonder if he has but don't know, is that it?" She smiled at some thought of her own, then said aloud, "And once upon a time I would have walked right into your net with the answer. But I'm glad you said that, Vivian. It's the first time you haven't been so icily polite that I've felt like some strange, unwanted guest." She flicked another glance at her sister, added a bit shyly, "You're all the family I've got now."

"I know." Vivian studied her thoughtfully. "But you are growing up, aren't you, sweet? That's really what I wanted to know. You—you aren't the same susceptible child who became so madly infatuated with Jack—"

"I was never infatuated with Jack, and I stopped being a child one September day five years ago."

Jane's color burned in two bright spots high on her cheeks, and Vivian characteristically returned to the subject of H and H as if they had never left it.

"You asked what Jack and Noel do. Well, Jack investigates the resources and conditions—water power, labor

supply, transportation facilities, things like that—in different parts of Brazil to see what industries they can support, either for Brazilian markets or export. Then he and
Noel go into a huddle. If they come out of it in one piece,
Jack dashes to New York or over to London to interest
clients—investment houses usually—in backing it. That
is, he used to. These last years he hasn't had to go personally. That's one reason he's so nervous, run down. He's
missed too many boats."

"And Noel?"

"Oh, he handles the organization of companies, super-
vises construction of factories and their management,
too, for a time. Sometimes when a textile mill or a cotton
fazenda—plantation—is going well they sell it. I wish
they'd sell everything. They have their fingers in so many
pies from paper clips to automobile parts, even stained
glass and railways, it's no wonder Jack's on the verge of a
breakdown. They're mixed up in everything made or grown
in Brazil, I think—except coffee."

"The one thing Brazil has the most of, isn't it? Why not
coffee?"

If I can keep this up, Jane thought, I have grown up!
At least twice she had dodged talk about Jack's health, a
subject, she knew now, inevitably led to Phil.

"Heaven knows! Jack's always been opposed to growing,
buying or selling it, but during the years they were burning it by the millions of sacks, to keep up the price, his
hatred of the stuff became an obsession. Lately it seems to
have become more than that."

"Yet Noel's his partner and he doesn't feel that way,
does he?"

"What makes you think so?" Vivian asked quickly.

"Perhaps I shouldn't have said that. I overheard him
and that banker talking about coffee one night, that's all."

"Oh, Tom Hughes." Vivian shrugged and again pushed back her chair. "When Tom takes the floor on any subject, my child, just listen and agree. We've all learned that—the hard way. Look at his wife Eloise." Vivian's eyes became round and wide; her mouth curved in a patient, placid smile. "Yes, Tom dear," she mimicked.

"Vivian, you're cruel!" Jane gasped, then laughed in spite of herself as her sister continued to sit demurely, gazing at her with round, marveling eyes. The impersonation faded gradually, and Vivian jumped up.

"Don't go," Jane urged. "You've no idea how much I've wanted to talk with you like this, darling. I have so many questions—I've felt so on the edge of things—"

From beneath her long lashes Vivian looked at her guardedly. "What sort of questions?"

Jane glanced round. Inah, who had been in and out noiselessly while they talked, was now busy at the buffet. "Well, for one, who is this Garcia that's giving Jack so much trouble?"

Vivian shrugged. "Just an H and H accountant. Honest and hard-working as the day is long, Noel says. But he's slow and Jack's impatient—and failure, any sort of failure—even turning over a report a few days late—is something Jack can't understand. He suspects Garcia of cheating or something."

As Inah left the room and Vivian prepared to follow she concluded lightly, "Jack's the one to answer such questions. He'll be delighted to find you so interested. Sure you don't want to go with us to Gavea?"

Jane rose too. "No. No, I'd rather stay here."

Before her direct glance Vivian's eyes wavered. She hesitated, moved swiftly to the door and closed it. For a long moment she stood before it, her eyes fixed appraisingly on Jane, then walked straight to Jane and faced her.

"You're thinking of Phil, of course. Well, I'm devoted to him. You will be, too, when you grow out of these small-town notions. Jack's a darling, but he's incessantly on fire about something. It's very wearing. I can lean back on Phil, talk to him as I can't to Jack . . ."

As Jane remained silent she put one hand impulsively on her arm, added urgently, "Jane, there's a reason. Phil helps me. He—he stands between me and Noel!"

3

The Owl Sang Three Times

Seconds fled away while Vivian's words repeated themselves in Jane's mind. On any other lips than Vivian's they might not have had such startling implications. On her sister's they recalled vividly scenes in the "big room" at home when Vivian, pinned down by some major folly her beauty and love of admiration had led her into, turned to her family to get her out of it.

"Oh, Vivian! Not Noel—Noel Hardwicke!"

Vivian nodded. Without speaking she returned to her chair and dropped into it hopelessly. Jane drew a chair to face her, prepared, yet afraid to listen.

When Vivian spoke again the bright-chatter notes of her voice were gone, so was the reserve she had maintained toward Jane since her arrival. If something more than despair had not been written so clearly on her wax-pale face, Jane could have smiled at the similarity between this Vivian of Rio and the old Vivian of Hudson.

And this impression was heightened when Vivian reproduced her old method of indirect approach. "I haven't made your two weeks here very pleasant, have I? But I couldn't talk with you, Jane, I didn't dare—for fear you wouldn't understand. Now you've got to understand. Be pleasant to Phil, accept him. Make it easy for him to join

us, natural. And why not? He makes an excellent fourth—
with Jack."

Jane shook her head stubbornly. "I can understand that
you're worried about Jack's health and"—she lightened her
tone, added in an effort to lighten the tension—"that you
had to feel a little jealous of me for a time, but—"

"Not without reason, darling." Vivian's voice lightened
too, became ingratiating. "You're much more beau—pretti-
er—than I expected you would be and more mature. Jack—
and I too—have never felt, well, right about marrying one
another under your nose. We could have waited a little,
managed the whole thing better—for you perhaps. That's
why I thought that—that he might have given you shares in
H and H companies. I know he feels responsible for you."

"He needn't. And he doesn't," Jane assured her promptly. "And it is neither Jack nor I nor—nor Phil—who is
worrying you now, Vivian. It's Noel. Why?

"Yes, it's Noel," Vivian admitted reluctantly. "Oh, Jane,
I don't know what to do. He—Noel loves me!"

Jane looked at her aghast. "Vivian, are you sure? He's
Jack's best friend, his partner!"

Vivian's gaze went round the room before she answered.
Had she felt also that sensation of listening ears? Jane
wondered swiftly. But she had no time to ask. Her reserve
broken, Vivian rushed into words.

"Jack and Noel were inseparable until Jack married.
It's a friendship that always amazes me—amazes everyone. Noel's so immovable and quiet, Jack so vivid and
swift. They don't think alike, do anything alike—yet they
are Rocks of Gibraltar for one another. Noel acquired the
habit at Madison when he came up to the States to go to
the University of Wisconsin. You can imagine how difficult a great, shy foreigner like Noel would find life—especially when he didn't speak English well and had very little

money—among thousands of students, more than half of
them coeds."

Jane nodded. The picture was all too clear.

"He met Jack there, working his way too. And Jack took
him under his wing, helped him, encouraged him. From
their second year they lived together, studied together,
worked together. And finally, when they were graduated,
Jack came to Brazil with Noel. They didn't find life any
easier here. They never speak of the first five years to
others, but sometimes when they think they are alone they
go back to them—with a sort of wonder that they sur-
vived. I know that once Noel scarcely ate, slept outdoors
somewhere for weeks when there was only money enough
for one. Jack never knew till long after. Perhaps it was
then that Noel saved his life; perhaps it was later."

Vivian's voice broke and she paused. Jane looked at
her wonderingly, apprehensively. Vivian must be deeply
stirred indeed when she would permit anyone else to see
more than surface emotions.

"Yes, darling?" she prompted gently.

"I'd never known friendship like theirs. I didn't understand it. Perhaps if I had—"

"Yes?" Jane murmured again.

"At first Noel's resentment of me was terrible. And I—
well, I resented him too. I wanted Jack for myself. And
then when even Jack at times resented my coming between
them I—I lost my head for a time. I don't need to tell
you." Vivian's voice grew hard, bitter. "You'll hear—soon
enough."

"That doesn't matter now." Jane moved her chair closer,
caught Vivian's restless hands in hers. "Go on about Noel."

"It's difficult to explain unless you know Brazilians.
And Noel is Brazilian—though he has Danish blood from
a grandfather in Rio Grande do Sul and American blood

from a grandmother who came down to São Paulo after the Civil War with a colony of Southerners."

"That's not difficult to understand. You know how Germans and Scandinavians have married Americans in Wisconsin—"

"It's a little different here. 'God is a Brazilian,' they say and in many ways feel themselves superior to the entire world. But in other ways they feel inferior. Some of them at times become so humble and apologetic that you could choke them; others feel that the only way to justify themselves is by overassertion. Noel's that way—the first way, I mean. Sometimes he feels inferior to Jack—"

"Poor Noel!" Jane exclaimed with understanding. "You used to make me feel that way too—remember?"

"When I—I realized that I was going to lose Jack unless I found some way of making Noel accept me," Vivian went on, unheeding, "I tried to use Jack's tactics, build Noel up as he did. I tried to make him feel he was as interesting to me—as attractive—as Jack."

Jane suppressed the words on her lips, turned her eyes from her sister. They sat in silence for a time.

"He—he believed me," Vivian murmured miserably at last. "He"—she groped for words, then repeated—"he believed me! And now he hates himself—hates me too, at times. And I'm afraid. I don't know what to do."

Jane clung to her twisting hands. "Does Jack know?"

"Jack suspect Noel of anything?" Vivian jerked her hands free, half rose. "Never! And he must never know. I don't know what he'd do. I think he would—kill me. Noel comes first—"

"But Phil knows?"

"Yes, Phil knows." Vivian relaxed a little, sank back in her chair.

"Vivian!" Jane leaned forward, her voice low but sharp with apprehension. "Let Phil go. He's nothing to you, really. Can be nothing. Tell Jack about Noel. He loves you. Understands Noel. He'll know what to do. Oh, darling," she urged as Vivian turned away from her, "don't you see? If you keep this between you and Jack—and Noel—it will be all right. It's Phil that Jack—Noel too—will resent. That you turned to him—"

Vivian was not listening. She smiled at Jane from behind the cool bright mask she turned to the world, then looked toward the doorway.

"Yes, Maria, come in. What is it?"

Jane turned too, to see the colored cook, a typical Bahian mammy, standing in or, rather, filling the doorway. Her ample form in a spotless white uniform and apron, the twist of white cotton about her head, always made Jane think of something for breakfast.

Usually a broad smile disclosed two ranks of shining white teeth, but this morning her full red lips were shut tight and her eyes were round and somber as she looked at Vivian.

"Minha senhora," she began in her rich, throaty voice, "you ain' aimin', as usual, to have midnight supper here?"

"Of course I am, Maria," Vivian told her impatiently. "What is the matter with everyone? You'd think that man in the gates was a member of the family the way you all act."

"I'm scare, minha senhora. Things don' look right to me." Maria waddled into the room until she stood beside the table. There, bending down, she said fearfully, "Minha senhora, trouble bird sat on this house las' night."

Jane found her voice and interposed quickly. "Trouble bird! You haven't told me that one, Maria. What is it?"

Maria's signs and portents had made her something of an oracle in the neighborhood. Jack suspected her of being a leader in one of the *macumba* cults—the Brazilian form of voodooism—scattered over the city, but Maria admitted to nothing save a sound belief in signs.

If a butterfly crossed her path, providing, of course, it was not a black butterfly, Maria was all smiles. Good luck was surely coming her way. When her right eye twitched she calmly stopped all preparations for dinner, knowing that shortly Vivian or Jack would send word that they would not be home after all. Expectant mothers, even fathers, were a not infrequent sight at the back gate, bringing an opened chicken heart for Maria to study and decide whether the child would be a boy or girl.

"Trouble bird is *coruja,* Miss Jane."

"An owl," Vivian translated.

"An' las' night"—Maria's voice lowered to a whisper—*"he sing three times."*

"In the United States we say owls hoot, Maria," Jane told her. "But I've heard owls around here ever since I came. You must have too."

"In trees by back gate, Miss Jane. An' they sing two times. They's a bird that knows trouble. Don' you smile. They *knows.* Didn' *coruja* sing three times on Ricardo's house, minha senhora, night before his brother bit by that snake? Didn' *coruja* sing three times—"

"Oh, be still, Maria." Vivian jumped up. "How you can listen to such nonsense, Jane . . ."

She left the breakfast room without completing her sentence but not before Jane had heard fear beneath the irritation in her voice and seen it in her face. She rose to follow her sister, paused uncertainly after a step or two. Vivian, as her clicking heels approached the library, was calling blithely to Jack, "I'll phone Varta not to expect us until luncheon."

"You no go, Miss Jane?"

Jane shook her head, aware that Maria's dark, unfathomable eyes were looking through and into her as if she were a pane of glass. Maria hesitated as if to say more, then, muttering to herself, moved her heavy body lightly through the door.

When she had gone Jane wandered to the open French doors to look across the lawns to the hedge. But their shadowed quiet only emphasized the tensions in the house. With a sigh she remembered that Jack was waiting for her in the library.

4
Jack Exacts a Promise

Jack rose from the huge jacarandá table that dominated the library as Jane appeared in the veranda doors. Without a word he placed a chair for her beside his own, walked swiftly to the corridor door and closed it securely, then to the veranda doors and closed them. Before he returned to her he scanned the veranda through the bars of one of the two broad windows.

Watching him, Jane was disturbed again. More closed doors! Because of what he had to tell her about that dead man in the gates? Or did he, too, sense the presence of listening ears?

Even though the house was filled with sunlight, secrecy and fear seemed to stalk through it. This silent, grave man was not the swift and vivid Jack of whom she and Vivian had been speaking. As his long lean body dropped into his chair she saw that his face beneath its tan was pale, even his lips were pale. For a man he had strange eyes, a sapphire blue that deepened in color according to his mood. Now they appeared dark, almost black.

She had only a glimpse of them, for he turned to the table, and his strong, well-kept hands moved purposefully among the letters and legal-looking documents there. One he tore suddenly to shreds and dropped them in the basket, already half full of similar shreds, beside him.

"Aren't you going to tell me what happened this morning?" she asked finally. "What was all that talk in Portuguese about? And why did you give those policemen money?"

"The police think some hit-and-run driver struck that chap, then placed him in my gateway to delay his being found. I gave them some milreis to encourage that line of thought." He spoke carelessly and continued to sort and shift papers.

"Isn't that true? You didn't know who he was, nor Vivian. None of the servants had ever seen him before."

"In a few minutes," he told her, swinging round to pull down the left side of the table and release a typewriter, "slip a sheet of paper in this machine and peck away while I talk, so that Vivian will think we are hard at work. Oh, my intentions are honorable, lady."

A brief smile crossed his lips, then he was serious again. "Jane, I must talk with someone I can trust. You did me a great service this morning. If it should be necessary, will you do me another?"

Questions and the qualified assent that rose to her lips died there. She said simply, "Must I say yes, or don't you know the answer?"

"I know." For a moment, as he looked at her, his brooding triangular face cleared; even his eyes seemed to lighten a little. "Later we'll talk, but first I want you to take this check. Don't look at it now," he interposed quickly, folding it and slipping it into the pocket of her blouse. "If you can resist the temptation, don't look at it till Monday. Then, if I haven't asked you for it, put it in your bank—"

"My what! You know I'm almost Cinderella."

"You're nothing of the sort. I didn't mean to tell you, but one day I've wanted you to know that I've always been grateful for your friendship—your— Oh, you know I'm no good at putting what I feel in words. Let it go. But in the Canadian bank here—" He turned from her abruptly as she started to speak, picked up a sheaf of what appeared to be letters and typed papers.

"I want you to know about these," he said, riffing through them. "Also about this. It's a secret that only the man who made this table for me and I know."

Jane leaned forward to place a restraining hand on his arm. Vivian's references to shares in H and H companies and now these evasive words of Jack's ran together in her mind. "Wait, Jack. You must explain."

"Later," he said with finality. Ignoring her protests, he leaned back and pulled out the table's one drawer, thrust his hand inside and brought out a second drawer, smaller and shallow. In it he put the papers in his hand, then returned it to its place. A moment later only the main drawer was left.

Now Jane could follow him only with her eyes; her attention was fixed elsewhere. Again she had that uncomfortable sensation of someone near her. "Jack, listen," she whispered.

"Later." He rose and pulled away his chair. "Run your hand along the bottom of the table inside the drawer," he instructed. "Find anything?"

Reluctantly she obeyed. "No."

"Move your hand off left center toward the back of the table."

"There may be something there, a small knot; something, anyway, that feels a little rougher than the rest of the wood."

"Press it."

Jane pressed. The little drawer dropped into her hand.

"Fit it into place and press again."

When they were seated Jack swung his chair to face Jane squarely. "If anything should happen to me, Jane—if Doctor Ames is right about this trick heart of mine—those are papers I want you to have."

"Me?" Her eyes escaped his to circle the long comfortable room with its simple dark furniture and well-placed lamps, the book-lined walls, the collection of Brazilian riding crops over the fireplace. These were Jack's choice of surroundings, his taste. If anything should happen to him! She brought her gaze back quickly.

"Shouldn't they be with your executor?"

A grim smile came and went. "Not these. They are instructions and letters for you—and only you. Follow them exactly and as quickly as you can."

She shook her head. "If this is what you wanted me to do for you, Jack, I can't do it."

One eyebrow cocked sharply. "Vivian?"

"I came in here this morning to tell you that I don't want to work with you again."

"I know, I know." A curious concentrated expression fled across his eyes. "She's a bit of a prima donna at times." The expression changed, became rueful. "Vivian's a gorgeous child really, and I'd like her to remain that way if possible. Your father did an excellent job of spoiling her, and I carried on. She's never known a day's responsibility in her life."

But fear, Jane thought, she's known fear.

Jack shoved some papers away violently, turned from her. The firm carriage of his shoulders, the assured pose of his head, sagging in some subtle way, as if from an inner drag.

Conscious of her eyes, he straightened, said crisply, "Forget Vivian—temporarily. Before I tell you about these papers I want you to remember one thing. Have I ever of my own accord mentioned coffee or shown the slightest interest in it?"

When she shook her head he continued slowly, tapping an accompaniment with a finger to each word. "If anything should happen to me, Jane, you're to remember that.

No matter what anyone says, refuse to believe it. I have never had, have not now and, so help me, never will have any interest whatever, financial or otherwise, in coffee. Is that clear?"

"Of course. But why? Shouldn't I know?"

He glanced at his watch. "It's a long story, but perhaps one reason will be enough. Brazil has led the coffee world for almost a century, has had practically a monopoly until recently. She could set the price—and get it. Today she has over a million square miles planted to coffee, can produce annually four billion pounds—that's more than the entire world can consume in one year. But today she does not have a monopoly. Thirty or more little competitors are also growing coffee; they can supply perhaps half the annual world consumption. That makes too much coffee, as you can see if your arithmetic is any good at all."

"Yes, I can see that, but—"

"Brazilian coffee-growers can see that too, but—they go right on growing coffee. It's difficult to convince a man whose father and grandfather made fortunes in coffee that he can't do it too—and to convince others that if the Mendonças and Albuquerques can live like kings on coffee they should not break their land to coffee too. That was a good theory while it lasted, but the high price the old fazendeiros set gave other countries ideas too; they began to compete—and the theory went overboard.

"The fazendeiros of last century formed a powerful political clique; they could force the government to help them maintain the price. The modern fazendeiros carried on, and the government finally, to reduce the supply, ordered a certain per cent—a "sacrifice quota"—of each harvest to be burned. In seven years some 67,000,000 sacks, each with 132 pounds of perfectly good beans, went up in smoke. And while Brazil burned, her competitors proceeded to grow more and more coffee."

Jack threw up his hands. "Lord, it makes me mad even to talk about it. And it's half-past eleven. I'll make the rest short. Three years ago—in 1937—a new government was established—the new state. It stopped the burning, allowed every bean in Brazil to flood the market. That's what the growers should have done years ago, of course. They'd have wiped the slate clean of competitors and would still have their monopoly today—"

Jane gasped and, when he stopped in surprise, exclaimed, "How ruthless you are! I mean you look that way when you talk about coffee."

"Why not?" he asked coolly. "Foreign trade isn't a game for pretty sentiment. To go on. The price of coffee hit bottom, and the fazendeiros shrieked to heaven. The government banned replacing old trees with new ones, did other things to keep production down, improve quality. Never mind that. The point is that Brazil began to get her markets back. During the past year she has been exporting more and more coffee—though at a lower and lower price. The situation might have worked itself out—given time. But last September this Second World War, or whatever they are going to call it, broke out in Europe. Next to the United States, Germany is Brazil's best market, then France and Holland. Germany's gone, the others will go. And if the war continues, all Brazil's European customers are going to have to do without their coffee. Meanwhile coffee is already piling up in warehouses on the fazendas and in the ports."

His eyes went back to his watch. "That's rather sketchy but enough to explain why I don't invest my own or other people's money in coffee. Unless a miracle happens there's always going to be too much coffee and there are always going to be emergencies—wars, depressions, increasing competition—a score of things to affect it. And the days of miracles, my child, are over. Now let's get on to these papers."

Jane looked at him thoughtfully as he dismissed coffee, war, the world in general from his mind with a wave of the hand. Perhaps it was the intensity with which he could concentrate on each thing that held his interest that made him successful at forty. That quality was part of his charm socially, she knew; it made each one feel for the moment that for Jack no one else existed. But it disturbed her too.

She sighed as she heard his impatient finger tapping the table above the little drawer. "I'm glad he's for me," she thought swiftly. "He could be rather terrible—as an enemy."

"If anything happens to me," he said when he saw that he had her attention, "go through these instructions carefully. All the information you need is here. Don't ask questions of anyone."

Is this the Brazilian way of doing things, the usual she asked uncertainly, a little frightened now at what she might have undertaken.

"Nothing in my life has been usual, has it? I came to Brazil when I was twenty-two or -three with only my wits to help me. Well, in twenty years I've made a good many men besides myself rich. In the course of doing it I've learned a great deal about Brazil, about people—Brazilians and foreigners—in Brazil."

Again Jane found it hard to follow him when her ears were straining to hear a faint sound somewhere—perhaps at the French doors, perhaps at a window—but something in his voice, rather than his words, brought her head up sharply.

"You mean you think some of these people may be enemies?" Suddenly relief flooded her and she laughed. "Jack, we're both so tired we can't think straight. I was even imagining that I heard dark footsteps! You know you haven't an enemy in the world."

"Nonsense. Of course I have enemies. Everyone has who has done anything at all. Sometimes they don't discover who they are, that's all—until it's almost too late."

Vivian's words came back to Jane. "Jack's incessantly on fire about something. It's very wearing." It certainly was.

"Give me a cigarette," she tried to say brightly. "This is pure melodrama, and cigarettes are always smoked when the villain enters."

"Don't talk like that." He rose to get his cigarette box from the small table that stood beside his reading chair. "Vivian's an expert at it, but it's not like you—any more."

She took the box from him hastily but not quickly enough to forestall the deep color rushing to her cheeks. "What kind of stones are these?"

"Stones?" His eyes followed hers to the lid of the box. Inlaid in shiny shell was a vivid pattern of small red-orange ovals, each flecked on one side with black. "They do look like stones, don't they? And they are almost as hard. Really they are seeds of some sort that grow in Brazil. Up north, probably. That box came from Pernambuco."

He sank into his chair and gleamed at her wickedly. "If you've recovered the composure you thought you were losing, I'll give you a light."

As he held his lighter for her, however, Jane was aware that his little finger, touching hers, was no more steady than her own. She glanced at her watch.

"Time is flying, Jack, and you still haven't told me—"

"Why I sent you to the gates?"

He swept some checkbooks into the drawer, then unexpectedly tore everything else on the desk to bits and dropped them in the basket. He sat looking down at them for a moment, picked the basket up and swung it round to set it down beside her.

"When everyone is gone," he asked, "will you take this basket out to the garage and burn these papers yourself? Lock them up in the meantime in your room."

Jane looked from basket to Jack in perplexity, nodded as if agreeing to the whim of a child.

"All right, you asked for it," he said grimly. "Jane, that man in the gates wasn't killed by a hit-and-run driver. He was murdered. I told the police I didn't know him. I do. His name is Sebastião Pinto, from São Paulo. He's been in my employ secretly for almost a year. He was in this house, in this room, with me for hours one night. You arrived on a Thursday, didn't you? He was here the following Saturday night—just two weeks ago. And he was on his way to see me here last night."

Jack was not on fire now, Jane knew. He was as cold as ice, and each word as clear and cold.

"If he had reached me, it wouldn't have been necessary for me to have told you about these papers in the little drawer. He didn't reach me. Vivian thought I was in the library reading. I was waiting for him, waiting for hours. Then I thought I heard a noise at the main gates—"

Even Jack heard now the sound at the window—a gasp, a sigh, a soft rubbing, something. He was out of his chair and across the room in two long, noiseless strides, but the veranda, the spread of lawns were empty.

"Funny. I could have sworn I heard someone there." He sat down again, half facing the window, and lowered his voice. "There isn't much more. I went to the gates myself, Jane, or near them. But I couldn't use a light. I was close enough to suspect what was there—and that someone else was waiting outside."

As an involuntary shudder ran over her he said quickly, "I hated to send you, but with the flashlight there was no danger, and it had to be done. The watchman was due, and I wanted that body discovered and taken away, if possible, before daylight. If the police found you there they'd accept the explanation that you had been awakened by some noise and gone out to investigate. If they'd found me— Well, it didn't suit my purpose to be connected with that murder—yet. Nor to have anyone know that I was the first one to reach those gates."

He stopped, his eyes fixed on some thought of his own. Jane, intent upon him now, was startled again at the ruthlessness, relentlessness his face revealed. The look was gone in a breath, and his whole face changed, smoothing out, even smiling a little.

"I had to deny knowing him," he said deliberately, emphasizing each word, "because he was murdered for telling me something I wanted to know that Saturday night two weeks ago."

"You can't say that!" Jane cried desperately. "You don't know—you can't know—"

"Hush! I do know." Jack's low, short laugh in the quiet room had the effect of a cracking whip. "The man who murdered Pinto took care to leave a small warning for me. You saw that little branch in Pinto's hand? That, my dear Jane, was a spray of coffee."

Coffee! The word formed on Jane's lips, froze there.

As he watched her incredulity change to understanding, to fear, a grayish film crept over his face, gathered in dark pools beneath his eyes.

"My dear, my dear," he said, taking her hands. "Don't look like that. I'm not worth it."

"How shall I look?" she demanded with stiff lips. "You're telling me, aren't you, that what happened to Pinto may happen to you?"

"Not if I can count on your silence. And I can." He pressed her hands, released them, forced a smile. "I'm not helpless or unprepared, Jane," he added in an odd tone.

"There's only one chance in a hundred against me. It's because of that one chance I've got to depend on you."

As he spoke Vivian rapped on the corridor door, opened it.

"If you two are just talking"—she smiled—"we might as well be on our way, Jack. It's almost one and the car's here."

Jane's eyes traveled from one face to the other in amazement. Vivian, stunning in a brown and green sports outfit, looked fresh and untroubled. Jack, by some magic, had forced life and color into his face.

"My lovely wife," he said, going to meet her and managing in three words an objective statement, a caress and a sting.

5

Wisconsin Interlude

Jane watched them leave the library arm in arm before, catching up the wastebasket of scraps, she slipped out the French doors and down the veranda to her room. As nothing there could be locked and she felt certain that no one would venture to enter the house at high noon to piece some bits of paper together, she simply swept back the counterpane of her bed, made the scraps smooth under it with her hand and covered them again. Feeling as if she were playing a bit part in some old-fashioned melodrama, she hurried back to the library with the basket.

"Good girl," Jack called as she passed the door of his and Vivian's room. He joined her, smiling, a worn brown sweater over his arm. "Forgot this rag and had to come back. Angelo blows up without it. That's what even lawyers come to in this land of signs and superstitions."

At the library he took the basket from her and stepped in to replace it. "I should have done something about those papers myself days ago," he went on when he appeared again. "But you'd be surprised how hard it is for me to do anything privately, even inside this hedge."

As they swung round the corner of the veranda Vivian rose from her perch on the rail and sent them a quick, questioning glance. Jack tossed the sweater to her gaily.

"I've done my bit finding the thing. You make the presentation. Give Angelo a chance to deliver one of his pretty speeches."

Before Vivian could reply he seized her hand and hurried her down the steps and into the sports car.

"Wait." Vivian turned to Jane standing on the steps. "If you change your mind, darling, just telephone the club and we'll send Arnaldo back for you."

Jane shook her head and waved them off thankfully. To be alone was the one thing on earth she wanted; to be alone and let the tumult of thoughts and emotions boiling within her find some sort of order and meaning. Although she stood quietly, smiling, she felt that she could hold that pose no longer than it would take them to reach the gates.

She did not hold it that long. As the chauffeur swung the car round the shrubbery and she saw that Jack and Vivian had forgotten her, were laughing together about the sweater, a memory so poignant swept over her that she turned and stumbled blindly along the veranda. In the first lounge chair she flung herself down to press her burning face deep into the cushions.

"I mustn't think about that, it's over," she told herself frantically. "I mustn't remember, I won't remember—"

But even while she fought with herself the old brown house on the corner of Hudson and West streets, that had been her home until she left for Rio, loomed so vividly before her eyes that she could see every curl of its gingerbread decoration. And on the steps she saw herself at seventeen, Vivian's bridal bouquet on her arm, watching her sister and Jack drive away, laughing together, on the honeymoon that eventually would take them to the home that was to have been hers in Brazil.

She could see how the shadows had lain that September afternoon beneath the elms on the lawns, how bright the last nodding heads of nasturtiums, of sweet peas and

cosmos had shone in the thinning sunlight. Even the
ambling figure of Tim Mahoney, the postman, came before
her as, homeward bound, he had paused to look from her
to the vanishing car. And again she heard the impudent
whistle that Jimmy, the newsboy, had tumbled off his
bicycle to send after Vivian before he turned to toss the
folded evening paper in the direction of the steps.

Before the car was out of sight she had fled up the steps
and into the house and up the stairs to the "big room" that
ran across the front of the house. It was the refuge her
father had made for himself when her mother died at her
birth and the refuge he had shared with her when Vivian
began to take over the lower floor for the entertainment
of crowds of high-school boys and girls and later for her
innumerable beaus.

There her father had sat beside her until her tense,
tearless silence had broken. Then he had turned on a light
and read aloud, as he had done every evening since she
could remember. She hadn't known what he was reading—
perhaps he hadn't either—but somehow that return to the
old familiar order had sealed over her wound and given
her the courage to face the shocked and critical town.

Jane struggled to regain that composure now, to dam
back her confused and fearful thoughts with memories of
her years as a child in the old brown house, particularly in
the "big room." But even there she could not shut out Vivian, the lovely older sister with whom she had identified
all the beautiful princesses and heroines of fairy stories
and even of the history and poetry her father read.

She saw herself slipping away from the reading to peer
through the banisters of the stairs at the sister who for
her was always the central figure, the only figure, in the
constantly changing groups below. Like a small camera she
would register every detail of the scene and return to tell
her father. And he would listen and nod gravely.

She must have been five when that strange dark-faced young man suddenly appeared at the house one summer to sit silent and unmoving in a corner, his eyes fixed on Vivian. Vivian was seventeen then, a junior in high school, and this man was older—much older—than the football and track stars surrounding Vivian.

As suddenly he disappeared. What happened Jane had never learned either from Vivian or her father. But that fall Vivian had been sent East to school, and from then on the house was quiet for nine long months of the year, more and more like a country club as Vivian entered college and returned to Hudson for the summers. Carloads of smart young people from Minneapolis and St. Paul, from Milwaukee and even Chicago, were constantly arriving and departing at the worn stone horse block that once had served her grandmother's friends arriving in carriages.

Finally had come the winter when Vivian had been sent home from college for daring to think of signing a contact to be glorified by Ziegfeld. "Your daughter's beauty is too great a responsibility," the dean had written to "My dear Mr. George," in declaring the college's intention of being relieved of it.

Hudson, a little worn also with her hectic romances and, to Vivian, perfectly harmless forays among the young married men of the town, no longer provided adequate appreciation for her now really breath-taking loveliness. Chicago—with New York and Europe in the offing—did. So Vivian had departed for Chicago to enter what their father had called a "decorative business," with Vivian as the decoration.

Before Jane reached seventeen Vivian had been engaged a dozen times, on the eve of marriage at least three and, if the rumors seeping back from Chicago to brighten the gossip of Hudson had any foundation, the center of one romantic adventure after another. But surprisingly she had never married. And the brown house had seen little of her except when she fled to its shelter for family support through some emotional crisis.

It was not strange, therefore, when one late June afternoon a tall and handsome stranger called to ask for Miss George, that old Martha, the housekeeper, had assumed he meant Jane and had invited him to wait until she returned from a tennis game. And there Jane, running up the steps to the vine-shaded porch, had found him. Conscious of her disheveled and flushed appearance, she had stopped short and he had come quickly to meet her.

"Vivian!" he had said, then, with a strange change of tone, "But you're not Vivian."

"Vivian's in Europe," she had told him. "I'm Jane." She had remained standing, staring too, as something in his blue, concentrated gaze set her blood racing.

"I'm Jack—Jack Houghton," he had said finally and added, taking the rather grimy hand she offered him, "I don't think you had reached this earth when I knew Vivian."

"No. No, I don't think I had," she had answered in confusion, for it had seemed to her then that at that moment her life really began.

He had been in Brazil for fourteen years, he told her, and now had returned for the first time to see his family. During dinner, to which he stayed, he had been gay and deliberately fascinating, holding her father absorbed with tales that ranged from the pampas of south Brazil to the jungles of the Amazon.

But when later she sat with him alone on the porch he had said, his voice edged with mockery, that he had come back with all the anticipations of a "local boy makes good" to find himself a celebrity among strangers. For his father's farm was now the suburb of a small new town, his parents were dead and his two sisters "married somewhere in California."

To Jane his disappointment had all the heartbreak of a small boy suddenly and tragically orphaned.

"I've lived and worked like a Moor to come back here to prove something to two people," he had added savagely, "and now neither one is here."

"But didn't you write them—ever?"

He shook his head, and in the dim light she had seen the effort he was making to keep his voice casual.

"One was my father. He was a farmer, not a very good one, and we were poor—some years desperately poor. By the time I was fourteen I thought a dollar was the only thing in the world that mattered. But money meant nothing to Dad; it was the land itself he cared for, and he wouldn't—couldn't—understand why I wanted to leave it.

"The day I told him I was leaving for Hudson to find work so that I could go to high school was a black day for both of us. He swore that I need never come back looking for a bed and food from him, and I swore to him then that the next time he saw me I would be rich—and that I'd give him a better roof and food than he'd ever given me. That hurt him to hear and me to say. I think I would have stayed if he had spoken a single word. He didn't. He simply opened the door wide for me and walked away. And I walked out. Sounds like one of the old dime novels or something, doesn't it?"

"And you never went back?"

"I never saw a member of my family again—though for the next three years I was right here in Hudson." He had sat silent for a time, seeing perhaps the years that had followed. "There were times when I think I'd have been glad to crawl back if I could have managed to swim several thousand miles of Atlantic Ocean. If it hadn't been for a friend in Brazil—"

He had risen abruptly and she had risen beside him—automatically, as if she belonged beside him.

"Well, I'm a rich man now, a successful man by the world's yardstick, but the house I came back to build for them isn't needed. Neither am I."

"You mean you're going away?"

"Tomorrow. Back to Brazil."

He hadn't gone back to Brazil until September. He had stayed in Hudson because of her. It was not until weeks later, when the date for their wedding had been set, that he told her the second person he had come back to see was Vivian.

"She was just a tyke when I first saw her—not more than eight or nine—but I thought her the most wonderful thing I had ever seen. I paid my way through high school working as janitor, and somehow I always found a reason for sweeping the walk or shoveling snow on the grade-school side just to see her arrive. She knew I did too—though she never looked at me or spoke. Then I went to Madison for four years, but when I knew I was going to Brazil I came back here—perhaps to see my family, perhaps to see her—I don't know. I saw her. She was something like you only—"

Jane had laughed in delight at his hesitation. "Beautiful," she had finished for him. "I know. I was only a tyke too then, but I could never believe myself she was a sister like other people's sisters."

"Beautiful!" he had exclaimed as if that were a pale word. "God, yes!" He had laughed too then. "But with a degree in my pocket I felt I was getting on. And I knew myself well by that time. I knew something about her too—we were much alike in some ways. I wanted success, to be recognized as a rich man; she wanted admiration. I gave her that—all she wanted."

He laughed, mocking himself again. "It was all she thought I had to give. I used to come here to give it—in a secondhand blue suit. I'd sit in a corner all evening, never saying a word, just looking at her."

"I remember," Jane had told him. "I saw you—through the banisters."

"If I had only known you existed . . ." He had turned that exciting blue gaze on her, drawn her close.

But she had resisted. "Tell me the rest—about Vivian." She had known then the first prickly fear that she was for him only a reflection of the Vivian he had remembered, but she had resisted that too. Vivian was in Europe, would not return until November!

"Your father still thought of her as a child, did not approve of me. But she was not a child. She had had too much attention not to know how lovely she was—and how to use her beauty. I was mad about her, frantic with fear, too, that I would lose her if I went to Brazil. And I was so sure that I could give her anything, everything, she wanted one day that I actually felt it was just a matter of waiting. I told her that—just that—that one day I would return rich and she was to marry me then."

Jack had sent such a rollicking laugh into the air that Jane, reassured, had laughed too. "What did Vivian say?"

He had sobered quickly. "I had stopped her on the street—in front of Palmer's old grocery store—to tell her," he said slowly. "There was no door there she could open as my father had done. But the effect was the same. She didn't say a word, just turned and walked away. I stood still on that very spot and promised myself that I would come back one day—the man she wanted to marry."

Again he had drawn Jane close and held her within hard arms to whisper, "Instead I found you."

Memories of the summer that had been for both of them a fantastic, delirious dream poured over Jane now. He had found her, and she had found in him, in his flashing gaiety and moods, in his high spirit of adventure, his quick, shy tendernesses, outlet for her own ardent emotion. But he was thirty-six, she seventeen, and her father, their friends, all the town had shaken doubtful heads, uttered warning words against their marriage.

Jack had listened, considered, offered to release her or wait two years, four, and return. "You don't really understand me," he had warned her. "I'm an opportunist—I've had to be—and pretty ruthless at taking what I want. I'm not a substantial citizen at all."

But she had not listened, would not listen. "I'm not sure what an opportunist is, but if it means that when you go back to Brazil I go too, then we're birds of a feather—and you know what they do."

And so they were to have been married in September, leave immediately for Brazil. In August Vivian had returned. A radiantly beautiful Vivian, mature, sophisticated and as ruthless as Jack in taking what she wanted.

They were married in September. Under her nose, as Vivian had said. And she had watched them drive away, laughing together, as she had watched them go this afternoon.

But in the five years since she had had plenty of time to wonder if it had been the memory of Jack and those sapphire eyes that had come between Vivian and the men she had been ready to marry. And now as she lay in her chair she began to wonder too if Vivian had not become a symbol to Jack—the tangible recognition of the success he had set to gain for himself in those early years of shattering effort in Brazil. With her he might have been happier than with Vivian, she thought honestly, but would he ever have been satisfied? Wouldn't marriage with her have been a perpetual reminder of failure? And failure was something that Jack never permitted himself or others.

She sighed and stirred, returning to reality as if from a deep and troubled sleep.

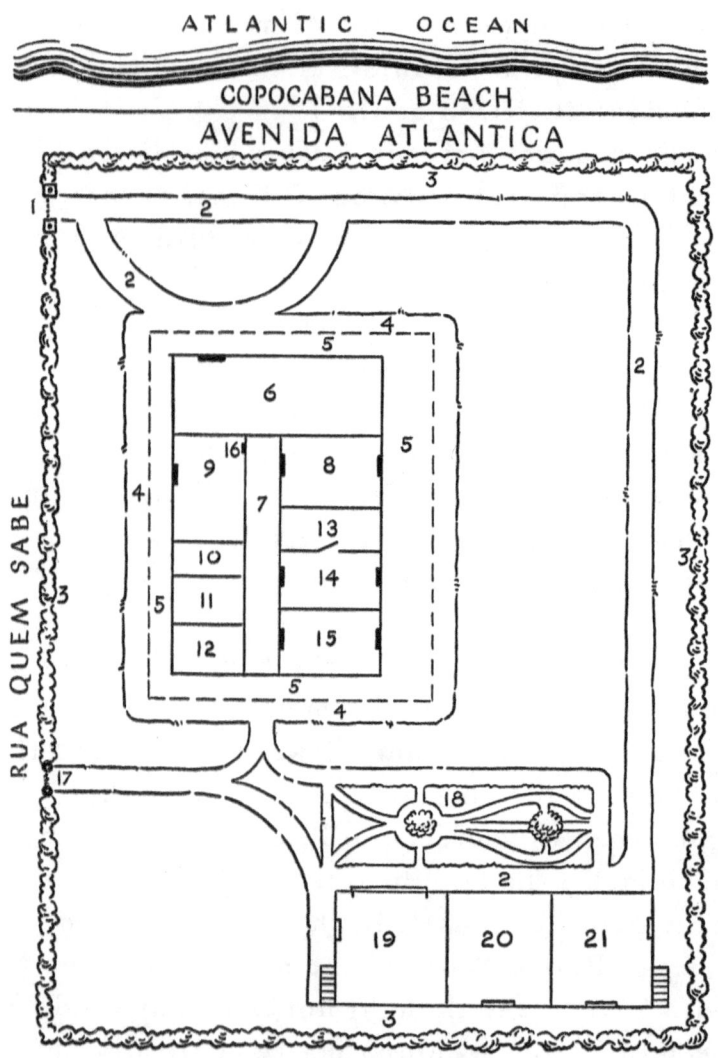

1. Main Gates. 2. Driveway. 3. Ficus Hedge. 4. Path. 5. Veranda. 6. Living Room. 7. Corridor. 8. Library. 9. Formal Dining Room. 10. Pantries. 11. Kitchen. 12. Breakfast Room. 13. Vivian's Sitting Room. 14. Vivian's and Jack's Bedroom. 15. Jane's Room. 16. Telephone Niche. 17. Rear Gates. 18. Gardens. 19. Garage. 20. Gardener's Storeroom. 21. Laundries.

6
Jane Burns Some Papers

"You wake now, Miss Jane?" came to her in a cautious whisper.

She opened her eyes to find Maria beside her, a formidable figure in a tight black dress, her head crowned with a red turban.

"I haven't been asleep, Maria, just thinking," she began and stopped at the deep look in the dark eyes. How long had Maria been watching her? Had she, as Jack had said she could, been walking around in her mind, following those hidden memories? She sat up, tried to say with something of Vivian's crispness, "Are you ready to go now?"

Maria didn't answer. She stood firmly, her hands on her hips, a worn black bag dangling from one. As Jane waited her expression became more strained and somber. "You think about home, Miss Jane? You go back, maybe?"

"Rio is my home now," Jane started to say but thought better of it.

"Rio is no good home for you, Miss Jane," Maria said slowly, as if in answer to her unspoken words. "You—I no think you be happy here."

Jane sat up, startled, to look into the noncommittal face, then looked round the veranda.

"Nobody else here," Maria said encouragingly. "Everybody gone now. Inah, Theresa, Ricardo, José, go out back

49

gates when the senhor and senhora go out front. Nobody lose no time today." Her voice dropped, became solemnly warning. "Trouble bird *mean* trouble, Miss Jane."

Jane was troubled too. Maria had something on her mind, perhaps something about that man in the gates, but she felt she couldn't listen, not with Jack and Vivian gone. Even with Maria it would never do to encourage confidences in their absence.

"He sing three times *las'* night. Never sing other time before you come." Maria shifted her weight, bent down. "Maybe he mean trouble for you, Miss Jane. Maybe better you go home."

Jane gazed at her helplessly. Her Anglo-Saxon mind had no means of bridging the gap that lay between it and a world where dreams and portents were realities. Jack, through his many years in Brazil, had acquired some insight into it and *macumba* practices. Whatever he thought of them, he had a healthy respect for Maria's powers. And the eyes gazing at her now were more pregnant with warning than the words the full red lips had formed.

She stood up, taking confidence from her height. "Don't worry about me, Maria. I've broken mirrors, walked under ladders, seen plenty of black cats. Yet here I am."

Maria snorted, gave her another darkly significant glance, then unexpectedly suggested, "You want I stay till the senhora come back?"

"Nonsense, I'm quite all right. In fact, I'm going to enjoy being alone for an afternoon. Run along, Maria, and have a pleasant week end."

But as she watched the black figure waddle to the back gate Jane was not so sure. When she had said she would enjoy being alone she had not realized just how alone she would be. One of Jack's unbreakable laws—whims, according to Vivian—was that from Saturday noon until Monday morning the servants should all leave the grounds. After five strenuous weekdays and an equally strenuous Saturday of relaxation he insisted on one day of complete isolation and rest.

Now, though the air was filled with the hum of Saturday-afternoon traffic on the Avenida, the roll of combers and shouts of swimmers and handball players on the beach, even sound became muted when it crossed the hedge. With only indigo sky and emerald lawns and gardens ablaze with sunshine about her, she was conscious that she was very much alone indeed.

The gate clanged, reminding her of her promise to Jack. Everyone was gone now, and she could burn those papers. She set about the task with relief; any activity would be better than sitting alone in this silence, thinking, listening.

When she had collected the scraps into her own basket she stood a moment looking down at them. Could they hold the secret of that man Pinto in the gates? In the stillness she could feel again the quiet of the night, see Jack in the darkness of the French doors, hear his words in the library. "Only one chance in a hundred," he had assured her—and perhaps someone else who had stood close to the window when he said it.

Afraid of the silence, her own thoughts, and cautious too now, she first visited both gates. Maria had locked the rear one after her; Arnaldo had closed and latched but not locked the main gates.

Should she return to the house for the key? After a long moment she decided against it. Jack's and Vivian's week-end habits were too well known for any friends to drop in. A substantial fee to the policeman on the corner every week kept his eye alert to turn away strangers. His eye was alert now, and he took a step or two away from his corner to see more clearly what she was doing.

Deliberately she watched a bather or two swing beachward before turning away with what she hoped was an idle air. If he saw her lock the gates and knew she had found that body, heaven only knew what he would make of two and two. Besides, Jack or Vivian might decide to return when they discovered how hot it was. On the veranda she had not noticed the heat; now it rubbed on nerves quivering from shock and lack of sleep.

She had arrived in late March, just after summer had become fall, and the days since had been Junelike. This unseasonable heat made her dizzy and dull, weighted her feet as she walked through the gardens that ran across the rear of the grounds, hiding garage and servants' quarters from the house.

Zinnias, shoulder high, blazing with color; roses on vines and bushes, red, pink, yellow, white; more masses of pagan color in the heavy heads of purple and crimson and gold coxcombs closed round her stiflingly. Perfume from carnation beds added its weight to the air. Even the dark shiny green of trees and shrubs seemed to absorb and diffuse a blare of hot color.

The luxuriant wilderness ended at a wide strip of gravel beyond which stood a low two-storied building with an outside stairway at each end. Only the double doors of the garage faced toward the house. Otherwise the wall was a tapestry of scarlet bougainvillea.

Silence was deep here too, with the servants absent and the doors of their quarters and those of the gardener's storerooms closed and padlocked. Could it be the eyes and ears of one of them she had felt constantly watching, listening? Now that they were gone, she wasn't conscious of that nagging sense of someone near her.

Maria and Arnaldo she dismissed without a thought; they had been with Jack for years before he married Vivian. They considered themselves, and were, established members of the household. Of the others José, the gardener,

and Ricardo, the handy man, were also beyond consider-
ation through lack of wit and opportunity. Remained only
Inah, the housemaid, and Theresa, Vivian's own maid; of
them she knew nothing except that they were excellently
trained and decorative.

Standing in the entrance to the garage, she was puzzled
as to where Jack had expected her to burn papers there.
Cupboards and a workbench filled the far end. One half
the floor was given over to the big closed car. The only
possible place, she decided, was in the drip pan of the
sports car in which Arnaldo had driven Vivian and Jack to
Gavea.

Conscientiously burning scraps a handful at a time,
to make sure that each was destroyed, she grew increasingly uneasy. To burn papers was a simple thing in itself.
To burn them secretly in a setting obviously designed for
secrecy took on a sinister significance when in spite of
herself words leaped to her eyes from the shriveling pieces.

One word stood out again and again, sometimes as *café,*
sometimes as coffee. Yet that very morning Jack had emphasized his complete lack of interest in the past, present
or future of coffee! And—she drew a sharp breath as she
remembered—Jack had said that spray of leaves in Pinto's
hand was coffee.

Silence and heat pressed round her like a presence as
she worked and worried. The feeling grew that she was
not alone in the garage. Yet no one else could be there.
Flushed and grimy, her eyes smarting from the sting of a
little plume of smoke some grease in the drip pan created,
she fought the feeling off. She would not turn her head.

Then, though she had heard no sound, she knew someone was there. She felt eyes watching her as she had that
morning in the library. Without changing position she
flashed a quick glance about her.

Phil Monroe, cool and immaculate in white linen, stood in the doorway. A tall, self-contained young man, behind whose broad, smooth forehead and deep gray eyes was the brain that made everyone exclaim at his ability and marvel that so young a man could be recognized as an expert on transportation. Vaguely she knew he was in Brazil in connection with the electrification of one of the railways. Definitely she disliked and resented him.

In comparison with the great Dane Vivian had once called Noel, Phil resembled a greyhound. Perfectly groomed always, perfectly controlled, he seemed endlessly at ease, yet his eyes were wary—even when he looked at Vivian his eyes were wary. He roused in Jane a tingling antagonism whenever she saw him.

As if reading her thoughts, he stood silent, half smiling. Then, his eyes on the ashes in the drip pan, he asked in his usual lightly cynical tone, "Why aren't you fanning a golf ball this stifling afternoon?"

"The same to you," she tried to say as casually.

"I'm on my way—just dropped in for a book Vivian—"

"How did you get in?" she demanded, making no effort to conceal her distrust and displeasure. And for all his nonchalant air, she knew he was viewing her with something more than curiosity.

His tone remained light however. "Oh, the johnny on the corner knows me now. I simply lifted the latch and walked in. Now that I'm here, can't I help? I knew a boy scout once. He could build fires without smoke. As a matter of fact, I was all set to do my good deed for the day. Saw the smoke and—here I am."

His smile, his spotless coolness, increased Jane's discomfort in her own heated appearance. "Thank you, no," she said with an effort. "You're the executive type. I advertised for unskilled labor."

Deliberately she scooped up another handful of scraps and dropped them on her little fire.

"Must you play with fire," he asked at length, "or can we talk somewhere?"

"Why?"

"Because we share a deep interest in Jack."

Through her thick lashes she looked at him distrustfully. Was he mocking her resentment of his friendship with Vivian or had he surprised her own secret? She could not restrain the telltale color surging to her face but hoped desperately he would think it anger. She was angry.

Something straightened his own lips an instant, then he smiled again. "Ah, youth," he commented ponderously, as if he were seventy instead of thirty-three. "Once it burned torches before its heroes; now it burns bonfires behind them."

She dribbled a few more scraps on her fire.

"You aren't at all like your sister, are you? She's an amusing and easy person to talk with. Or don't you find her so? Five years is a long time, isn't it?"

Silence.

"You like Rio, I hope," he offered then, politely. "Though dead men do upset one."

At her start of surprise he smiled. "My child, you found him in the gates ten or twelve hours ago. Ancient history in a city where the year-round sport is gossip, hot off the servants' grapevine. Most of us are pretty good at it."

Was he warning her? And for her own good or his? She flung back her head and straightened to face him.

"Don't be like that," he advised. "Look here. I came up so quietly that I startled you, and now I've been teasing you. I'm sorry—even ashamed of my behavior. Can't we start again? I think I know better than anyone how you feel—strange, cut off from people, as if you were drifting round somewhere by yourself on a raft. I felt that way too when I first came. The long ocean voyage does it; some people take weeks to get their land legs again. How's that for a diagnosis of your faraway don't-touch-me manner?"

"Perhaps you're right," she admitted unwillingly.

"Shall I go on? I can tell you what comes next."

"Maria's just told me what to do next."

"Go home?" he asked quickly.

"Yes, or else . . . It seems an owl sang—"

"So Maria has advised you to go home," he said thoughtfully. "Well, if the Number One Oracle has spoken, you'd better begin to pack. She has second sight or something, you know."

"I'm glad I'm not sensitive," Jane answered coldly. "This enthusiasm for my departure might undo me. What is your reason for—"

"But I don't want you to go. On the contrary. I was merely giving Maria's powers a testimonial. And perhaps her idea is better than the one I came to suggest."

"That you came to suggest! You expected to find me here?" Jane's subsiding irritation revived with a bound.

"Well, not here," he corrected, looking about the garage, then pointedly at the dwindling fire. "But I suspected you wouldn't arrive at Gavea with Jack and Vivian." As her expression grew stony he added hastily, "Wait. I haven't finished."

He stepped into the garage to say seriously, "I know you don't approve of me, Jane. There's no reason why you should. But it's important to Jack, to Vivian, to all of us, that you and I put up our guns." He swung round to draw out a bench from beneath the work shelf. "Please sit down and listen, at least. We may not get another chance—"

"Not now," Jane protested. "In the house, later, if it is really important."

"Later is just another way of saying *amanhã*—tomorrow—and tomorrow never comes."

Reluctantly, as he waited, she seated herself and he dropped down beside her.

"You make it difficult to begin," he said, his eyes on her unresponsive face and the long black smudge that ran down one cheek. "Especially when I want to suggest that you and I become—friends."

"Why?"

"Why not? Here we are in Rio, perhaps the most beautiful city in the world. All sorts of things to do and see, marvelous scenic highways, trails for riding. I've had very little time to see anything, and this crowd of Jack's and Vivian's might as well be in Timbuctoo for all they know of it. Why not join forces, see everything, do everything, find out what Rio outside the foreign colony is really like?"

Jane's face lighted eagerly, then became stony again. "Why?"

"How about inferring that we might enjoy it? You're lonely. So am I!"

For a moment her eyes misted. To have a life of her own, to get away—even for a few hours—from the tensions of the house. The invitation was tempting—but it came from Phil. Vivian's friend, not hers.

"You said it was important to Jack and Vivian," she began uncertainly, "that we talk here, now. This moment. What does it matter to them whether you and I see Rio?"

"I'm torn between desire to choke and to admire you," Phil said after a pause. "Now I see why Jack brags about that head of yours. And why, if I may say so, Vivian finds you a bit of a thorn in the flesh. You must puncture some of her best effects."

Jane and her anger rose together. "If this is a sample of important—"

"Sit down, Jane." Phil stood beside her, his glance steady, compelling. "I hoped to persuade you to accept my suggestion or invitation on faith. And I rather sold myself the idea, as I talked, that it might be rather nice going places together. Well, that's out. But the reason why I suggested it still remains important, and if I must put it in words, I will."

7

Phil Rewords an Invitation

He waited until she perched again on the edge of the bench.

"You've seen for yourself what a curious existence members of the foreign colony lead here in Rio. It's the same in the foreign colonies in India, China, Africa, everywhere. Isolated from their own backgrounds, without roots or responsibilities in the new, foreigners, the women especially, are cut off from all their usual props and conventions. They have more servants than they ever had before, fewer interests, more leisure—"

"Are you quoting something?" Jane asked icily.

"I'm trying to answer your eternal whys in general terms. I did sound a bit pompous, perhaps. If you prefer, I'll get down to cases—namely, Vivian. She's very beautiful, Jane—fascinating. You don't need to be told that. I hate to use the word intoxicating, but that's the effect she has—on men. She doesn't want to make trouble; she doesn't need to. All she wants is attention and admiration, lots of them, all there are."

"She's always had them."

"And she's had them here. The difference is that if she were married to Jack in the States she'd have a thousand demands on her time. And she'd have more competition. More checks and balances on her way of living, if you know what I mean."

"I'm afraid I don't."

"Good lord!" he exclaimed in exasperation, "if you can't be open-minded about what I'm saying, we're sunk."

Jane looked at him in surprise. Phil Monroe capable of losing the perfect control that irked her beyond endurance!

"I'll try," she said quietly. "Go on."

"When Vivian came here as a bride she was lonely—naturally. Jack, after months of absence, was absorbed in H and H, away from home a lot of the time. So she turned to other men, who were only too delighted to entertain and amuse her . . ."

He paused to study Jane cautiously but, when she made no protest, went on more easily. "Angelo Barassa's marriage with Varta was postponed a year because of Vivian. Tom Hughes lost head and heart completely over her the year Eloise was in France with the children. Mercer Todd—that little Viennese menace you see about everywhere—was here when her husband, Russell Todd, fell for Vivian. To impress her, entertain her royally, he took money from his firm. Vivian paid no attention to Noel until two years ago when he returned from a trip to New York—"

"I know about Noel," Jane murmured. "Vivian told me. And I'm trying to be open-minded about this, but I don't like it. When are you coming to the point?"

"I'm practically there. One point is that Vivian is constitutionally unable to see any other characters on a stage except the hero and herself. I'm sure that she was completely ignorant of the fact that there was a Mrs. Todd when she knew Russell. Three years ago Mercer was just a pretty little housewife, so she says herself, hidden away in the Rio Comprido section somewhere. Tom and Angelo came out of their affairs with Vivian badly enough, but Russell Todd was sent back to England when it was discovered that he was using company funds for private purposes.

On the way he jumped overboard. Mercer returned to Rio a year later. No one knows just why."

Jane stirred uneasily. Was this what Vivian had said so bitterly that morning would reach Jane's ears soon enough?

Phil rose, uncomfortable too, moved to the door and back. "It's no pleasure to me to tell you all this. I certainly wouldn't be telling you now if I didn't think—know—that unless something is done, and quickly, we're all going to find a volcano erupting under us."

He paused again, obviously to choose his next words. "I don't know how much you have read into my friendship with Vivian. It is friendship, a very real one on my part. And I'm thinking of her now and Jack and Noel. Jack is on the verge of a collapse if he doesn't take a rest. The point is that if you and I take ourselves out of the picture as often and as long as possible, it may clear the atmosphere, give them a chance to work out a solution. Don't think I'm suggesting this out of nobility of soul," he concluded hastily.

"I don't," Jane told him. "Why are you making such a sacrifice?"

His lips straightened for a moment, and he looked at her with unconcealed displeasure.

"I came down here to investigate an application for a loan for the electrification of the São Joaquim Railway. That's done, but there is something else I must do before I return to New York. I'm sorry, but that is as far as I can go on that. The reason I'm making the sacrifice, as you call my invitation, is that an eruption in the social circles of Rio, with Jack, Vivian, Noel, you, me—not to mention the Hugheses, Barassas and Mercer—blasted into the headlines, isn't going to be any better for me than for anyone else."

"But one of them—of us—would have to do the blasting. Do you think anyone of us is going to—"

"I've either said too much or too little," he interrupted. "I'm not an alarmist, Jane, and by headlines I don't mean scandal. I'm afraid, I'm afraid to say what I do mean."

She turned away to look at the charred papers on her dead fire, more disturbed than she was willing to admit. Phil certainly was no alarmist. If he were, she thought illogically, she might have been persuaded. But she couldn't shake off her distrust of him, her feeling that under the guise of concern for Vivian and Jack the brain behind that smooth forehead was trying to manipulate her for its own ends.

And she could place no faith in her own judgment. Nothing and no one she had known in Hudson had equipped her to understand or cope with the situations and people she was meeting here. She rubbed her forehead, trying to rouse her own brain to function, but it lay heavy and numb like a dead weight in her throbbing head. Certainly Vivian was afraid. Jack, if not afraid, was in danger and preparing to meet it. Now Phil . . . Now herself, for that matter; she was afraid, terribly afraid—

"Jane," Phil's voice said gently, "forgive me. I've made a great mistake in talking to you about—all this."

"It's all right," she told him wearily. "Vivian said I'd hear it all soon. But what makes you think that if you and I went up Sugar Loaf or swimming we could prevent— what you're afraid of?"

"I offered no guarantee. But you and I are additional and unnecessary causes of strain in these parts at this moment. If we remove ourselves, we may make things easier. It's a naive idea, perhaps, but realistic, practical."

Realistic, practical! Jane's anger boiled again. Pinto crumpled in the gates! Vivian, white face, murmuring, "I'm afraid. I don't know what to do." Jack assuring her with gray lips, "Only one chance in a hundred . . ." And now this mastermind on transportation suggested a practical solution!

"I think the whole idea is fantastic!"

"You refuse?" Phil's voice was level, but his face showed sudden pallor.

"Unless you have a better reason than you've given me so far, yes."

Phil was silent a moment. As he looked at her she was startled at the directness and clarity of his eyes. But they told her nothing.

"There is another reason," he said quietly after a moment, "but it must wait until you have grown a little older—in years or experience."

Confused, startled again by something in that clear glance, she turned and picked up her now almost empty basket of scraps. "Then if you don't mind . . ."

"Not in the least." With a wave of his hand he was gone.

Vexed with him, still more with herself, she stood in the doorway watching his lithe shoulders swing up the path, disappear among the flowers, after a minute saw his head rise as he ran up the back steps and into the house. Then, with the uncomfortable sensation of having acted like the most ignorant country girl to be found in all Wisconsin, she seized a handful of papers and once more started her fire.

When the little plume of smoke rose again she stepped back, staring. A moment later she was hurrying up the path, turning every few feet to look back toward the garage.

Shortly where the path swung round a large bed of rosebushes she stopped, her brows puckered. At no point had the smoke from her fire been visible; from that point she could not even see the garage. Whatever had brought Phil out there, it had not been the smoke, she knew then.

The papers burned at last, the ashes swept up and dropped in the *lixo*, she returned wearily to the house. While she bathed and changed she could fend off doubts and misgivings, but when she dropped again into a lounge chair outside her own French doors she found them all there waiting for her. Jack's health. Jack and Pinto. Jack and coffee. Vivian and Jack. Vivian and Noel. Vivian and Phil. Vivian's intermittent hostility toward herself. Maria's warnings. Phil's invitation—now possibly his enmity.

Question after question whirled into her mind without relation or solution until heat and exhaustion bore her mercifully away in sleep.

Sometime later she woke, chilled and cramped, to find a cold breeze blowing in from the Atlantic and masses of soft white cloud shutting away sun and sky.

As she sat up, however, she knew that neither cold nor cramp had waked her. The house behind her was silent the lawns empty, but in her ears echoed the sound of a sharp rap—an exclamation—something unusual somewhere.

8
"I'll Do It Just Once More—"

Feeling more and more like a hysterical old lady as she hurried from room to room, Jane made a swift but thorough search, opening every door, looking into every corner, even behind furniture. No one else was in the house; nothing out of the ordinary was to be seen. Even the three cigarette stubs in an ash tray on the table beside Jack's chair in the library could not be considered unusual. Hollywoods—the popular Brazilian brand that Phil smoked. He was perfectly at home in the house, must have left them there when he ran in to get the book he had mentioned. Nothing else, however, suggested that he had lingered or why.

With the early tropical darkness creeping over the lawns, Jane pressed switches as she went until finally, in her own room, every light burning, her doors closed and curtains drawn, there was nothing to do but wait for Jack and Vivian. On previous Saturdays they had all returned together about six, usually with two or more guests in tow, for cocktails and the canapes for which Maria was famous. But her little clock was dragging toward seven when she heard the car on the driveway and a moment later her sister's heels beating an agitated tattoo on the corridor floor. Alarmed, her first thought for Jack, she hurried to open the door.

Vivian rushed in. "Jack—Jack knows!" she cried wildly and flung herself on the bed.

If Vivian had not seized her arm in a feverish grasp to pull her down beside her, Jane could have laughed aloud in relief. "About Noel?" she asked.

"Yes. At luncheon. I tried to keep a place beside me for Phil. He didn't come, and Noel took it. He—he said he wasn't another Jack and ordered me to stop seeing Phil. Jack heard!"

For the first time Jane looked at her sister with detachment, without charity. "Well, that's that," she said coolly.

"Don't look at me like that! You haven't any right," Vivian began angrily, then her voice broke on a sob. She caught up a bit of folded paper from the bed and jerked it in and out of her fingers until she could control it again. "Jane, Jack has some mad idea. He's going to do something. I know it. And you must help me. He's giving a dinner tonight—and I'm afraid."

"A dinner!" Jane repeated in amazement. "Vivian, you're acting like a child. There has scarcely been a night since I came that we haven't had guests or gone out—"

"Small, private, eight o'clock dinners. This is to be at Copacabana Palace, the largest hotel in Rio. Jack loathes public dining; you can't drag him to a night club."

"Where is he now?"

"Dressing, I suppose. Jane, he wouldn't let Arnaldo drive us home. He drove. I never was so frightened. I—I thought he was trying to—to kill us all. I'm afraid of him—really afraid."

Her hunched shoulders spoke more convincingly than her words. Only under great stress would she have assumed such an ungraceful position.

"But he brought you home safely," Jane said after a moment. "What is there to fear now?"

"I don't know, I tell you. But Jack never does anything without a reason. Never. You must help me."

"Have you forgotten that I love Jack too?" Jane sat a long minute, following her own thoughts. "And now you've failed him—you want my help."

"No, I haven't forgotten. I've never forgotten," Vivian said slowly. "I think the day I can forget you standing on the steps at home with my bouquet on your arm will be the happiest of my life. Darling, I—I didn't really think till then that you loved Jack. You'd always seemed such an infant to me. I thought—have tried to make myself believe ever since—that it was just infatuation—first love."

She sprang up nervously. "But there's no time for that now. Jane, I'm in earnest. You must help. You're the only one who can do anything with Jack now. He loves me—not you—as much as he can love anyone. But he worships you—up on a pedestal somewhere. Stay close to him, try to get a chance to talk with him, get him to wait until we—I—can explain—"

Before Jane's unresponsive gaze she broke off. Only her rouged lips and her eyes, feverishly bright now, gave color to her face.

"If you don't, something is going to happen. You don't know how ruthless Jack can be, how dangerous. I do. Oh," she cried, beating her doubled fists together, "I wish I were dead! Or he was. Or—"

"Vivian!" At the limit of her endurance, Jane rose and gripped her sister's shoulders, shook her. "Stop dramatizing—"

Vivian stepped back as if Jane had struck her. "Dramatizing! You call it dramatizing when I am trying to save my husband from doing something that may wreck us all. Forget me. Forget yourself. Think of Jack, if you really love him. He's the head of one of the biggest companies in

Brazil. Hundreds of people—thousands, for all I know—
depend on his judgment. What will that judgment be
worth tomorrow if tonight—"

"I still think you're being dramatic, romanticizing,"
Jane told her with more calmness than she felt. "I'm one
of the hundreds who believe in Jack's judgment."

Vivian twisted away from her; her hands, with interlaced fingers, crushed against her mouth. When she turned
again to Jane some raw emotion—terror—shame—anger—
glittered in her eyes.

"The guests," she said almost in a whisper. "I can't tell
you now. There isn't time to make you understand." Her
voice sank lower still as she went on speaking her thoughts
aloud. "I—I think I'm just beginning to understand myself. Jack—he's known all the time—about everything.
He's been waiting to strike at me—as I've watched him
wait—for others."

Dread crept over Jane as she gazed back at Vivian, a
helpless dread of something deadly and malignant hidden
beneath the surface of this gay life about her. Was this
truth that Vivian was speaking or only more of her histri-
onics? "Angelo and Tom Hughes came out of their affairs
with Vivian badly enough. . . . Russell Todd jumped overboard." Phil had said that, but he had not said that Jack
was involved or even aware. Had he been? Was that what
Vivian was realizing now?

"Oh," Vivian was moaning in despair, "he hates me!
You hate me—"

Jane's arms went round her then. "Darling, darling,"
she murmured, "you're ill, imagining things. We both love
you—you must believe that." As her sister's wracking sobs
quieted she said softly, "We won't go to the dinner. You
stay here, lie down for a while. I'll tell Jack."

Her arms, holding Vivian tight, dropped and she
stepped back. Vivian drew away from her too, to stand for

a moment with compressed lips. Then without a word or glance for Jane she walked to the dressing table, smoothed her hair, dusted her face with powder. Steadying herself with one hand, she turned, while with the other she continued to roll and crumple the bit of paper she still held.

"You're right," she said, looking at it, not at Jane. "I've been dramatizing myself. I've done it all my life. I'll do it just once more—if I can."

"But there's no need," Jane protested. "You're not fit, Vivian, to go to a dinner or anywhere but to bed. Jack wouldn't force you—"

"Everyone at that table tonight will be there because Jack told them to be there. And so will I."

Vivian walked lightly back to Jane and stood beside her, her face a mask but smiling. "Jack and I are pretty much alike in many ways. We've both taken what we wanted without much regard for others. Well"—she shrugged her slender shoulders—"if he can see this through, so can I."

She moved on to the door, to turn as she opened it. "Perhaps he counted on me funking it. Perhaps that is what he wanted. You said I'd failed him, didn't you? Well, I haven't failed him—yet."

The door closed behind her, but Jane was not reassured. Vivian and Jack *were* much alike. And if Jack could be dangerous, so could her sister. She had known that during the moments when Vivian's body, within the circle of her arms, not suddenly but with slow and definite resolution, had grown tense and hard.

With fingers that fumbled as if tipped with ice she opened the door of her wardrobe and began to lay out her evening things.

9

Jack Gives a Dinner

As he descended with his guests the wide steps to the illu-
minated glass dance floor of the ballroom in Copacabana
Palace, Jack appeared the only one among them completely at ease. Vivian's vivacity was stilled for once, though
perhaps she had never appeared more beautiful. In a black
and green bouffant gown, her shining hair rolled high
about her fine head, she walked and looked like a queen.

The immense gold and white and mirrored room, the
orchestra playing on a dais at one side, the flowers, even
the crowded tables, it seemed to Jane, became merely a
setting for her sister's progress. Conversation slackened or
stopped and heads turned as Vivian approached, rose in a
buzz when she had passed. But Vivian looked at no one,
ignored the nods and greetings Jack and other members of
the party acknowledged.

At their table just off the dance floor Jack, with a smile
that did not reach his eyes, waved Noel to a chair on Vivian's left. Noel sank into it without a word. A rock of a
man, thrust awkwardly into dinner clothes, he was out
of place in that conventional setting. He should always
be seen as she had seen him first, Jane thought, sitting
a horse like a Tartar, skimming hedges and ditches with
wide and wild country behind him.

Even in formal dress he managed to suggest the rolling pampas from which he had come. The strong, regular features, the clear eyes trained to face great distances, the impassivity of his face, revealed a man accustomed to taking hard blows, shoving them down somewhere within him and raising his head to what came next.

With his blond hair and light blue eyes he appeared as foreign to Brazil as Jack, but beneath that blocklike exterior, Jack had said, beat a fiery Brazilian heart, fantastically proud of Brazil and all things Brazilian. Jane admired and respected him though seldom felt at ease with him, perhaps because he was so ill at ease himself—with her, with any woman.

On Vivian's right Jack left an empty chair. "For Phil," he said, smiling again. Vivian smiled too, a brilliant metallic smile that remained fixed on her scarlet lips.

Jane stepped forward quickly. "And I'm going to sit beside you, Jack."

For a moment, as he looked down at her, a shutter seemed to open in his eyes and she saw again the tortured, driven man she had faced that morning in the library. Then the look was gone, and he told her softly, "Five years too late, my child."

She set her chin and slipped into the chair on his left, and Tom Hughes stationed his tall figure firmly at the next one. Jane knew him as Jack's banker, an American who, as head of the North American Bank and Trust Company, was a potent factor in Rio. He studied her a moment gravely before he stooped to say in her ear, "Well done. And I'll do what I can."

"What do you mean?" Her eyes were on the empty chair beside Vivian, and she missed his gesture of surprise.

He seated himself before he answered. "Aren't you here under duress too? Don't you know that this is a command performance, that all of us have been dragged from home and fireside to share some fatted calf or sacrificial lamb with Jack?"

"It—it looks just like a dinner party to me," she said as casually as she could.

"Well, there's something cockeyed about it," he told her bluntly. "I don't like it, and my guess is that no one else does either. I'm glad Eloise couldn't leave the children. Our new son is just at the teeth-cutting stage, you know." He flicked a disapproving glance about the table. "That's what all these women should be doing."

"Cutting teeth?" Jane asked, her eyes scanning the guests too.

"I was about to say rearing children," he corrected her, then chuckled in his throat, "but cutting wisdom teeth will do as well. My wife is a Frenchwoman of the old school; so are Brazilian women—that is, those trained on the old European pattern. They are happy in their homes, with their children, busy with their church and charities. You don't see any of them here, do you?"

Fortunately he didn't expect an answer to his question but, having announced his topic of the evening, continued to develop it to his own satisfaction. Jane had only to murmur or nod occasionally when he paused. Her attention remained on the table.

He was right about the guests not liking this dinner. Their gaiety was forced, and as they talked and laughed their eyes crossed one another's in that blank fashion that says so much more than words.

Beyond Tom Hughes sat Mercer Todd, exquisite as a doll and blithe as a child, her gaze roving incessantly to Noel. In any other group she would have been enchanting, but Vivian's beauty, the luminous effect she always achieved and tonight superlatively, dulled Mercer's color,

sapped her charm. Usually she hardly touched cocktail or
wine, but tonight, Jane noticed with surprise, her glass
seemed continually empty.

Angelo Barassa, Jack's lawyer, an Italian with a long
saturnine head and gallant manner, sat on Mercer's left.
As Jane's glance reached him he lifted Mercer's glass and
placed it beside his own, shaking his head and murmuring
something that heightened the flush on Mercer's prettily
tinted cheeks.

Varta, his wife, an Argentinian of great chic and ani-
mation, watched them too, from her chair on Jack's right,
and nodded approval at her husband. Her smooth black
hair and eyes, her olive-toned skin, shone in the brilliant
light, but her flashing wit and sparkle were stilled too . . .
though that might have been because of her interest in
what Jack was saying.

On Varta's right sat Dr. Hamish Ames, also an American
though born in Brazil. The only small man in the group
and the oldest, he perched among them like a bright-eyed
bird, his twinkling glance beneath bushy gray brows missing nothing. He was telling now about a horse that one of
his sons had just acquired. "The finest piece of horseflesh
in Brazil, Noel," he was saying. "And I think you're probably the only man in the country who can ride her."

Noel did not answer, but Angelo and Mercer hurried to
cover his silence with questions and exclamations.

Jack's partner, banker, lawyer, even his doctor—there
was something significant about this impromptu dinner
after all. Noel, Tom, Angelo, Russell Todd's widow and—
still to come—Phil. Perhaps there was something even
more significant about it.

"Don't worry," Tom's bland voice said startlingly in her
ear. "If Jack's going to stage a show, it will be to a one-
night stand. Most of the people here are tourists—out to

see native life. What they see are other tourists or members of the foreign colony paying off social debts."

Again his eyes flickered distastefully to his left, touched Mercer and Angelo. "You'd never see this table together in a private house. Few Brazilians come to a place like this, and few old members of the colony either. That's one reason I suspect that Jack is up to something."

Jane did not know him well enough to judge, but his narrowed eyes and hurried words suggested that he did not feel as bland as he looked. While he talked she was struck with the isolation of Vivian. Usually the center of attention, she sat now apart, Noel's silent bulk on one side, Phil's empty chair on the other. Her eyes, tonight enormous and limpid, looked beyond the guests to the dance floor.

As course followed course and alert waiters hovered over the glasses Jane became uneasily aware that Jack's talents as a host were too perfect. His wit and high spirits were doing something to Noel. While Angelo and Tom and the doctor rose to him, fighting back at whatever challenge he was offering them, Noel grew more uncomfortable and rigid. Varta and Mercer were silent, their glances meeting, Varta trying, apparently, to reassure or restrain Mercer, who by the moment was becoming more flushed and resentful.

Suddenly Mercer's glance turned from Varta to Jack. "Now I know who—whom—who you remind me of, darling," she said sweetly. "Mephisto—only you don't—"

"The devil you say," drawled Angelo, his voice amused but his eyes sharp.

"My favorite character—in fiction," Jack told her. "But you flatter me, lady. I'm a simple man who bargains for men's goods, not souls."

"That's what I was going to say," she explained naively. "I mean—even if you aren't interested in souls—perhaps there is no profit in them—why don't you give men credit for having them? I—I mean you'd make more profit on their—their goods, wouldn't you?"

So far as Jane had observed in her two weeks of seeing Mercer about, the little widow's function had been purely ornamental. Everyone seemed to like her, pet her, include her, but never under any circumstances to expect her to think for herself, let alone for others. Now an amazed and bewildered silence met her words.

"As Mercer's physician, I think she means," Dr. Ames said with a twinkle, "that you're a very material devil, Jack, who should keep his horned hoofs off other and more sensitive people's toes."

Suppressed emotions found relief in a gale of laughter. Mercer turned indignantly on the doctor. "That's what I said, exactly what I said."

"Any defense, Jack?" Angelo asked.

Jack laughed and shook his head. "Not guilty, your honor."

"Yes, you are, Jack," Varta broke in. "You're guilty of bringing us together here for some purpose of your own, then keeping us on tenterhooks. Not only our toes but our ears are tingling. I'm a nervous woman—Doctor Ames will tell you so—and may have a crisis any minute now."

"For heaven's sake, come clean then, Jack," Tom Hughes urged. "Angelo's in no condition to finance the luxury of Doctor Ames' services at present. None of us," he added blandly as Angelo's head thrust round at him, "are, with this war playing havoc—"

"Sss-cipth the war," Mercer interrupted and sneezed like a kitten. "Skip the war, I mean. Go on, Mephisthto."

Jane looked from one to the other quickly. Outwardly all were at ease, amused and a little surprised perhaps at the effect of wine on Mercer but prepared to manufacture this innocuous pitter-patter until they could go home. Yet

though their voices were low and casual, their lips prop-
erly curved, their eyes were not amused. Veiled or emptily
clear, all were watching Jack tensely.

"You do me wrong," Jack assured them. "I'm not Mephisto but Cinderella." His glance went round the table, paused
on Vivian. "And even that poor girl had until midnight before she became a pumpkin."

"A little mixed but clear," Angelo said, and relief
warmed his drawl. "It's Vivian who holds the secret."

For the first time attention swung to her. She looked
straight at Jack, her eyes alight as they pressed her for an
explanation, then smiled and held up one hand.

"It's really Jack's party," she began deliberately, her gaze
still on him, "but I don't enjoy suspense either. He's shy
because he doesn't like to talk about—his heart. Though
we've all been talking about it and trying to make him take
a rest for a year. That man killed by a car at our gates this
morning was the last straw. Jack ran out when Jane found
him, ran in and out a dozen times—"

Jack's face did not change as Vivian spoke; he watched
and listened as intently as the rest, but now abruptly he
rose and made his way round the table.

"This change of plan calls for a little rehearsing," he
said, lifting Vivian to her feet, and to her, "Shall we dance?
And talk?"

Laughter and protests swept the table again as they
moved out on the dance floor.

"My mistake in swinging the spotlight to Vivian," Angelo apologized. "This is Jack's show. Nothing to do but
wait till he's ready to ring up the curtain and announce
the great departure. About time, too." He lifted his glass
to Noel. "Here's luck to you, old man, while you carry on
alone."

Noel made no answer. His eyes were on the dance floor,
and the others, one by one, turned to look also. Jane last

of all. Her confusion over the turn of events was heightened by meeting the penetrating but enigmatic glance Dr. Ames had fixed on her.

Jack and Vivian, moving slowly to the music, were obviously not rehearsing. They appeared unaware of where they were, to be moving together as if through space, freed of everything but rhythm and spirit.

As Jane glanced across the floor to other tables she saw that more and more eyes were watching them with increasing absorption. Jack somehow did resemble a modern Mephisto, his slender body lithe as a blade, his dark face intent, unsmiling. Vivian, her lustrous head just beneath his, her bouffant skirt drifting about her, suggested one of Brazil's radiant butterflies. And the changing light—ruby, gold, sapphire, emerald—playing over them as they moved from square to square of the glass floor gave an eerie, other-world remoteness to the scene.

Something swelled and tightened in Jane's throat. Hot, dry tears burned against her eyelids. She turned away, reaching for her glass of water, but she did not pick it up. Noel, watching still, faint lines of white about his mouth, startled her. As she looked at him the music bore Jack and Vivian past the table. Noel half rose.

"Vivian!" he said hoarsely.

He sank back immediately, but it was too late. Jack stopped, his arm still supporting her. Then, smiling, he led her back to her chair.

"Jack," she implored there, clinging to his hand, "take me home now."

He did not answer. Over her head he was looking at Noel. Jane felt as if the room had grown empty and cold. "I'd like to go home too," she said.

Jack lifted his hand, restraining the others who moved quickly to rise. "No," he said, not turning from Noel. "No, we must wait for Phil."

As if on a cue, Phil appeared. He had come up unseen, and in the tensity of the moment his cool greeting was electrical. He did not speak but nodded swiftly about the table, then fixed his eyes speculatively, warily, on Jack.

Mercer giggled nervously. "Black magic!" she cried. "Do it again, Mephisto."

No one heard her. Noel had risen, and attention was focused on the three men facing one another over Vivian's lovely head. During that brief but timeless instant she sat like something done in marble. Then Jack laughed and drew out the chair beside her.

"Reserved for you, senhor," he said to Phil.

"You are mistaken, my good man," Phil told him.

"No?" Jack's voice rose clearly in the stillness. At other tables men and women were turning to watch. "A man after my own heart. No, my error. A man after my own wife's heart."

No one moved or spoke. Yet some wave of emotion rose from the table, hung over it ominously.

"Your error again, Jack." Phil's voice was low but, in the quiet, as clear as Jack's.

A smile flickered across Jack's lips. "My next will not be an error," he said.

His open right hand swept up and struck Phil across the mouth.

10
Vivian Wakes Early

Long after midnight, while Vivian's sobs still echoed through the corridor, Jane stood at her window gazing into the black night. Helpless to aid either Vivian or Jack, she longed to get away. But there was no place she could go, no one to whom she could turn—now.

Her ears still ached from the silence that had fallen over the ballroom as Jack's hand had cracked like a whip against Phil's face; from the silence in which they had all somehow made their way to the steps, the silence in which Jack's guests had gone their separate ways, the silence in which Arnaldo had driven them home.

How could Jack, with his passion for privacy, have staged such a scene in public? she asked herself for the hundredth time. Why would he do it when he knew that before morning the entire city would ring with it?

The stillness now, as Vivian abruptly became quiet, started a new thought. Had that been Jack's purpose? Had he wanted to center attention on that scene or group? For itself or to divert it from something he didn't want known or talked about? But what could be so important that he would sacrifice his wife, his partner, himself, to protect?

The gardens offered the only refuge from such thoughts, and she caught up a wrap and slipped silently out the back entrance. The gardens, however, could give neither solace nor reassurance. Incessant jabs of coppery lightning webbed the sky, illumining the ragged edges of whirling black clouds. Wind rushing in from the sea rocked and twisted the branches of mango trees and filled the air with the roar of waves crashing on the beach.

The tumult released thoughts that lay like numbed things in her mind. They poured over her, a senseless chaos from the hours since the owl had waked her to find Jack in her doorway and death in the gates.

Heedless of time, of the gravel piercing the thin soles of her slippers, of the flowers weaving patterns of light against the darkness when the lightning ripped through it, she walked back and forth. Fear for Jack tortured her, for Vivian, fear most of all for her own helplessness and ignorance.

Suddenly she found herself held fast. A rose stem, whipped free of its trellis by the wind, had laced its sharp thorns into her wrap. As she stooped, loosening them, somewhere near her gravel creaked.

Someone else was in the gardens! Slowly she turned her head, waiting for the lightning. It came, to flash over solid black clouds in long, quivering tongues. But it revealed nothing about her save the swaying masses of flowers and behind them the darker mass of the deserted servants' quarters.

Arnaldo had locked the gates before he left. The hedge was as solid as granite. Nevertheless she turned uneasily back to the house.

After a few hasty steps she walked more slowly, reassured. Against the light of the corridor she had seen Vivian's figure outlined for a moment. Perhaps she too had come to the gardens, for refuge or to look for her, Jane thought.

But when she entered the house Jack's and Vivian's door was closed. Only the corridor lights and those in her own room were burning.

Dreading the long night, she entered her room. Sleep, of course, was out of the question. But before the heavy black clouds opened and rain deluged the city she was asleep. When she heard Vivian calling her the early morning sun, sifting between the bars of her windows, was laying a design of broken light on her floor. As she sat up Vivian threw open the door.

"Quick! Come!" she cried. "I can't wake Jack."

Vivian did not stop at their bedroom door but sped on to the library. Jane, entering a moment later, found her on her knees beside Jack's chair, just inside the French doors.

In his black silk robe, pajamas and slippers Jack sat there motionless, his head bent toward her, but to her frantic repetitions of his name he made no answer. He might have fallen into the deep sleep of physical and nervous exhaustion, but when Jane touched his hand she knew he had not. Even in the shock of that moment her sister's hysterical voice, coming to her from far away, seemed a false or artificial note there.

"He is not sleeping, Vivian," she heard her own voice saying quietly. "You must know that."

"He must be," Vivian insisted. "He must be."

Jane looked into the dark, handsome face, into those strange, fixed eyes. Perhaps there was no expression there, perhaps it was his attitude, the way one hand gripped the chair, that slowly, irrevocably, gave her an impression of horror, of horror and something else.

"Vivian," she whispered, "it's as if he saw death coming to him like a person, isn't it? He couldn't believe it."

Vivian nodded. "I don't think he ever really believed Doctor Ames."

"Have you called the doctor?"

When Vivian, relieved to be able to do something, had gone to telephone, Jane remained in the library, grateful for those few moments alone. That Jack should die—other people, yes, but not Jack!

Rising quickly, she opened the French doors and let the fresh blue day, sparkling after the heavy night rains, flood the room and Jack. As she stepped back light flashed in the sun from a sapphire that Vivian had once called Jack's third eye. It shone from its deep bed in the ring on his left hand, now flung out over the arm of the chair next the door.

Jane looked uncertainly from ring to hand. The long fingers were folded closely, as if they held something that even death could not take from him. Perhaps a note, a message, Jane thought swiftly. He might have had warning, time— With trembling but sure fingers she stooped and forced it open.

Pressed to the palm, so tightly that it had cut its irregular outline into the skin of his hand, was a bit of broken Venetian glass. As she picked it up the sun glittered on its gold and greens and peacock blues.

The colors were vaguely familiar. Somewhere about the house she had seen glass like that. But how could this broken bit have come to Jack in those last minutes of his life? Why, at such a time, should he have clung to it? Seeking explanation, her eyes went back to his hand, dropped from it to the floor. She saw no other pieces of glass, but there was something—

On the shining wood mosaic almost directly beneath his hand was a film so faint that if she had not opened the doors to the strong light she might never have noticed it. A small patch of some yellowish-white powder had drifted there.

Crouching over it, she could see that in some places it was thinner than in others, that the thin parts formed the broken outline of a curve. Within the curve were two tiny dots of clear floor.

Although sunlight streamed over her, Jane shook suddenly with cold. "Death like a person" must have stood very close to Jack to have made that strange impression.

"If anything should happen to me . . ." Jack had said. But he had meant death like—like Pinto's. He sat there so quietly now, surely and only because his heart, already fatigued, had been unable to beat longer after the strains of Saturday.

She sprang up, her hand pressed to her lips. Pinto had lain in the gates just as quietly, the victim of a hit-and-run driver, the police had said. But Pinto had been murdered because of what he had told Jack. And now Jack was dead!

Vivian's footsteps sounded in the corridor as Jane stooped to touch her finger to the powder. Instead she drew the chair toward the door an inch or two necessary to cover it. The change was not enough to disturb Jack's body, but something crashed like a clap of thunder in her ears.

When Vivian entered Jane was on her knees picking up scattered cigarettes and red-orange seeds from the floor.

"Jack's box," she murmured. "I knocked it off the table."

"Doctor Ames is coming at once," Vivian told her, unheeding. "He was just leaving for his fazenda. I called Noel's apartment and left a message. He always rides till noon on Sunday, but perhaps they can reach him somewhere. And Phil is coming . . ."

She seemed reluctant to stop speaking, but under Jane's gaze her voice trailed off into silence.

"Phil!"

"Of course. He's the best friend I have in Rio. Why not?"

Jane rose and turned the bit of glass in the pocket of her robe before she spoke. Then, "When did Jack come to the library?" she asked carefully.

"Soon after we came home. I—I went to sleep." Vivian paused, added defensively, "I had to, Jane. I couldn't bear any more. I took some powders, more than enough. I didn't care if I never waked again."

"What woke you? I mean when—"

"About six. Even with the powders I didn't really sleep, and I had dreadful dreams. I thought I was tied to a moving belt that was carrying me into some roaring machinery, and above the noise I could hear Jack's voice shouting orders—"

She stopped again, horror-stricken.

"Oh, Jane, perhaps I did hear his voice. Perhaps he was calling me—when he felt—knew—"

"And then?" Jane was startled at the coolness of her own voice, her sense of detachment. She seemed frozen somehow. But Vivian was not, and tears came readily to her. Why didn't they come now? Why was Vivian staring back at her, dry eyed and tense.

"When I woke up, you mean? Jack wasn't in his bed, and for a minute I was so—so dazed I couldn't remember anything. Then I remembered—last night. Sometimes lately Jack came—used to come—here to read when he couldn't sleep. So I . . ."

Her voice trailed off again as Jane's eyes sought the clock above the fireplace. Ten minutes of seven.

"Then you knew a little after six—you knew when you came for me that Jack was dead."

"Yes, I knew—in a way." Vivian shivered and drew her robe more tightly about her. "But I—Jane, he must have died here—alone—in the dark. There were no lights on when I came in. I was so stunned. I've been such a fool, such a crazy fool. I just sat here and thought of the miserable failure I'd made of our life in Rio. I didn't think of him as dead then. I can't now."

"But later—almost an hour later—you said you couldn't wake him."

"What does it matter what I said?" Vivian cried despairingly. "I wanted you—"

Jane understood the appeal in Vivian's voice but she could not respond to it. She was seeing again that glimpse of her sister running out of the night into the light of the back door.

"You—you didn't leave your room at all last night?" she asked finally.

Vivian shrank away from her, her eyes darkening. "No. No, I went to bed, I tell you."

As she spoke another voice, soft and familiar, spoke behind them.

"Minha senhora."

Maria stood there, immaculate as usual in white uniform and turban.

"Doctor Ames here."

11

Dr. Ames Gives an Order

The next three hours passed before Jane's tearless eyes like scenes behind dark glass. After a nod and a word to each of them Dr. Ames bent over Jack. Shortly he motioned first Jane, then Vivian, aside. He worked silently and, when he straightened, paused to look from one to the other before directing his questions to Vivian.

She stood with her back to the windows, her eyes as tearless as Jane's, and answered his questions in her clipped, smartly accented voice without looking directly at either of them.

No, Jack had not complained of his heart or anything else when he returned from the Copacabana. He had not spoken a single word, had simply prepared for bed, then gone to the library to read, as he had often done during the nights of the past two weeks.

No, she did not believe he had consulted any other physician or had medicines of any kind in the library. Dr. Ames knew how difficult it had always been to persuade Jack to take any care of his health.

No, so far as she knew, Jack had not intended to announce at the dinner that he was going to take a rest. She did not know his reason for giving the dinner. Perhaps he had simply wanted excitement and amusement; he had been overwrought and upset as a result of the commotion caused by Jane's wandering out in the night and finding that dead man in the gates. She did not look at Jane but the doctor did.

No, she had heard no sound in the night, but Jack could have called without her hearing him. She had taken three sleeping powders—

"Three! You know one was enough," the doctor had broken in sharply. "You're to go to bed yourself, Vivian, and stay there until I can see you again."

Phil, appearing in the doorway at that moment, had put an end to the questions. Dr. Ames greeted him with relief, and together they carried Jack to his bed. Vivian, following close behind them, had shut the door just as Jane, following her, reached it.

Thereafter, literally and figuratively, doors closed wherever Jane turned. She had remained desolately in the corridor, her presence restraining the servants who, wide eyed and mute, watched from the kitchen door.

Only the doctor addressed her, and that briefly, when he emerged to find her there.

"I'd like a word with you," he said and led the way into the living room whose black and silver decor, with electric-blue and scarlet accents, appeared cold and bizarre now in spite of the morning sunshine.

Dr. Ames obviously was upset, too, by the death of his friend. He took quick short steps up and down the room, stopping only once to tell her irritably to sit down somewhere.

"I'm sorry that I must get up to my fazenda as soon as I can," he said jerkily as he paced. "Tony—my youngest son—has had an accident. Tried to ride a new horse— My wife telephoned just before Vivian called me."

He came to a stop in front of Jane. "But I've signed a certificate of death from natural causes, and Phil—and Noel when he comes—will take care of everything for Vivian."

His bright eyes studied her from beneath the bushy brows, then he drew up a chair. He did not sit down, however, but remained standing, one hand gripping the back.

"There are two things I want to say to you. One is that your sister is in a very serious condition. Those powders, for one thing. Strain, for another. We won't go into that now."

As Jane neither spoke nor moved he sat down, leaned forward, to say less brusquely, "This may seem hard to you, but you must believe I mean it for the best. You can make Vivian's life—and your own—for the next few days much easier by keeping out of her way. I've ordered her to bed, and you must see that no well-meaning friends are allowed to rush in on her. That's your job. Let her maid—Theresa?—take care of her."

"You mean I'm not to see, to speak—"

He broke in briskly again, his voice a tone or two higher. "This isn't easy for me either, Miss George. I've known Jack for years. I—I'm shocked too at his death. Let me finish."

Jerking up his wrist, he looked at his watch, went on even more hurriedly. "I not only advise you, I order you, as Vivian's doctor, to see as little as possible of your sister. And"—again she met that penetrating, enigmatic glance—"and I suggest that you yourself take the first ship available for Buenos Aires. You're none too fit yourself, and the trip will do you good. This has been no experience for a child like—"

"Hardly a child," Jane murmured bitterly.

"No? Good. Then you can understand what I'm saying. When you return, if Vivian feels more like herself, come back here. If not, my best advice is that you go on to the States."

"Doctor Ames!"

Jane tried to rise, but he stopped both words and movement with a gesture.

"Remember what I've said about Vivian and think seriously of what I'm saying to you. I'll be back tomorrow—tonight, if possible. We can talk further then."

Jane watched him catch up his hat and bag, hurry across the room and out the wide-open doors without another word. His head bent forward, his short legs taking short twinkling steps on the gleaming mosaic floor and skittery rugs, he almost gave the impression of scuttling.

And she had the curious feeling that he had been saying one word for Vivian, two for himself. How different he was, even though a friend of Jack's, from the old family doctor who had stood by her when her father died.

Dr. Ames wanted her to leave. So did Maria. So did Phil—at least, she corrected herself, he wanted to get her away from the house. So must Vivian, or would the doctor have urged it?

She set her chin stubbornly. Vivian and Jack had invited her here, had made their home her home. She would not leave it now unless Vivian herself suggested it.

The shrill bell of the telephone roused her, and she rose unsteadily. Surely it was too early for anyone to have learned of Jack's death yet! She heard Inah's swift patter up the corridor, her voice answering almost in a whisper, then her swift return to the kitchen. And silence.

For a moment she wished it had been some friend calling. This silence of the servants, usually so voluble over the slightest happening . . . This stony silence of Vivian . . . Now the brusque haste of the little doctor whom she had liked on first sight . . . And Phil—she could not tell about Phil. He had quietly taken charge of Vivian, of the house too, she realized suddenly, as she heard him at the telephone asking central to close the line until further notice. She sank deep in a chair, unwilling that he should see her there.

A moment later she knew that if the doctor had ordered Vivian to bed she had not gone. Jane heard her join Phil at the telephone, urge something in a low, feverish tone. She was aware that they came to the living room, turned away at sight of her. She heard Vivian's voice again but not the words, then the doors of the dining room closing together. Numb and dry eyed, she sat on until Noel arrived.

Still in riding clothes, his eyes dim and dull with pain, he walked into the living room and stood waiting, a huge silhouette against the light of the day outside. He did not answer her low greeting or move until she touched his arm. Then he followed her heavily across the room and down the corridor to the dining room. He made no move to enter until she stepped inside herself and again, with her hand on his arm, drew him in.

Phil rose and spoke, but Vivian only looked at him, her eyes shiny and tight in a face as white and finely drawn as a cameo's. Jane drew out a chair for him beside the long jacarandá table where they sat, then, after a brief hesitation, drew out another and seated herself beside him.

Sunshine did not reach this formal room until afternoon. Now, with its dark paneled walls and dark, heavy carved pieces of old colonial Brazilian furniture, it was dim and cool. Vivian hated the room, used it only for entertaining. She would never have brought Phil there if the living room had been unoccupied, Jane knew.

Listening, she offered no suggestions, was asked for none, as they discussed in low tones the arrangements to be made. Though everything else in Rio moves at a leisurely pace, death and the events that follow it are the exception. Within twenty-four hours, according to Brazilian law, the body must be interred.

Phil, giving no sign of what he thought or felt about last night's scene, took skillful charge here too. Vivian clung to his arm, seldom speaking except to second, in that feverish whisper, every suggestion he made. Noel, quiet, almost bewildered, agreed docilely to whatever they decided and accepted, with a slow nod, the arrangements assigned to him.

Jack's oldest and best friend, Jane thought, watching him—and he was alone, also, now. Vivian and Phil. . . .

Silence, awkward and pregnant, fell when they had finished. Jane knew that Phil's gaze had turned on her occasionally, felt it now as he rose, loosening Vivian's clasp on his arm, but she kept her eyes on Noel.

"I must see Doctor Omlie at once," Phil was saying. "This is Sunday, you know. He'll be on his way to church soon."

Noel rose stiffly, and Vivian sprang up between them. "I'm going with you, Phil. I— Don't leave me here."

She might as well have put into words, Jane felt, shrinking, that it was not the presence of death in the house that terrified her. Hostility, mistrust, even fear, were all apparent in that one swift glance Vivian gave her.

Without a word Jane rose and left them. She sought automatically a deep chair on the side veranda and there, shortly, she heard the two cars drive away.

Behind her the house was silent. About her the lawns and gardens were warm with sun sparkling on the rain-refreshed grass and trees. Hardly a sound, save the beat of the waves, came over the hedge. Even Jack lay on his bed as if sleeping. Outwardly she could see no difference between this Sunday morning and the others she had spent in Rio.

Here it was fantastic to think that the man who had built himself so firmly into her life was gone—suddenly and alone. And that the sister whom she had adored so passionately was gone also and in a way even more cruel than by death.

The idea that Vivian feared her she thrust aside as absurd, and yet in some deep corner of her mind she knew it was not absurd. She was afraid herself of the memories moving dimly there—words of the day before, actions, implications. "I wish I were dead. Or he was." That resolute tautening of Vivian's body against hers as she held her sister in her arms . . . That glimpse of Vivian running into the light of the back door after midnight . . . Vivian's assurance that she had not left her room . . . Above all, Vivian's words at the Copacabana, pointing a reminder that all might hear and remember about Saturday's strain on Jack's already overstrained heart . . .

She fought off each memory as it rose. She was overwrought herself, imagining things as Vivian was. When the funeral was over, when they had time to rest, they would forget these dark suspicions and frictions, understand one another again. She was all Vivian had now, Vivian all that remained to her. "I must wait, stand by Vivian," she told herself over and over.

The shaded panes of the open French doors of the library caught her reflection as she lay back in her chair, so like and yet so unlike her sister—the same eyes, straight nose, lips. But she looked younger than Vivian now and, because the glass did not catch fully her rounded, sturdy chin, more helpless and bereft. It did catch her loneliness and aloneness—and registered her startled movement as she realized that the time had come when she must open the little drawer!

12

Garcia Brings a Report

The thought alternately terrified and reassured her. At least it was something she could do, something that might put an end to all this mystery. Yet she made no move to rise and remained gazing with unfocused eyes across the lawns to the hedge.

When that dark figure came between her and the hedge, she did not know. But suddenly her eyes, refocusing, met the probing stare of a pair of small black ones.

A heavily built man stood on the path below the veranda. His dark florid face sloped down from a narrow forehead to pouchlike cheeks and jaws and on to a thick bare throat. His hair, brushed straight back, passed through a variety of shades from dark brown to light, almost yellow at the ends standing upright in the morning breeze.

Although she was accustomed to see men, women and children in all sorts of bathing costumes making their way to and from the beach, this man in trunks and vividly striped bathrobe was like no one she had ever seen before. Incredulously she stared at him; coolly he studied her.

"Bom dia, senhora," he addressed her, omitting the deferential *minha*. "My name is Garcia. I bring a report Mr. Houghton wishes to have."

From the pocket of his robe he drew out a long envelope. Jane, rising, held out her hand for it, but he did not place the report in it.

"Give it to me, please," she ordered, controlling her voice with difficulty. "Mr. Houghton has been expecting it."

Still he withheld it. "I could see him for a moment? I did not bring it yesterday because I come to Copacabana today to swim with friends."

Yesterday! If he had brought the report yesterday, at least one of the strains Jack had been under would have been removed. "Mr. Houghton sees no one on Sunday. Give me the report," she repeated coldly.

His small eyes slipped over her slyly, insinuatingly, almost as if he shared some secret understanding with her. With a gesture, indefinable but insolent, he placed the envelope in her hand, then, with another Bom dia, turned away.

Jane called Maria. "See that that man leaves the grounds and have Arnaldo lock the gates. No one else must come in until the senhora returns."

Shocked and angry that Garcia should have brought the report now, too late, she walked back firmly to the open doors of the library. On the threshold she hesitated. The rich tones of the room, the arrangement of the furniture, were just as she had always seen them, but now they appeared faded, desolate.

Stepping in at last, she closed and locked the doors behind her, crossed to the corridor and locked that door also. Then, remembering that Jack had done the same thing less than twenty-four hours before, yet some eyes had watched and ears listened, she drew the heavy curtains and turned on the lights. Only a little more than half-past ten, the clock over the fireplace recorded. She had plenty of time. Vivian would not hurry to return.

But when she had taken Jack's chair before the jacarandá table she could not bring her fingers to press the little knot. Garcia's report offered a moment of respite, and, taking it up distastefully, she slipped it out of the

envelope. How could Jack have had such a repellent creature in his employ? No wonder he distrusted him!

The report, however, was merely a statement of the
income and expenditures of the Santa Maria and José Coffee Company for January, February and March. She had
expected something much more interesting and important
after the fuss Jack had made about it. So far as she could
see, only two things were significant—the final figure in
red, showing in contos a substantial loss, when both Jack
and Noel took pride in the fact that all their companies
were solvent, and the fact that the Santa Maria and José
was a coffee company.

Coffee, like a macabre theme, had run through the
past twenty-four hours—in the branch in Pinto's hand, in
Jack's words in the library, on the scraps of papers she had
burned, now here!

She dropped the report as if it had stung her, sat erect.
Jack had said Pinto had been murdered. He had seen no
more than the police. Yet he had seen in Pinto's death a
threat to his own life, to something that meant more to
him than his life. The little spray of coffee in Pinto's hand
had told him, he had said. Could it have been information
about coffee, then, that Pinto had brought him two weeks
ago? Information about this Santa Maria and José Coffee
Company, perhaps? Yet Jack had warned her never to believe anyone or anything that asserted he had any interest
in coffee!

The answer must lie in the instructions and papers he
had left in the little drawer. With fingers that trembled,
though partly with eagerness now, she felt for the knot.
The little drawer dropped into her hand.

As she took up the papers and laid them aside one by
one her hand trembled still more. Jack had not shown
her that sheaf of papers he had placed here, but she had
glimpsed typewriting and had thought them to be letters

and pages of typed instructions. And he had assured her she would find in them all the information she would need.

These pages were printed! And again they concerned coffee! Pages torn from reports of the São Paulo Coffee Institute and of the National Coffee Department. World coffee production by countries. Coffee production in Brazil by states. Records of daily shipments from Santos, Rio de Janeiro, Victoria and other ports for February and early March. Not one word that offered instruction or information for her.

The figures blurred and jumped before her eyes when she went through the pages again. As she dropped them one by one to the table a tiny tick caught her ear. And when she picked them up something caught her eye. In the roughly torn edge of the bottom sheet was a crumb of glass so small that when she held it under the table lamp only a single glint of green and gold flashed.

For a moment the room whirled darkly around Jane. When it cleared, leaving her white and shaken, a cold flame of anger burned steadily within her. With firm fingers she separated the bottom sheet, with its fragment of glass, from the rest and placed it in an envelope. Then she faced the fear that had been gnawing at her heart.

Jack had not died of heart failure. He had been murdered!

The hand that had caused his death, that had stolen the information which would have led to discovery, had held a bit of the same glass she had taken from Jack's hand. The owner of that hand had left these substitute printed pages—and he had left something else. That curve in the powder on the floor beside Jack's chair could be the curve of a heelprint!

But when she sprang to move Jack's chair the filmy patch was gone.

For a time she sat huddled in that chair, drawing some obscure comfort from the fact that it was Jack's, while she tried to order and answer the questions swirling in her mind.

A light sound, a rubbing, brought her to her feet and noiselessly to a window. No one was on the veranda. Swiftly she made for the corridor door, flung it open.

Inah, on her knees, brushing about the feet of the wall table that stood beside the library door, looked up apprehensively. Almost white skinned, with provocative eyes that had completely subjugated the usually unsusceptible Arnaldo and a pert manner that amused Jack and annoyed Vivian, Inah was neither provocative nor pert now.

"I didn't do it, Miss Jane," she said instantly. "I found it. Just now."

"Do what?"

Inah held up the slender base of a Venetian glass candlestick. "It was behind that door, Miss Jane, see?"

Scrambling to her feet, she swung out the right half of the living-room doors that always stood folded back into the corridor. In the angle formed by the doorjamb and wall lay a golden candle and a few pieces of glass.

"Yes, I see, Inah," Jane told her. "Just an accident."

She longed to pick up each piece herself but, restraining the desire, turned to the table. In its place beside the library door stood the mate to the broken candlestick, its golden candle held high.

"Give the pieces to me," she ordered, "and if you find any more, bring them to my room. Oh, and if you find any seeds in the library from Mr. Jack's cigarette box, I want them too. I broke it this morning."

Inah picked up the glass cautiously but calmly, now that she was not to be blamed for breaking the candlestick. When she had finished Jane carried them to her room.

From her door she glimpsed Maria busy in the kitchen and crossed the corridor to ask, "Why are all the servants here on Sunday, Maria? How could they have known so soon that we would need them?"

Maria lifted grief-filled eyes from her work at the table. "I send Arnaldo for them," she said simply. "I have bad dream."

Again Jane stood helpless before that barrier behind which Maria moved so surely. After a moment she started, turned hastily back to her room, hoping that the quick tears filling Maria's eyes had hidden from them the resolution which had formed in her mind in the library.

Jack had been murdered, and she was going to find his murderer.

13

Noel Receives Coffee Leaves

During the almost silent dinner, while Vivian infrequently sipped her wine and Noel ate steadily through whatever was served him, Jane was conscious of Phil's veiled scrutiny. From time to time, also, Vivian's eyes skimmed over her and away. But she was too occupied with her own thoughts to wonder. She had a decision to make. Everything else must wait.

From the moment Vivian had returned with Phil and the gates had been opened and the telephone reconnected she had had no time for thought, no time for anything but to receive the friends, messages and flowers that arrived from all parts of the city and later the telegrams from other parts of Brazil, even from such distant points as Buenos Aires and Santiago. Word of Jack's death seemed to have sped over the continent on light waves.

With Vivian sealed away in her sitting room, Noel wandering blindly in the gardens, Phil absent on some final arrangements about the service, she had been submerged in a thousand unfamiliar details. She had welcomed the activity and now, though physically exhausted, found her mind clear and alert. She knew what she was going to do; all that remained was to decide how she was going to do it.

She waited until they were at last in the living room. Vivian lay back in a deep blue leather chair, the black lace of her gown accenting her whiteness, the lamp behind her making an aura of pure light of her hair. Noel sank on a divan and remained as if carved there. Jack's death was too severe a blow for him to raise his head easily, but he was making a great effort. Feeling her eyes upon him, he lifted his own, and Jane turned quickly from the naked sorrow she saw in them.

Her glance moved to Phil, and for a moment she resented his presence as Noel did. He leaned back in his chair, apparently watching the smoke of his cigarette curve toward the ceiling but aware, Jane knew, of every movement or change of expression in the room.

With her eyes on the clean line of his jaw she spoke quietly and distinctly. "Is it possible to postpone the service? Shouldn't we have an autopsy?"

The minute hand of the crystal clock on a table behind Phil jerked from six minutes past ten to seven, to eight. Had she really spoken aloud? Vivian had stiffened in her chair; Noel remained as though he had not heard; Phil had not moved except to flick ashes from his cigarette into a tray. And no one spoke.

Inah, entering with tiny cups of Brazilian coffee, broke the undercurrent of emotion that flowed among them. When she had gone Phil leaned forward, crushing out his cigarette.

"Why, Jane?"

Aware that Vivian's head had turned slightly, that Noel's eyes again had lifted to hers, Jane hesitated, then answered slowly, "Because I do not believe that Jack died of heart failure."

"Jane!" Vivian's voice was barely audible.

"I'm sorry, Vivian. I wanted to talk with you first, but you gave me no opportunity. I had to speak before it is too late. I think we should be sure—"

"Sure of what?" Noel's deep voice asked.

"Sure of what—killed him."

"Killed is not the usual word, Jane," Phil said. "Did you use it intentionally?"

"Yes."

Silence curtained them again. Noel broke it.

"It is possible to ask for an autopsy," he began in his slow, precise English, "but do you realize what it would mean? We will place Doctor Ames in a most difficult position—and ourselves—if his diagnosis is proved correct."

He paused but, when no one came to his assistance, went on reluctantly. "Assume it proves him wrong. Your position, yours and Vivian's, would be even more unfortunate. You are living in a country that operates under different laws than those of the States. To secure an autopsy, we must first ask the police for a permit. We must give the police the results of that autopsy. Do you want that to happen? The newspapers—"

"No! No!" Vivian cried. "It's unthinkable, Jane. I won't allow it."

Phil's eyes had not moved from Jane's face. "You mean suicide, of course," he interposed quietly, "and you may be right. Everyone knows that Jack was exhausted from overwork and worry about his health. But what would be gained by proving suicide?"

Jane tried to draw her eyes from his, to speak, but his eyes held hers.

"And much might be lost," he went on, directly to her. "Jack was not only one of the best-known foreigners in Brazil but in all South America. If you destroy the prestige of a man in his position, you affect the whole foreign colony here. That may not seem possible or important to you, but Noel will tell you that it is."

"Yes," Noel agreed, "Phil is right."

Phil still held Jane's eyes. She could not turn from him though she longed to ask why a man whom Jack had struck publicly should defend his reputation so eloquently now. For each word he said aloud she felt he was saying another to her, warning her, compelling her to silence.

"One more thing. Noel may not feel that he can speak of it, but I can. In South America, in the States and Europe, the house of Houghton and Hardwicke has a reputation for the highest financial integrity. Word of Jack's death in tomorrow night's papers will be a sensation. From suicide it would be a catastrophe. Scores, hundreds of people's investments would be jeopardized."

"I won't allow it," Vivian said again.

Jane looked from one to the other. "I'm sorry," she offered finally. "I hadn't thought of all that. I simply thought that an autopsy would make it easier."

"Make what easier?" Phil asked quickly.

"To find out who killed Jack. But there must be other ways. I intend—"

Vivian, with a stifled cry, rose and moved toward her, swayed, fell.

Noel somehow was beside her, caught her. Even as she led the way to her own room, for Vivian to be put to bed there, Jane marveled at the swiftness of that slow, awkward man and at his gentleness.

Theresa arrived in a moment. "You go, Miss Jane. I know what to do."

"Does she faint often?"

"Plenty times."

In the living room Noel and Phil were waiting.

"You must get some rest too, Jane," Phil urged. "Have you any idea how white you are, how you're trembling? Please go. Noel and I will stay here."

Perhaps because she wished so keenly for a friendly, understanding word Jane thought she heard a note of genuine sympathy in his voice, read concern in his face. Noel too. As he towered over her his lips moved as if he would like to find a phrase that would help her. Failing, he placed a hand awkwardly on her shoulder.

"It isn't necessary, really," she said gratefully. "The servants are here, and we're quite all right."

Reluctant as they were to leave her, each of them, she could see, was even more unwilling to go without the other. At last she moved them both to the doors, across the veranda to the steps and down to their cars, Phil's behind Noel's in the driveway.

She stood on the lawn beside them until their engines started, then turned back toward the steps. A hoarse exclamation from Noel swung her round. He was half standing over his steering wheel, ripping something from it with violent hands. With a furious gesture he lifted it high and hurled it to the ground. Then his car swept out the gates.

Phil was out of his car instantly, drawing Jane back as she stooped to see what it was.

"It—it's only a coffee branch," she told him shakily.

"That's all," he said, picking it up. "Noel seems to have inherited Jack's hatred for the stuff."

He said no more until they reached the steps. As he took her hand again he added urgently, "Jane, I'll be back in one hour. Have Arnaldo open the gates for me."

Before she could speak he was gone. And the coffee branch with him.

14

Arnaldo Makes a Discovery

Arnaldo did not open the gates for Phil an hour later. Jane never thought of him again until she saw him at the service Monday morning. His car had hardly cleared the gates when Arnaldo stepped out of the shrubbery and locked them. Then he came swiftly to the steps where Jane still stood.

Trim and straight in his green chauffeur's uniform, very Brazilian, no one would have recognized him as Maria's son. The white and Indian blood of his father had made of him a different type entirely, brown and taciturn.

"Come," he said. "Come, Miss Jane."

Deep in thought, Jane did not hear him. Jack gone, the coffee branch had come to Noel! And he had understood its message. If not, why had he cried out like that, hurled it away as if it were a poisonous snake?

"Miss Jane, come," Arnaldo repeated.

She looked down. "Come? Where?"

"I show you. Come quick, Miss Jane."

Once Jane had thought his faithful imitation of Jack amusing. Now, as she followed him, it was disturbing. He walked like Jack, moved his head and hands in the same short, swift gestures. She was even more disturbed when he did not stop at the gardens but moved rapidly down the paths to the garage.

Only a single light burning above the closed double doors illumined the darkness there. Arnaldo did not step into the light. Circling round by a dark path, he stopped before the little door that opened into the garage at the side. Before he unlocked it he waited for her to reach him.

"Go in," he said when she hesitated. "Do not have fear."

Jane stepped into blackness in which the masses of the two cars were blacker still. Arnaldo stepped in after her and locked the door.

As she heard the key turn her heart leaped to her mouth. Someone else was in the garage with them! Then the bright eye of a small flashlight glowed in Arnaldo's hand, swept downward to the floor.

Sitting there, tied to the rear wheel of the sports car, his feet stretched out before him, bound too, was Garcia. Above an old towel tied about his mouth his black eyes gleamed in the light.

"I find him," Arnaldo said. "He try to go in libry."

Placing a box in front of Garcia, he rolled his eyes significantly toward the rooms above. "Sit down, Miss Jane. I talk low."

Jane stared from the stern-faced chauffeur to the twisting accountant. Her head ached, her whole body ached, with the shock and emotions of the past two days. Now this dark garage, these strange and alien men in the little circle of light before her, seemed like some fantasy her weary mind might have created.

But the box was real enough. So was her anger that this man should have dared approach the library where Jack now lay among flowers and greens.

"Garcia not bad man," Arnaldo said after a moment. "Jus' big fool. This morning he give you paper. It wrong one. He come—"

"Let Garcia tell me." Jane took the flash from Arnaldo, trained it on the accountant's face.

Blinded by the light, he turned his head, was silent. Jane lowered the flash.

"It is true," Garcia admitted then. "I brought two reports to Copacabana this morning. One was the H and H report for Mr. Houghton. The other was a small one I made for a friend. I gave that one to you."

"Why didn't you come to the door and ask for it?"

"I did not know when I gave it to you that Mr. Houghton was dead. When I came back Inah told me. Many people were there. I was afraid you would say for me to come back later. I—I must have that report for the morning. All day I have worried. Tonight I think to come—"

His glib words choked off apprehensively. Arnaldo, too, was gazing at Jane in alarm.

She was unaware of them. The flash and her eyes were fixed on Garcia's shoes. In their worn rubber heels were four round nubs. At the base of each nub was a pinhole perforation. A heel like that could have made a broken curve in powder; those nubs could have picked up a grain or two. There had been two tiny clear spots on the floor within the curve.

"Take off his shoes, Arnaldo," she ordered, gesturing with the flash. "Take them off," she repeated when the chauffeur stood amazed and motionless.

"Arnaldo will not take them off."

She swung the flash upward quickly. Garcia was peering up at Arnaldo, some intense message or threat in his eyes. Before it Arnaldo wavered, then anger burned in his face and he flung himself down beside Garcia's feet.

"I take them off, Garcia," he said, "but first I tell." He looked up at Jane, his face expressionless but his eyes shamed and mournful.

"Las' night I do very bad. Because Garcia is husban' of sister of Inah, I do him big favor. He live far—in Bomsuccesso. He want to swim here this morning. I say he can stay in my room las' night."

"You went home and left this man locked inside the gates with us!" Jane demanded incredulously. "But why—how did he expect to get out this morning? Surely you did not let him have your key!"

Arnoldo's eyes were proof enough of the power of Inah's wiles.

Jane fixed her own on Garcia until he writhed in the bonds that held him. She resembled Vivian only slightly now. Arnaldo, familiar with the fireworks of Vivian's anger, was unprepared for the authentic fire he felt beneath Jane's. Garcia, too, appeared to shrivel before it.

Her voice was quiet, terrifyingly quiet, as she prompted him. "And last night, Garcia? What did you do?"

"I did not do it," he whispered, twisting away from her gaze. "I swear by Our Lady of Penha I did not."

"Do what?"

The man stared, as if paralyzed, at her. He moved his lips, but no sound came from them.

"Who did?" she substituted.

"I do not know! I do not know!" he cried then. "He was dead."

Arnaldo, torn between rage and fear, leaned over him threateningly. In that moment's pause Jane knew again the sensation of someone near by, watching, listening. But the doors were locked; the walls contained no windows. She shook off the feeling impatiently. Before everything else she must know what Garcia knew.

"What he do, what he do?" Arnaldo was demanding of her. Frantically he tore at Garcia's shoes, loosening them, pulling them off.

One after the other, as he held up the heavy soles to the light, Jane studied the rubber heels. She could see nothing in the pinhole cavities of the nubs, but something might be there. Garcia had admitted too much.

"You do not need to tell me, Garcia," she declared, getting up. "But you must tell the police."

The heavy face grew ashen. "Listen," he implored. "Before God, I will tell you the truth."

"I'm listening."

His voice, her own, sounded far away. This man with evil eyes, this dark, locked garage, the dark gardens cutting them off from the house where Jack lay dead, could not be real. Things like this didn't happen in real life to real people! But she continued to hold the flash steady with a very real hand, to keep her eyes on the cowering man, register each word he said.

"I do not come here last night because I want to swim this morning," he began eagerly, the threat of the police unsealing his lips. "I have something Mr. Houghton would pay well to have. If I can say one word to him, he will listen, I know. But I cannot find a way to say it to him. So I think to come here and see him when he is alone. When Arnaldo went home I go down into the gardens—"

A quick shudder ran over Jane. It was Garcia, then, not Vivian, she had heard. Garcia saw that shudder and misinterpreted it. He paused to slip his tongue about his dry lips while he studied her furtively.

"You came out. Mrs. Houghton too. You were in great trouble. You did not see me when I stood close to you. And Mrs. Houghton—she ran to the small gate and unlocked it and ran back to the house."

For a moment the garage reeled around Jane. Had Vivian admitted someone to the grounds last night? She had said she found Jack dead about six o'clock. Had she known before that? And Vivian had refused to permit an autopsy, had fainted when she had declared her intention of finding out who killed Jack.

Garcia's gleaming eyes, watching her, brought her back. "Go on."

"I waited. Perhaps Mr. Houghton would come out. But soon all the house is dark, and I think I must see him in the morning. I am going to bed when I hear a small noise like someone who walks on gravel. I look out but see nothing. The lightning is strong but the night is dark."

His eyes were pinned on Jane like shiny beads now, and his voice had lost its cringing tone. For some reason, she felt, she no longer had the upper hand.

"Maybe I sleep. I hear the noise again. The wind has stopped. It is very quiet. I am not mistaken. Someone walks on gravel. I go out quickly. From the top of the stairway I see a man pass like a shadow to the gate. Then he is gone. I think he has talked with Mr. Houghton. Perhaps I can see him too."

Garcia's voice was facile now; obviously he was appreciating the dramatic qualities of his tale and his own skill in telling it.

"I hurry to the house. Everything is closed and black. But when I come to the steps that go up to the library the lightning flashes and I see the door is open. When it comes again, I see Mr. Houghton. He is sitting in a chair. I think he sleeps. He will be angry to find me there but not when he sees what I have. I speak to him. He does not answer. I touch his arm. He does not move. There is a lamp there. I turn it on for one moment. He is dead."

Dramatically Garcia paused.

"And then?" Jane prodded.

Cunning moved in his eyes; a hint of insolence crept into his voice.

"The house so quiet. Mr. Houghton dead. You in such trouble, Miss Jane. Mrs. Houghton running in and out. I do not know what has happened. All I think is to get away. I—I have my key to the H and H offices. It is raining very hard, but I go there and wait. In the morning I think I

must come back here in the day to show you I do not know
Mr. Houghton is dead."

"Then the H and H report was not finished?" Jane
asked suddenly.

"No. I took my—friend's. I think someone will tell me
Mr. Houghton is dead and I can bring it away. You do not
tell me. You take it."

His manner now puzzled Jane more than his words.
"The man you saw at the back gate," she asked, searching
his face, "did you know him?"

Garcia's eyes became blank. "No."

"Would you recognize him if you saw him?"

"No. No. It was very dark. He was far away."

She had asked the questions while she tried to flog her
weary mind to find some way of extracting the truth from
him. He was lying, but what else? What had she done or
said to change his fear to insolent self-assurance?

"What information did you expect to sell to Mr. Houghton?"

"It has no value now."

"But you were in his employ. He did not need to buy
information from you."

"This was—did not concern the office."

Jane was silent. Most of what he had said he could have
learned from Inah. Yet Garcia alone knew that she had
been in the gardens, that Vivian had run out of the house.
And—she understood his change of front now!— cunning-
ly he had tried to use that knowledge to link them with
Jack's death. He was trying to threaten her—blackmail—
her and Vivian! Then he too must think—or know—that
Jack had not died of heart failure!

A hissing breath spun her round. She had forgotten
Arnaldo. Tense as a panther, he stood glaring at Garcia.

"You want me kill him?" he demanded.

"No. Give him some sandals and let him go."

"And the report?" Garcia asked when Arnaldo reluctantly and roughly freed him. "You will give it to me now?"

Jane studied his dark face, struck by his insistence on getting this report for a friend when he had delayed almost two weeks in delivering an urgent report to Jack, his employer. Could there be something in that Santa Maria and José Coffee Company statement that offered a clue to Jack's death? Could it contain the information he had hoped to sell Jack? Certainly she would be foolish to let it go without looking at it again.

Certainly, too, Garcia was in earnest about wanting it for his friend. Yet as she read the increasing anxiety in his eyes his use of the word friend seemed odd too. Why should he call friend someone whose displeasure he was so afraid to arouse by delay?

A little of his own medicine might do no harm, she decided, might result in forcing him to say more. He had threatened her and Vivian; why not threaten him? She could lose nothing, at least, by taking a shot in the dark.

"No," she announced, looking straight into his small eyes. "I'll return the report to its owner myself."

Garcia did not speak. Instead his face turned livid. Only Arnaldo's iron grip saved her from the flailing arms of a man beside himself with fear and rage.

"Go. Go," the chauffeur urged from the darkness beyond the flashlight's small beam, where he was fighting to thrust Garcia back against the wall.

Somehow Jane got the door open, fled through the gardens to the house, aware that she had aroused the enmity of a dangerous and unscrupulous man.

She locked the back doors behind her and her own doors when she was safely in her room, then waited at a window until she heard the back gate clang. A moment later swift, light steps on the gravel sounded and Arnaldo ran up the steps, came down the veranda to her window.

"Miss Jane?" And when she answered he said quickly, "Garcia go now. He very mad, very scare'. Maybe you give me paper in morning, I give him."

"Maybe," she repeated, "and thank you, Arnaldo. Good night."

But Arnaldo lingered. "Miss Jane, maybe you better stay inside gates or I drive you when you go out—"

"If everything is all right, go to bed," she told him. "We'll talk in the morning."

In the morning! In the morning they would carry Jack away and she and Vivian would be left alone in this silent, listening house.

15

"I am Not Mistaken"

Early Monday morning she heard Maria marshaling the servants but, still half asleep, aching with exhaustion, she made no move to rise. When she roused again Mercer was bending over her, eyes sleepy but overflowing with sympathy and not a little curiosity. Tears misted them as soon as she saw that Jane was awake.

"There, angel, I'm here," she said, stooping to kiss Jane's forehead. "And I've brought your breakfast. You're to stay right here till half-past eight. There isn't a thing you can do. And I'm going to stay right here with you."

"You're kind," Jane told her after a moment. "But do you mind if I say I'd rather you didn't? And don't cry, Mercer. Please."

"I can't help it." Mercer dipped before a mirror and dabbed at her eyes with a powder cotton. "A good cry would help you too, angel, make it easier for you, for all of us. Vivian hasn't shed a tear either, I hear."

"Vivian!" Jane sat up. "No one is disturbing her—"

"Not a soul," Mercer assured her hastily. "Except Doctor Ames, of course. He came shortly after seven, I believe, and has been with her ever since. He won't let anyone in. Poor darling . . ."

Tears filled her eyes again, and Jane said firmly, "Mercer, please go. I'll stay here if that is what you want, but I must stay alone. Please understand—"

"Of course I'll go if you don't want me." Mercer stood up, looking like a slapped child. She hesitated, however, and gazed at Jane earnestly, as if to make sure Jane too was in earnest. "You are so strange, Jane dear, you and Vivian. So cold and calm. As if Jack had meant nothing to either of you. Don't you see, darling, it makes his *friends* wonder."

Her face, rosy as a child's, her pretty hazel eyes dewy, her voice soft and compassionate, revealed nothing of the anger and resentment she had turned on Jack at the Copacabana. But as the door closed behind her Jane wondered suddenly what she had really intended to say with those blurred words and glances. She moved to call her, then lay back, ignoring the breakfast on the table beside her. "Later," she decided, "later I'll talk with her."

But there was no later. At nine Varta came for Jane and led her to the library to sit between her and Angelo, just behind Vivian, with Noel on one side, the doctor on the other. Dr. Ames never took his eyes from Vivian throughout the brief service, and when it was over he hurried her away, before anyone else moved, to be put to bed by Theresa and to sleep with an opiate administered by himself. Not for a moment had Jane been permitted a word with her sister,

And throughout the service she had been conscious of almost no one else. Vivian's drooping head, her alabaster face and almost closed eyes alarmed her more and more. Her beauty now was so startling, unreal, that she appeared to be the work of some artist's hands rather than a woman of flesh and blood.

There was no music, nothing but the low, diffident words of Dr. Omlie, minister of the Union Church the American colony maintained. He was new to Rio, too, and in any city would have lived a life apart from a man like Jack. In the silence of the group seated about him he seemed to feel his remoteness; he fumbled for words, hesitated, came to a quick conclusion with a prayer.

Even this simple service Jack would have resented, Jane knew, and her eyes sought Noel's face, gray beneath the brown. Perhaps he was thinking, as she was, that Jack would have preferred above all things to have had Noel alone beside him now.

A murmur of voices and a rustle recalled her. Vivian and Dr. Ames were gone, and as she rose with the rest she saw Tom Hughes and Eloise moving toward her and Phil with Mercer clinging to his arm, then other faces dimly. For the first time she became aware that the room was almost entirely filled with men, managers of Houghton and Hardwicke departments, she guessed as she saw them look first at Noel, then move forward to take up the casket.

She watched them go slowly, carefully, out the French doors with their burden, saw others follow, Noel almost the last, silent, pitifully alone; Phil, grave and noncommittal, facing the battery of curious eyes with unshaken composure. She heard the murmured words of the Hugheses, Barassas and other friends and associates of Jack's, equally grave, equally remote in their manner as they pressed her hands, then left quietly, almost hurriedly, she thought. Only the men would go on to the cemetery. Only Vivian, the doctor and herself remained at the house.

As she walked down the corridor to her room Dr. Ames's small gray figure appeared in Vivian's door. Seeing her, he closed it and stood before it as inflexibly as a guard. "You must not go in," he declared, shaking his head. With a hand on her arm he turned her back to the living room.

There, in his neat gray suit, perched on the edge of one of the big chairs, his bright eyes regarding her from beneath those bushy brows, he appeared to her grief- and fatigue-strained eyes like some strange gray bird that had lighted there. And if a bird had spoken, its words could have been no more strange.

"If you will have Vivian's things packed," he was saying, "I will charter a plane for New Orleans for tomorrow morning." His was the courteous, professional tone of a physician addressing someone he had never seen before.

"I don't understand, Doctor Ames," Jane managed to say without a tremor. "You must explain to me why Vivian must leave Rio immediately. Why won't you let me see her?"

"She needs change and complete quiet. Rest. We must get her to a new environment where no one or anything suggests Rio to her. She's had a bad shock, you know; several of them."

"I know. But I'm her sister—all she has now. Let me talk with her—help her."

He shook his head. "Vivian is mentally ill, really. That will pass, too, when she's rested. She's obsessed with a sense of some guilt or failure. Like a child who has played with a gun, ignorant that it could kill." As though alarmed by that last word, he shifted his position, went on swiftly. "And, like an undisciplined child, she now wants to place the blame on someone else."

"On me, you mean? For what?"

He was taken back by her directness. "Well"—he floundered a little—"you see, unfortunately, all her troubles came to a head after your arrival in Rio. She associates you with them, mistrusts you, fears you—"

"That can't be true!"

"No?" He studied her coolly. "You told me yesterday, I think, that you were not a child, and you aren't, are you? But as little more than one you developed a romantic passion for Jack; you brought it with you—into this house—"

He stopped, shrugged.

"You are keeping something from me, Doctor Ames," she accused hotly. "I insist on seeing Vivian, hearing her say this herself. I *will* see her unless you tell me why you want her to leave Rio and why you suggested yesterday that I should go to Buenos Aires."

"I've answered your questions about Vivian. My answer to yours is almost the same. It is the best advice I can give you. Go to B.A., return from there to the States. The long ocean voyage will give you a chance to rest and to prepare to take up your old life at home."

"Forget, you mean?"

"Do you want to remember?" An edge crept into his voice. He rose and walked to a window to stand, his back to her, looking out. From there he said after an interval, "Jack was one of my best friends. I'm extremely fond of Vivian. Because of them I've tried to help you."

"Help me?" Jane sat forward eagerly, brushing aside the implied warning in his words. "Oh, Doctor Ames, you can."

But when he turned she found it difficult to phrase the question trembling on her lips.

"Well?" he asked, watching her closely.

"Would it—could it be possible—for you to have made a mistake in the cause of Jack's death?"

As he returned to his chair he gave no sign that her question had stirred him, but she could feel some change in him.

"I am not mistaken," he assured her quietly. "Why?"

"I can't believe that Jack died of heart failure. I know he didn't."

"You know?"

Jane bit her lip, thought despairingly of her two fragments of glass, of those clumsy shoes of Garcia's. They were the only tangible evidence she had, and they proved nothing yet. She had gone over all she knew a dozen times.

Everything could be explained away naturally or denied. The powder patch and the heelprint, Jack's instructions to her, had disappeared. And Jack himself had pledged her to ask no questions, to remain silent.

"I know," she declared, "but I have no proof."

"No?" Again, as he rose, his voice wore an edge, yet he seemed relieved too. "Think over my advice. You must see that you—a young woman without family or friends—cannot stay on alone in Rio."

"This house is my home—until Vivian decides what she wants to do with it. I can stay here with the servants, and I can get someone to stay with me."

His glance ran over her skeptically, challengingly. "Don't decide now. Think it over. You can let me know this afternoon or evening, when I come back to see Vivian."

Jane watched him go as if he were a ship that had set her down on a deserted island. Then, with head high and chin set, she hurried to the telephone.

But Mercer, who lived alone in a tiny apartment, had no desire to talk with Jane now. She was so sorry, she *never* left her own "little nest," but there were others, of course, though at the moment she couldn't suggest . . . Eloise Hughes and Varta Barassa were sorry too—they understood, of course—would love to help her, but they couldn't think of anyone at the moment free to stay with her; perhaps someone else . . .

Hurt, bewildered, but not defeated, Jane turned from the telephone. She still had the servants; if she must, she could—and would—stay alone. But as she moved through the house she began to wonder uneasily about the servants. She felt their glances slipping over her, slipping away. When she spoke to them they did not look at her directly. When she left them she could hear their voices rise in an agitated buzz.

She did not long remain in suspense. Hardly had she returned to her room when Maria appeared at her door.

"Miss Jane," she said from the threshold, "Inah, Theresa, everybody wan' to go away." Her veiled eyes offered no explanation.

When Jane asked why, she merely shifted her feet. Jane walked over and closed the door. "Now tell me," she ordered.

Maria's eyes wavered. "Everybody scare', Miss Jane."

"Of what?"

"They say what for *coruja* sing in trees, sing three times on this house since you come, Miss Jane? What for the senhor die, the senhora sick—mus' go away? Everybody scare' of *you*, Miss Jane."

"You too, Maria? And Arnaldo?"

A shadow crossed the sober face, then Maria said stoutly, "We is diffrunt. Me an' Arnaldo is—is members of the famly, Miss Jane. Famlies helps each other. You say stay—we—we—stay."

Impulsively Jane seized a broad, soft hand and pressed it over her heart. "Feel my heart," she urged. "Look in my mind. Mr. Jack said you could, Maria. Do you see anything there to be afraid of?"

Perhaps it was her wan young face that touched Maria's own warm heart or that in her despair she had reached Maria in terms she could understand. The dark eyes plunged into hers intently, growing more and more intent as they did so. Then, far back, two little lights began to glow in Maria's eyes and her face softened curiously.

"You do what I say, Miss Jane?" she asked in an odd, hushed tone. "You do what Maria say? I show them you no have bad heart."

"What shall I do?" Jane asked, touched, startled too. "Maria, I must stay. Mr. Jack asked me to—the day before he died. But I can't stay here alone without the servants. They must stay with me and trust me."

"Suppose Maria make *macumba* for you? You no have fear? No talk?" The soft voice spoke cautiously through lips that scarcely moved.

Macumba! Jane knew nothing of the weird rites of voodooism except that they were weird. The dark face gazing at her allowed no questions, no compromise, and Jane asked none. If *macumba* could make it possible for her to stay in Rio . . .

"No. No, I will tell no one, Maria. And I'm not afraid. Make *macumba* for me."

Maria seemed to withdraw within herself, to commune with some other Maria; her fingers moved as if she were calculating.

"Tonight," she announced dramatically at last, "when young moon is high, I make *macumba* for you."

As she turned to leave, Inah rapped on the door, opened it.

"Policeman is here, Miss Jane. He have questions. He mus' talk to everybody, he say. Now he talk with Arnaldo."

Jane's heart skipped a beat, then raced ahead. "He must not disturb the senhora," she said quickly. "When he comes to the house take him to the library. I'll see him there."

"He say," Inah added slyly, "somebody murder that man in gates."

16
Senhor Diego Asks Questions

As Jane entered the library the Brazilian detective, a slender, dapper and apparently casual young man, rose courteously. But when he indicated the chair he wished her to sit in, and she found herself facing the light of the two windows as well as the observation of two sharp black eyes, she knew she would need all her wits to cope with his lacquered assurance.

"We will speak in English, Miss George," he began, smiling, his glance raking her from head to foot. "My name is Diego Machado—of the *Policia Central.*"

He placed his card before her and adjusted his chair—Jack's desk chair, rather—to face her more directly. "It is very necessary, or I would not trouble you on such a day. Early Saturday morning a man was found dead here, killed by a car, our men thought. Our autopsy proves he was not. He was smothered."

She had steeled herself against the word murder; when he used smothered, she jumped.

"And tortured," he went on quickly. "There were burns on his body, rope marks on his arms, many bruises. Can you tell me, Miss George, why on Saturday evening the ashes of burned papers were found in the *lixo* of this house?"

He spoke so smoothly, moved so lightly from explanation to question, that Jane did not grasp its significance.

"Why, I—I put those ashes there myself Saturday afternoon," she answered, confused.

"With so many servants? Why was it necessary for you to burn papers yourself? Why to burn them at all?"

"Perhaps it wasn't necessary," she told him slowly, while her mind, alert now, spun an explanation. "I—the papers I burned were personal letters. I didn't know how else to dispose of them. Oh," she concluded artlessly, "it was just one of those things. I was here alone, had lots of time."

"So you were here alone. Then no one saw you burn them."

Her discomfort grew as she realized this Senhor Diego could be as artless as herself. "Yes. No. Philip Monroe, a friend of Mr. Houghton's, dropped in for a book. He saw me, talked with me while I burned them."

She was offering up belated thanks to Phil for his unappreciated arrival when the detective swung into another unexpected question. "Perhaps you can explain also, then, why this same Philip Monroe tried to enter your grounds after midnight last night."

"I forgot him!"

Her spontaneous exclamation set his eyes sparkling. "Ah, North American young women are so very different from Brazilian!"

To her surprise she found herself smiling in return and relaxed a little under the warming effect of the interest and admiration in his glance.

"Mr. Monroe did not think my sister and I should stay alone here last night. When he left after dinner he said he would return—"

"And you forgot such a considerate gentleman? Why?"

"I can answer that question, of course, but is it necessary?" she countered after a moment. "What has something that happened Sunday night to do with a man found dead early Saturday morning?"

Senhor Diego's attention was no longer on her. He was listening—as she had done so many times in this house! She said hastily, to divert him from the subject of Phil, "You feel it too—that someone is trying to hear? I've felt that many times too, but there never is anyone."

He rose swiftly to open the corridor door and look up and down, then, closing it, crossed to the windows to scan the veranda. "These old houses . . ." As he returned to his chair he smiled and shook his head.

"Several nights during the past two weeks," he began briskly, seating himself and smoothing back black hair already so smooth it might have been inlaid on his head, "men have come and gone after midnight by the rear gate of this house. As long as they came and went safely and quietly, we could suppose many things. But when one of them is tortured and murdered we feel it is time to ask questions."

Jane's tension returned though she sat motionless, staring at him as if to make sure he was not some figure from a nightmare speaking nightmarish gibberish. Several nights! Jack had mentioned but one—the night Pinto came two weeks ago.

Two weeks ago! Everything seemed to date back to two weeks ago—Jack's impatience with Garcia, Vivian's moods and nerves, the owl hooting . . .

Maria had never spoken of seeing the owl, only of hearing it. Had there been an owl to see? Or had those calls been signals between the men who had come and Jack? Was it on the nights the owl called that Jack—unable to sleep!—had gone to the library to read?

In the intensity of her thinking she had forgotten the detective.

"Our men reported that they found you bending over the body in the gates."

She started, nodded.

He leaned forward, his black eyes tightening on hers. "What took you to the gates at that hour of the night, Miss George?"

Bound by her promise to Jack to say nothing, she could only fling out her hands helplessly. The gesture was a master stroke. Senhor Diego's glance softened.

"I was asleep," she told him, "and some noise woke me. Perhaps it was foolish, perhaps Brazilian girls wouldn't have done it, but I—well, at home I would have gone out to see what happened. I did here. There was nothing to see until I reached the gates. Then he—that man—was lying there—"

His eyes were skeptical again. "But you remained there, bent over for some time—"

"I couldn't do anything else!" she cried, "I couldn't move! "

That seemed to be the right answer. He nodded, then tacked to another angle. "Why did Mr. Houghton deny that he knew the man?"

Tired, confused and now afraid of him, she shook her head.

"And the papers you burned? What were they?"

"You jump around so," she protested then. "What is it you really want to know?"

"What you know."

"I! Do you think that if Mr. Houghton had really known the man he would have told such things to me?"

As her indignant, involuntary words rang in her own ears a small quiver of doubt and resentment of Jack ran over her. He *had* told such things to her.

"I am sure he did." Senhor Diego's voice was low, confident. "Wait. I will be very frank. There is nothing in Mr. Houghton's office to tell us who the dead man is or why he came. We went through it this morning. Mr. Hardwicke knows nothing. I feel sure there is nothing in this house now to tell us, or your eyes—some gesture—would have betrayed it when my first question made you aware of your position."

"My position?"

"Let me finish. Either that man was killed, after he left this house early Saturday morning, in revenge for something he brought to Mr. Houghton or he was killed to prevent his bringing something here. Nothing was found on his body. Therefore it was either taken away from him or what he brought was information and he was killed to prevent him from speaking."

An inarticulate murmur from Jane interrupted him.

"The burns, the bruises . . ." she said hesitantly.

"I did not say he was killed in the gates," the detective pointed out. "He was killed on the beach somewhere, smothered with sand. I'm willing to accept for the moment your statement that you—a young woman in a strange country—would venture out before dawn with a flashlight to investigate a strange noise"—he cocked an eyebrow at her—"but I cannot accept Mr. Houghton's statement that he did not know the man. He had some reason for that denial. It is more than possible, Miss George, that that reason was the cause of his own death."

"No! Oh no!"

"What could be more possible? For years Mr. Houghton has had a weak heart, yet he lived with it until now. Couldn't the shock of finding dead in his own gateway a messenger whose information was so confidential that he could not receive him by daylight in his office be a severe one?"

"How do you *know* he knew? I mean—"

"Isn't it still more possible that a man who had received such a shock, who knew he might die of it, would tell someone what had happened, prepare someone to act for him in the event of his death? Surely you must say yes to that."

Feeling as if she were being led forcibly down a dark and deserted beach herself, Jane nodded.

"Good. Now—no one left these grounds from the time the body was discovered until almost one o'clock, when Mr. Houghton and his wife drove out to the Gavea Golf Club. No calls of any importance were made or received on this telephone. At the club Mr. Houghton talked with no one privately. We can eliminate the servants here. They heard nothing Friday night, were chiefly interested Saturday morning to finish their work and leave at noon.

"That leaves you, Miss George, and Mrs. Houghton. She spent Saturday morning in her own rooms, resting and dressing. You spent it in this room behind closed doors with Mr. Houghton. All your servants know that. Mrs. Houghton drove to the club with her husband. You remained here to destroy some papers. You must admit that."

"Yes," Jane admitted, "we did talk here—Mr. Houghton and I—but only about casual things. He was cleaning out old letters and papers from this drawer. I burned them with my own letters."

The detective pulled out the drawer, glanced at the neat piles of stationery, the three checkbooks. The checkbooks he picked up and riffled through the pages of one of them.

"I'll take these with me if you don't mind. They seem to have been used chiefly for household and personal expenses, but they may—" He stopped at one stub, then dropped them all in his brief case. "Is it true, Miss George, that some years ago you and Mr. Houghton—"

"Some *years* ago, Senhor Diego," she emphasized coldly, but her cheeks flamed with sudden color.

"You say you and Mr. Houghton spoke of casual things on Saturday morning," he said, swinging bewilderingly to another subject. "We Brazilians do not consider murder a casual subject, Miss George. Nor should you. Think! One man has been killed; another is dead of heart failure.

Why? Because they knew something that someone else did not wish them to know."

He thrust forward in his chair, his black eyes fixed on her significantly. "Do you realize this? You have that information now, Miss George. *You have that information now!*"

All the apprehensions and doubts of the past days churned about in Jane until they merged in one all-absorbing fear. It ran over her body like electricity, swelled her tongue in her mouth, set her heart beating stiflingly.

And there was no one to whom she could turn. Alone in Brazil—a young woman without family or friends—she understood Dr. Ames's warnings to the full now. For a moment she thought longingly of the boat for Buenos Aires that would carry her away from all this mystery and terror.

Her eyes strayed despairingly round the room, found the clock. Almost twelve. Two days before, at this same time, Jack had sat in this room, facing the threat she faced now, telling her of Pinto . . . Yesterday, at almost this same time, she had found that second crumb of glass and the substituted pages in the little drawer. She fought down the fear throbbing in her throat and stood up.

"I cannot help you," she said. "I know nothing."

Senhor Diego studied her a moment, then held out his hand.

"You have very clear eyes, Miss George," he said gravely. "They tell the truth when your lips do not. And I have very great patience. The dead man's photograph is appearing in tonight's papers. We may learn from it who he is. In the meantime take my advice. Remain here inside your own locked gates. Somewhere someone may think as I do—that you know too much."

17
Jane Delivers a Message

Senhor Diego departed, leaving Jane to pace restlessly about the library. The intervention of the police was something she had never anticipated; its implications were frightening. Now she must either follow Dr. Ames's advice and go back to the States while she could or she must find the solution for Jack's death and the mysteries that hung over the house—and quickly. She must know before the police did who had killed Pinto—tortured, smothered, burned . . . When she knew that, she would know who killed Jack.

Blind to the incongruity of such an undertaking by a young and innocent stranger in a foreign land, she walked back and forth, shivering with the chill of fear and excited resolution. A few months before she had thought herself a self-reliant, coolheaded young American, capable of managing her father and their home; now she felt helpless and bewildered, uncertain of everything she did.

Should she have told Senhor Diego why she was found in the gates bending over Pinto? Should she have told him that Jack had not died of heart failure? Hardly, when Vivian, Noel, Phil, even Dr. Ames would deny it and Jack himself had warned her to silence.

If only she had those instructions he had left her . . . Suddenly she was pulling out the table drawer, feeling for

135

the little knot. She knew what to do as clearly as if Jack had told her. She must get those instructions back. It was as simple as that.

Someone had stolen those instructions, someone who had been in the library. And Garcia had been! For a moment her newborn confidence wavered at thought of facing him again, of his evil eyes, his sly attempts to bargain with her. They were evenly matched, he with his knowledge that Vivian had unlocked the gates, that Jack was dead before anyone else had known, she knowing his fear of the police, his even greater fear of the man for whom that Santa Maria and José coffee report was intended. But thinking was dangerous. . . .

With half a dozen of the printed pages that had been substituted for Jack's instructions in the envelope in which the Santa Maria and José report had come, she rushed to dress, calling to Inah to have Arnaldo bring round the sports car for her.

Less than an hour later she stood for the first time in the foyer of the H and H offices in the A Noite Building and a young Brazilian receptionist was saying, "These offices are closed today. Mr. Houghton is dead."

"I know, but I thought someone might be here—Mr. Hardwicke, Garcia—"

"Senhor Garcia is here."

Surprised, a little dubious, the girl opened a door into a long room aisled with desks. At the far end, silhouetted against high windows, a man bent over one of them.

"Your name, please. I will call him."

"Thank you, don't bother. I just want to give him a message."

Before the receptionist could protest Jane stepped into the room and hurried down a long aisle between the desks.

At the sound of her footsteps the man looked up, then thrust back his eyeshade and rose, his back to the light.

Not until she was close to him could she see him clearly. She stopped.

In height, in breadth, in feature even, this man was Garcia and yet he was not. The light pouring over him revealed no variation in the even brown of his hair. His face was full but not florid. His lips too were full, but weak in comparison with the ugly strength of the Garcia who had given her the report.

Under her increasingly astonished and puzzled gaze he moved uneasily.

"You wish something?" he asked, and his light voice was not Garcia's though he added, "My name is Garcia."

"You have a brother who is an accountant here?"

His hands gripped the desk as he stared at her. "No. No, I am Garcia, the accountant here."

"But you are not the Garcia who brought this envelope to Mr. Houghton yesterday morning," she declared flatly. "Where can I find him?"

He took a step forward, his eyes on the envelope. "I do not know. I am the only Garcia in this department. Perhaps he was some messenger Mr. Hardwicke sent—"

"He told me he was Garcia—from this office—when he gave it to me," she interrupted and turned away, but slowly.

"One moment." When she turned back he was nearer her, his tongue moving nervously about his lips. "You can leave the report with me. I will give it to Mr. Hardwicke."

"Report!"

He stepped back, consternation in his face. "I—I thought it might be a report. That is one of our envelopes. Mr. Hardwicke often sent reports to Mr. Houghton at his home." Holding out his hand, he added, "It is possible that I know the man you mean—or can find him."

"I did not bring a report," Jane said carefully, watching, from beneath her lashes, disappointment flash in his face, "but some papers I want him to have." Holding out the envelope, she added, "Tell him that if he will return the original papers from the place where I found these I will give him the report he wants."

"I do not understand." His hand shook as he took the envelope, and his voice was uneven too.

"Just give him the envelope and my message as soon as possible."

This time she turned quickly and sped back to the reception room and elevator. She shook a little herself when she reached her car, but she had taken the first step on the road she meant to follow and she was not dissatisfied. Next Jack's banker, then his lawyer . . .

A few minutes later she stopped the sports car before the "after three o'clock" door of the North American Bank and Trust Company on the Avenida Rio Branco.

"I have an appointment with Mr. Hughes," she told the guard there and followed his directions back through a maze of private offices to a door marked *Gerente*.

The Tom Hughes who rose to meet her was not the Tom Hughes she had sat beside at the Copacabana Palace. The room was large, with enormous barred windows; the desk and chairs were massive. Yet against them he appeared even broader and taller than on Saturday night and, as she moved toward him, much older.

"You have come about the transfer of your account?" he asked immediately. With distant courtesy he indicated the chair before his desk, then sank into his own and pulled a folder toward him. "It will not take long. You have only to sign—"

"Mr. Hughes! Don't you recognize me? I'm Jane George. I have no account here."

"I am not mistaken in you or the account. Don't you know that Jack Houghton has carried one in your name here for years?"

"No! No, I didn't know it."

Incredulity increased his reserve. "For the past five years Jack has deposited from one to two hundred contos in your name," he said briefly. "Today your account stands at something over eight hundred contos. Roughly forty-five thousand dollars."

"Forty-five thousand dollars!"

Jane gazed from him to the yellow sheet he laid silently before her. It was an ordinary bank form, headed by her own name and Wisconsin address. Beneath hers was Jack's. Between its perpendicular lines ran two columns of type-writing: one a series of monthly dates, covering the past five years; the second a series of corresponding amounts, ranging from eight to fifteen contos, occasionally more. At the bottom was a total—830 contos.

Through her shattering surprise crept a realization that Jack—in spite of his marriage with Vivian—had continued to think for her, to plan for her. His words as he slipped that check into her blouse pocket came back to her now. She had forgotten them, forgotten the check too!

She looked up to find Tom Hughes's eyes narrowed on her and for a moment was annoyed. Was she always to find someone watching her?

"I remember now," she tried to say casually, "that Jack did speak of an account last Saturday. But I understood him to say it was in the Canadian bank."

Something flashed across the banker's eyes before they became blankly attentive again. "It is possible that Jack held an account there in your name too."

"But why would he do anything like this? How could he do it without telling me?"

"It seems he did tell you—the day before he died."

Jane's head lifted swiftly, but his face told her nothing. He had dipped a pen in ink and was offering it to her.

She shook her head and motioned it aside. "If there is no mistake—I'm sure there is—I can sign these papers later. I really came to ask—"

If he had been reserved before, Tom Hughes became stony now. Unexpectedly he rose and walked to one of the windows, then to another. Disturbed, Jane moved to rise, then sank back, forcing herself to sit patiently.

As abruptly he returned, but he did not speak or sit down, and after a moment she stood also.

"I am sorry there is nothing I can do to help you, Miss George," he told her then, "nothing I can do or say."

"How do you know, until you hear what I came to ask?"

"I assume you wish information about some affairs of Jack's or his wife's. Noel Hardwicke is the man to see."

"But the offices are closed today. And Mr. Hardwicke is not at his home. I've tried—"

"Is that so strange? Noel—all of us are shocked at Jack's sudden death."

Again, though his face revealed nothing, his tone stung her to resentment. So did the fact that he was courteously but no less definitely moving her toward the door.

"Mrs. Hughes and I feel Jack's death deeply," he told her there, opening it. "And now we hear that Vivian is ill. Is there anything we can do?"

"Nothing, thank you. Doctor Ames is keeping her in bed until she leaves by plane tomorrow for New Orleans."

If she expected to surprise him, she was unsuccessful.

"Very wise," he murmured and bowed her out.

As she wove in and out of the flow of traffic on the Avenida, on the way to the Nações Building, a brown sports car slipped past her. Phil was at the wheel but apparently too absorbed in his driving to see her.

She slowed down, longing to find Noel, yet unwilling at the same time to intrude on him even if he were to be found. Angelo Barassa, as Jack's lawyer, however, should know the answers to some of her questions at least. Swinging left, she had soon parked her car and a few minutes later was facing him.

A tall, reserved man too, now his expression was curiously reminiscent of Tom Hughes's. When his secretary had announced her he had come to the door of his private office to remain standing as he talked.

"There is nothing we can do today, Miss George," he said promptly. "We must wait for Noel. He is Jack's executor."

"Are you talking about Jack's will?" she demanded, flushing hotly. "Of course I'm not here about that. I want some information."

"Why not wait for Noel then?" he suggested smoothly. "Give him a day or two, Miss George. He and Jack were more than partners, you know."

"I can't find him, and this is urgent," she persisted.

"I'm sorry. We must wait for Noel." He spoke with finality and drew back from the door as he spoke.

Bewildered, shocked, angry, Jane returned to her car. Where now?

Phil's car slipped past hers again, and again he did not see her. Or had he? He was the one person she had not intended to see, but with every door closing so mysteriously in her face she changed her mind.

Her chin set hard as she moved out into traffic and followed him—in and out of a web of streets, between high walls, past small parks and praças and out into the suburbs. Where was he going? she puzzled when small vegetable farms began to alternate with tiny settlements in the valley on her left and a tree-deep mountain to rise skyward on the right.

As they mounted steadily she knew he was aware of her though he gave no sign. The valley fell further and further below them; mountains rose higher and higher about them. At any other time the views of city and sea sparkling in the sunshine would have delighted her, but she could not enjoy them now. A waterfall cascading into sight became a silver flash as she ran by. Just ahead the road forked, and she had to make the right choice or lose time and perhaps her quarry.

She made the right choice, but as the road rose still more sharply misgivings crowded into the car with her. Stay inside your own locked gates, Senhor Diego had warned her, yet here she was, a few hours later, racing up a lonely mountain highway after the man whose name led all the rest in her mind as Jack's murderer.

She slackened speed a bit, then, as the brown car disappeared around a bend, flung prudence to the wind and rushed after it. Too late she saw that the bend led to a dead end. The mountain slope had been cleared and leveled there to form a small lookout over the valley and harbor. Around the edge ran a strong stone railing.

Phil waved her to a stop as she coasted toward it, and she brought up beside his own car which he had already swung round to face back toward the highway.

"Nice driving," he applauded, walking over to open the door beside her. He looked at her curiously, then added, "I admire your courage, Jane, but not your judgment."

"My judgment!"

"From the moment you began to suspect that Jack did not die of heart failure you have considered me his murderer. Yet you follow me up to this Godforsaken place alone. Look down there."

He waved a hand toward the railing that rimmed the gorge. "That's a several-hundred-foot drop—to trees and rocks and snakes and ants and who knows what. If anyone ever had the misfortune to fall down there, nothing but a few bones would ever be found."

18
Phil Displays a Check

With that challenge quivering between them Jane sought to conjure Jack's face for reassurance, but it wavered and blurred. All she could see was the lonely clearing, patched with thin, withdrawing sunlight. The mountain slope above, its trees already deep in shadow. The gorge below, deceptively soft with the green of massed branches. Guanabara Bay, far beyond, shimmering, dotted with islands and tiny craft. And beyond it more ranges of Organ Mountains, blue and purple now in the late afternoon light. Not a leaf stirred. Everything was drowned in silence.

Some small birds darting noiselessly from trees on the mountain to trees in the gorge, a pebble, carrying with it a fine sift of dry earth, trickling down from the brink of the raw clay wall cut in the mountain slope to make room for the road, broke the spell.

"Why did you bring me here?" Jane asked. "And where is here?"

"This is Excelsior." Phil slipped round and into the seat beside her. "Noel brought me up here to see the view when I first came to Rio; this is a favorite retreat of his too. And now I've brought you here because we are going to need all the privacy we can get for what we have to say. I didn't want to go or to be seen going to your house

143

today. Somehow lately I've thought that Jack hadn't
secured the privacy he wanted for whatever he wanted it
for."

"You're not the only one to feel that way—"

"More anon about that," he said hastily. "It's getting
late, and we must talk fast. And, Jane, you and I must
trust one another. You need a friend, don't you?"

She hesitated, then suggested quietly, "You brought me
here for some reason—what is it?"

"To ask you why you think Jack was murdered, for one
thing."

"I know he was murdered."

He waited and, when she remained silent, smiled a little at her obvious attempt to appear composed and cool.

"The foreign colony, at least, believes Jack died of heart
failure. And God help us if we don't manage this so that
they can continue to think so." His eyes were not wary
now but intensely alive.

"But they—some of them must be talking or thinking.
Tom Hughes and Angelo, at least. I saw them this afternoon; it—it wasn't a pleasant experience."

"That's what's worrying me—the general situation, I
mean. There are several people in Rio who had stiff grudges
against Jack. Take that group at his Copacabana show.
With the possible exception of Doctor Ames, everyone at
the table had at least one."

He gave her an appraising look before he added, "Remember our talk in the garage Saturday afternoon? Well, I
expurgated my remarks a bit. Jack had more than his share
of admirable qualities, Jane, but he had others too. He
took a malicious pleasure or pride in Vivian's beauty—its
fascination for other men."

"Must we talk of that again?"

"Wait. Vivian didn't realize until just before that dinner—she told me this herself—that Jack had known all the

time about Tom, Angelo, et al. He not only knew, but he read Vivian like a book. Why not, when in many ways she was a carbon copy of himself? He never revealed his hand to Vivian, but he brought it down heavily on Angelo and Tom. Before he finished he had both of them just where they were most useful to Jack. And to have one of the cleverest lawyers in Brazil and the leading foreign banker in Rio pulling his chestnuts for him was all to the good for H and H. It was through Jack that Russell Todd was exposed."

"Tom and Angelo and Jack were friends," Jane reminded him. "And what has Russell Todd to do— Oh, you're thinking of Mercer."

"Yes, I'm thinking of Mercer," he agreed. "That pretty little head never rattles when she shakes it. But friends is hardly the term for the crowd at that dinner, Jane. Business allies describes them better. I'd never seen them isolated like that before. Usually they meet only at big affairs.

"At that dinner Jack turned on Noel and me. I think he was acting, creating that melodrama for some obscure purpose of his own. From what I've heard, the others thought so too. Mercer didn't get that warning out just to be amusing. They'd lived through one hell of Jack's making, were in no mood to go through another."

"And you," Jane broke in pointedly, "what about you?"

He smiled, shook his head. "I'm not in love with Vivian."

Hurriedly she asked, "And you think Tom and Angelo had other grievances?"

She didn't really care to know. She felt drained, exhausted, sick at heart. Phil's voice, so dispassionate and impersonal as he stripped away Jack's life and Vivian's, left her little room for doubt. And she had known too personally Vivian's instantly roused competitive instincts where men were concerned; at such times her sister was something more than the "prima donna" Jack had called her.

"Business," Phil was saying. "Tom is one of the most ambitious foreigners in Rio . . . for himself and his bank. His fingers itch to make H and H the investment service of the North American. Noel sees certain advantages in such a merger; Jack wouldn't hear of it. With Jack gone—"

"Phil, you don't know what you're saying! Tom Hughes wouldn't kill—" She stopped, remembering the deadly cold eyes she had faced that afternoon.

"Coffee is the basis of Angelo's grudge," Phil continued. "He owns a coffee fazenda he can't maintain profitably now that Brazil has lost her monopoly—to say nothing of this war. He wanted H and H to finance him until—as he believes—Brazil will recover her leadership. Noel would help him; Jack not only refused, but his warnings against coffee prevented others from helping him. Angelo couldn't hold out much longer. Perhaps he can now!"

Coffee again! And Angelo, standing in the doorway of his office, coolly turning her away.

"And Noel?"

"I don't know," Phil confessed. "He's proud, very sensitive. Jack's treatment of him Saturday night must have cut deep. Noel loves Vivian with a curious passion, hates himself for it as passionately, I think. Incredible as it seems, I've tried to imagine that he killed Jack, put those coffee leaves on his own car. But his surprise and anger when he found them there were too real to be pretense, and this morning he sat through that service like a man who had seen a ghost. I'm sure of this: if he didn't believe last night that Jack had been murdered, he does now."

And Vivian, Jane thought, Vivian who had touched so disturbingly the lives of all these men, who could be ruthless too, Vivian had reason for wishing Jack dead.

She shuddered away the thought and turned again on Phil. "And your motive?"

"If I had one, it would be business too," he told her surprisingly. "I'd like to head up H and H, believe it or not.
Jack and Noel have done a magnificent job, but they've
scattered their fire, spread too thinly over too great a variety of industries. I'd like to reorganize them, concentrate
on transportation—"

He broke off and for the first time lost his poise. "What
am I saying! Forget it. I've never put the idea in words before."

"Then no one would suspect that motive?"

He looked at her oddly. "No. If anyone were to imagine
me the murderer of Jack Houghton, he'd suspect Vivian
was my motive. Wouldn't he?"

She turned away from his searching eyes. "Wouldn't
anyone who saw Jack strike you believe that?"

"Ordinarily I believe anyone would," he said gravely.
"But no one—except you—does think that. You see, someone else entered the picture, someone whose motives are
known, who had opportunity—"

His voice was dispassionate and level but his eyes were
not. From a face as pale and strained as her own he was watching her with pity and concern. But she did not see. Horror
seized her as the significance of his words struck home.

"You mean—me!"

She shrank away from him, her face pinched and white
in the fading light, and sat rigid, staring at nothing.

"People think—think I killed Jack! That's why everyone avoids me—why Doctor Ames won't let me see Vivian,
is sending her away—"

"Jane, Jane, don't take it like that. You didn't kill Jack."

"Then why torture me?" she asked in a choked voice.

"Someone had to tell you."

"Yes, someone had to tell me," she repeated stupidly.
"Though all day people have been telling me—the servants,

Doctor Ames, Mercer, Tom Hughes, Angelo—and now you!"

"Because I know you didn't kill Jack and I want to help."

Some change in him convinced Jane more than his words. He had changed subtly, so subtly that she could not explain the difference. "You can lean back on Phil," Vivian had said. She thought she understood now.

Afraid to trust anyone, yet eager too for someone she could depend on, she turned away to hide quick hot tears. "Oh, I don't know what to do, whom to believe," she murmured miserably.

"I know." He took her hands and drew her gently round to face him. "But we must talk of this, Jane; you must understand the evidence against you."

"I want to know," she said quietly, releasing her hands.

"You aren't at all like Vivian, are you?" He did not smile, but some deeper tone in his voice warmed her. "You may walk like her, carry your head as proudly, but underneath you're incredibly young—and sweet."

Before she could control her surprise his tone changed, was cool and level again. "Now for the case against you. First there's this." He laid a bit of folded paper in her lap.

She opened it with stiff fingers. It was a check, made out to her, signed by Jack, for five hundred contos.

"Where did you get this?" she demanded. "I've never seen it before."

"No? Vivian found it on your bed Saturday night." That scrap of paper Vivian had twisted and jerked through her fingers! Jane remembered now. It must have fallen from the pocket of her blouse when she scrambled for a shower after burning Jack's papers.

"Jack did give me a check Saturday morning," she admitted. "I didn't look at it then. I forgot it—until this afternoon. But, Phil, this can't be it. Five hundred contos—that's twenty-five or thirty thousand dollars, isn't it?" "Why not? You already have something like seventy-five thousand in accounts he held for you in Rio banks. That's a lot of money for a youngster like you."

"But I knew nothing about it," she burst out angrily. "I don't want it. I won't touch it."

"But others know."

"And they think I killed Jack—for money!"

Her face grew whiter still as she heard Tom Hughes's cold voice saying, "It seems he did tell you—the day before he died," remembered Vivian's scantily veiled hostility, her suggestion that Jack had given her stocks.

"What shall I do?" she whispered. "How can I make them understand?"

Phil did not answer. His eyes were on another drift of pebbles and leaves sifting down from the brink of the clay wall on their right.

Without warning he turned and took Jane in his arms, holding her close, his lips to her ear.

"Trust me now, Jane," he urged softly. "Do exactly as I say. My car faces the highway. Walk over to it quietly and start the motor. Don't hurry until you reach the turn, then drive home as fast as you can. Wait for me there. Promise?"

He held her tightly until her head moved on his shoulder in agreement, then his lips brushed hers lightly and he released her. One glance at his set face and she slipped from the car.

As she started the motor she glanced round. The clearing was dim now and as silent and empty as before. Mystified, she answered his wave and drove away. But when as she turned into the highway she looked back her car stood alone in the clearing.

19

The Gates Clang

During the long drive home Jane tried to order her incoherent thoughts—and emotions. Away from Phil, his quiet voice, the warm pressure of his hand (deliberately she closed her mind to that long moment when she lay in his arms and his firm lips touched hers), his words and actions took on new meanings. She hadn't asked him if he knew about the unlocked back gate, hadn't told him about Pinto or the missing instructions or Garcia, yet somehow she felt that she had been disloyal both to Jack and Vivian.

"We must be friends, trust one another," he had assured her in one breath. In the next he had admitted that if she hadn't entered the picture he himself might have been suspected of Jack's murder. She stood as a shield between him and the doubts that might ruin his work in Rio, prove even more disastrous!

Struggling blindly to extricate herself from the morass into which she was sinking deeper and deeper, she remembered, too, that although Phil had suggested everyone except Vivian as a potential enemy of Jack's he had made no direct accusation. And he had said nothing to explain why he knew murder had been done when no evidence of murder was visible.

And that check he had shown her—it could not possibly be the one Jack had given her. Five hundred contos!

Jack was generous, always giving Vivian checks for ridicu-
lous trifles, but he was never careless. She stepped on the
gas in her eagerness to reach the house; she was sure she
would find the original check in her soiled blouse. Theresa
laundered the silk things, but she had had no time since
Saturday to do more than care for Vivian.

Vivian! She slowed down again as she realized that
wherever Vivian got that check it must have shocked her.
Was that why she had called Phil among the first Sunday
morning, talked so long and feverishly to him, sealed herself away? Did Vivian really suspect her of killing Jack?
Did the others? The car swerved, and she brought it back
to the road unsteadily. She mustn't think of that.

But Vivian clung to her mind. Could it have been Vivian who had listened at doors and windows? Jealous, afraid
of her own sister? She herself had spoken of jealousy to
Vivian, but merely to recall an old family joke. Their
father used to say that Vivian was even jealous when old
Martha gave cookies to the young men who followed their
noses to the kitchen.

Smiling a little at that memory, she found herself before the gates and swung through them automatically to
stop in the driveway. A new moon, frail and white, hung
just above the ficus hedge, bringing new apprehensions.
Only a few hours now and it would be high and Maria
would be making *macumba* for her. Voodoo rites at midnight—to prove her for the benefit of the servants!

Well, nothing Maria could do now would frighten her.
And if this were the only way she could keep the servants,
she would go through anything—perhaps come out a little wiser too. She would see them all in a new relation;
perhaps one of them might reveal some grievance against
Jack.

His hot temper, his total disregard of others when he
was intent on accomplishing something, his impatience

with failure or delay—something might well have injured someone's pride or sense of individuality. She had heard of discharged or disgruntled servants taking vengeance on employers—stabbing, accusing them to the police, spreading malicious gossip.

Arnaldo worshiped the ground Jack had walked on, yet in defiance of Jack's strictest orders he had admitted that creature who called himself Garcia to the grounds. Maria must know more than she had revealed; no bad dream, surely, could have moved her to return on Sunday morning and bring all the servants with her. And Inah—Inah had induced Arnaldo to let that false Garcia use his room. Inah seemed eternally underfoot . . .

Behind her the gates clanged faintly, rousing her, dispelling suspicions of the chauffeur at least. "Faithful Arnaldo," she thought as she ran up the steps to the door.

Only there did she realize that veranda and house, usually so hospitably lighted at this time, were dark. While she flashed on gate and porch lights a sharp sense of Jack's absence touched her, went with her into the dark living room, into the corridor, impelling her to turn on every light she passed.

The house was very still, but that was not strange with Vivian shut away in her own sitting room and the servants preparing dinner in the kitchen. Yet when she reached her own door she saw that the little breakfast room, kitchen and pantries were all dark too.

Maria, at least, should be there. Impatiently she pressed one after the other of the various bells that connected with the servants' rooms outside. But though she waited longer than usual, no answering signal came back from any of them.

Alarmed now, she sped to Vivian's door, listened, rapped gently. Then she was pounding on the door, calling Theresa, her sister. Silence. Under her fumbling hand the door swung inward to darkness, and when her trembling fingers found a light she saw only an empty room. In perfect order. She sped across it to Vivian's sitting room. It was empty and ordered too. In a frenzy she turned on every light, searched everywhere for some message of explanation. There was nothing.

Back in the bedroom she opened drawer after drawer, once heaped high with exquisite lingerie. One drawer was empty, others disturbed as if hasty hands had sorted through them. She flung open the doors of the wardrobe that ran in sections across the width of one wall. Vivian's evening gowns and wraps still filled one section, but others showed gaps where suits and coats and dresses were missing. The shoe case told the same story and the cabinet for hats. And when she slid back the picture above the fireplace she found the little jewel safe open also and empty.

The smart room, so typical of Vivian's taste for bright, striking color in her surroundings, looked like a shambles when Jane had finished. The open drawers and doors—everything—shrieked that her sister had gone, left without a word, but not so hastily that she had not made ample provision for remaining away some time.

What could it mean? Was this Vivian's way of telling her that they could no longer remain under the same roof? Impossible! If Vivian had really wanted her to go, she would have said so plainly. Had Dr. Ames taken her away? Then there would have been a message from him, a servant at least waiting to tell her—

The gates—the gates had clanged! Arnaldo, she remembered; he must be waiting in the garage—with a message—to take her to Vivian. But why hadn't he spoken to her when she came in, or come to the house? As she hurried to press the garage bell she knew something of Jack's irritation. Brazilians and North Americans frequently differed on what was the obvious thing to do.

No answering signal from Arnaldo reassured her. Unlocking the back door, she called his name again and again.

The sound of her own frightened voice, coming back to her from the now dark gardens, frightened her still more. She drew back quickly, shut and relocked the door. Someone else must have closed the gates! Someone else was in the grounds. Perhaps in the house. The front doors had not been locked.

Afraid to remain where she was, afraid to move, she stood, her back to the door, staring fearfully up the brilliant corridor to the living room. Phil! Phil had said he would come, had asked her to wait for him. If he would only come now. Surely it was time. Hours seemed to have passed since she had left him.

Her lips went suddenly dry. Phil had lured her up the mountain, kept her talking there, sent her home without explanation. Had that been a ruse to keep her away from the house while Vivian— Had he taken the sports car—Vivian's car—to Vivian? Perhaps he did not intend to come.

She shrank back against the door. Perhaps he had come! The sports car was faster than his. And he might know a shorter route to the house.

Perhaps he had arrived before her, had closed the gates, was waiting—beside his car—in the grounds—in the house—

From the first she had mistrusted him, and he knew it. When she knew Jack had been murdered she suspected him first. He knew that too. Now she alone stood in his way!

With lightning speed the terrified thoughts flashed through her mind, yet it seemed as if she had stood with her back to the door for hours. She must move, thing. Her eyes crept up the corridor, past the doors standing open on either side, to the telephone niche. If she could reach it, call someone—but whom?

Her wildly beating heart told her. So it had beat when Senhor Diego had warned her, "You have that information now!" If she could call him . . .

She moved along the wall on her left, past breakfast room and kitchen and pantries and dining room. Each door, as she reached it, marked a milestone. At last, in a silence that seemed clarion, she stood in the niche, her hand on the dial, her eyes turned fearfully on the dark library.

It wasn't completely dark, and now, with her hand gripping the cold round face of the dial, she remained still—staring. In the edge of the light penetrating it from the corridor some dark mass lay on the floor.

"Vivian!" she sobbed and sprang forward.

But when she pressed the switch just inside the door the quick light did not reveal Vivian lying face down in front of Jack's chair. It was Noel!

For only a moment she remained rooted to the floor, then she was kneeling beside him. His outflung hand was not as cold as Jack's had been. His great shoulders moved slightly with his breathing. But he made no answer to her urgent repetitions of his name. Pulling the cushion from Jack's chair, she tried to turn him on it, but he was too heavy for her.

"I seem to have arrived just in time."

Dr. Ames came swiftly into the room, his eyes keen as he knelt beside her. For a time he ignored her as his hands ran over Noel, lingered about his head. Then he motioned for her to help him.

As they moved him Noel moaned, opened his eyes to turn them blankly from Jane to the doctor, then closed them again.

"He's all right. Just a bad knock on the head," Dr. Ames said irritably. "Get some brandy, will you? Bring two glasses."

When she returned with a decanter and glasses he poured the first full for her. "Sit down in that chair and drink it all," he ordered. "You look like a banshee."

"But Vivian," Jane wailed. "She's gone."

"Drink that," he ordered and bent again over Noel with the second glass. "Not another word until you get some color."

He lifted Noel's head, helped him drink the brandy, then let him sink back on the pillow. Rising, he walked to Jack's chair, stood looking from it to Noel, tried the veranda doors. They were closed but not locked. Suddenly he returned to Noel, stooped, his back to Jane. When he stood up he held a heavy riding crop in his hand.

Tapping it lightly against his leg to test its weight, he turned to Jane. "So Noel told you," he began.

Jane did not answer him or open her eyes. The strong brandy had been too much for her exhausted mind and body. She lay back relaxed in her chair, drifting further and further from reality among confused thoughts of her own.

20

Maria Makes Macumba

Hours later Theresa's voice roused her. But when she opened her eyes she saw no personal maid beside her. Instead of a trig uniform Theresa was wrapped from throat to foot in some odd white garment. Silhouetted against the light of a tall white candle, holding in her hands a small metal tray on which stood a curiously molded metal cup, she might have stepped straight from an ancient frieze depicting mystic rites.

For a moment Jane thought she was still dreaming. Then as she realized she was in her own room, her own bed, memories of the day rushed over her.

"Vivian! Where's my sister?" she demanded. "Oh, Theresa, where were you all? What happened?"

"Do not talk, Miss Jane. The senhora all right. Doctor Ames send her away on plane. An' the young moon is high now. We mus' go."

"Why didn't he tell me?" Jane thrust her hair back from her flushed forehead in bewilderment. "Oh, Theresa, I was so frightened."

"Hush, Miss Jane. He take Mr. Noel home an' he say not to worry. He come tomorrow, tell you everything. Drink this."

Jane motioned her aside. Her head was spinning, partly with relief, partly because there was something else to

159

remember. Phil! Those awful moments when she had cow-
ered in the corridor, seeing him as a sinister figure lurking
behind dark doors, accused her now. She shivered as she
recalled them. Only fright, hysteria, could have made her
think such madness.

No, Mr. Phil had not come to the house, Theresa assured her. No one had come since all the servants returned
at nine o'clock. But why they had gone or where, she would
not say. Dr. Ames would explain in the morning. Again she
urged the little cup.

Jane took it reluctantly, wishing her head were clearer.
But to delay longer, she knew from Theresa's manner,
would be to increase the servants' doubts of her. She had
promised to go through this ceremony, and she must do
it in good faith. If Vivian were all right, Phil—everything
else—must wait.

She drank the cool, strange liquid, responding at once
to its soothing, penetrating force. Her head stopped spinning as Theresa folded a soft white dressing gown about
her, placed slippers on her feet. When she stood up she
felt so peaceful, so feather light, that she seemed to float
to the French doors. With an effort she restrained her
buoyancy to dignity.

Phil liked dignity, she remembered and suddenly saw
his face clearly. Odd, when she couldn't recapture Jack's.
And Phil was all right, she felt sure now;

everything was all right now.

The night and the rapt quiet of the maid, perhaps the
potion she had taken, awakened all her senses. She delighted in the soft darkness of the lawns, the cool touch of
the grass, the measured rhythm of the waves; even the dew
from a dahlia head that touched her lips as they passed
through the gardens seemed sweet to her. High above them
the new moon, golden now, lay on the sky, guarded by
brilliant stars.

As they crossed the gravel she had the impression that she was crossing, too, the tangible barrier that separated her world from Maria's. And again she caught herself. She must keep her head clear of fancies, watch while she was being watched.

Yet when Theresa's hand stopped her in the open doorway of what she knew by day to be the gardener's storeroom her imagination accepted at once the cavernous shadows there, the dry earthy odor of roots, as essentials of the drama she was to share.

Luminous in the heart of the shadow was a pattern of lighted candles, set in some geometric arrangement on a tawny cowhide spread over the center of the packed earth floor. On one side of it sat three solemn figures—Arnaldo, Ricardo, José—wrapped like Theresa in white; opposite them a young boy, an old man, and between them Orminda, a neighbor's housemaid. And on the far side of the group, alone, sat Maria. The candles' light caught odd planes in their faces, shone into dark, unfathomable eyes.

At Theresa's warning pressure Jane looked down. Crossed one above the other on the doorsill were two curiously shaped knives. Startling symbols—a twisted serpent, interlaced triangles, other designs unknown to her—were crudely traced in chalk on their broad blades.

As they stepped over them Jane's ears vibrated to an intense humming. The semicircle, chanting together in undertones, drew her forward to sink down with Theresa in the open space across the cowhide from Maria.

Spread on the skin she saw then a small open square of red cloth and around it bright feathers, scarlet and yellow, and bits of ribbon in vivid shades. At intervals were tiny piles of different leaves and roots, a bottle of wine, another of perfume, a saucer filled with farina.

Though enclosed by darkness, lulled and rocked by the monotonous chant, Jane for a time was of, but not a part

of, the group. Her different background, her conscious
desire to remain aware, made her alien. Gradually—how
long she did not know—she felt her body swaying lightly to
the rhythm, her lips moving to repeat unknown syllables.

Not until then did Maria stir. Then her broad hands
took up with delicate precision some of the leaves and
roots, mixed them in a metal pot and held them over a
flame she lighted with a candle in a flat dish before her.
When they were all charred she poured them into a bowl
and pounded them in time to the beat of the chant.

Arnaldo rose quietly then and brought the knives from
the door. Effortlessly he sank them deep in the ground,
one on either side of Maria. When he had returned to his
place the old Negro, gray hair twisted in tiny buttons all
over his head, drew a scarlet cape about his shoulders,
picked up the bottle of wine. Filling his mouth, he sprayed
the cowhide in all directions.

While the chant and Maria's pounding beat on he took
up, one by one, the leaves remaining, traced on each a
symbol with white chalk and placed it on the red cloth.
On top of them he set a crudely carved wooden symbol
and, to Jane's astonishment, a lock of her own hair. Over
everything he poured the thick black powder Maria had
prepared and a dusting of farina from the saucer.

Jane's eyes clung in fascination to Maria's face, though
it was not the round benevolent face she was accustomed
to see. A strange, stern woman faced her. Sometimes her
cheeks were so indrawn that the outline of her skull was
visible, sometimes so puffed out that her head lost all pro-
portion.

Slowly the chant faded into silence. Only the candle
flames moved. Through the darkness from bins and rafters
came earthy breaths to weight the stillness.

Maria rose. Face uplifted, arms outstretched, she appeared to grow taller and taller, larger, to fill the room,

to dominate both the light and darkness. At last, whirling round three times, she flung herself full length on the ground, her lips to the earth.

Again that silence. Jane sat transfixed, holding her breath. The preliminaries were over, the moment coming when she must play her part, she felt dimly. As Arnaldo rose again and, slipping past Maria, lighted one by one a row of candles fixed in the ground there Jane's wonder was transformed into understanding. If she had any guilt to confess, she knew she would have shrieked it aloud then.

A low, improvised altar, spread with one of Vivian's lace tablecloths, was revealed by the candles. In its center stood a little wooden pole. About its crossbar twisted, somehow, a live snake, its back brilliant with a coral stripe!

Spread beneath it were some curious stones, clusters of brilliant beads, mounds of fruit and vegetables, of bread and little sweet cakes. At one end stood three or four bottles. At the other a mound of farina, topped by an egg.

A new chant began as the old Negro, rising, took one of the two knives from the ground and traced on the earth between Maria and the altar a simple design—a long straight line from which brief forked lines sprayed out. At each end of the line he drew a circle and on a short line drawn at right angles to the center a third.

From the cowhide he lifted the red cloth, folding the ends tightly about its contents; stooping, he held it before the snake. The creature's head swayed toward it, and Jane, closing her eyes, swayed in her place.

When she looked again the red packet rested on the altar at the foot of the little cross and the old man, eyes intent, had turned to face her. Maria did not move, did not seem to breathe.

No one spoke. No glance told Jane what to do, yet with her heart still as ice in her breast she rose, moved toward the old man until she stood facing him across Maria's body. He held out his left hand to her, palm upward, and she extended hers to him.

From the tensity of the silence round her she knew that this was the moment of her final test. She set her lips; even when she saw the knife in his hand she let no protest escape them—nor when he drew it swiftly along the line that circles out and about the mound of the thumb.

Her heart beating wildly and some pulse in her throat beating with it, she held her hand firm while the old man caught a small quantity of blood in an earthen bowl, took from the altar the red packet and placed it on the wound. Behind her another chant rose then, low as before but with a new tempo, fast and stirring. It excited yet steadied her.

One by one, as she stood rigid, the old man took up the bottle of oil, the saucer of farina and the bottle of wine and emptied each slowly into the circle he had drawn at the left of the altar. Into the circle at the right he poured rum and ashes. And into the center circle water.

When he had finished he lifted the packet from her hand, returned it to the altar. The blood had ceased to flow. Only a red line something over an inch long remained on her hand.

Jane felt Theresa's touch on her arm and moved with her to the door. There the small boy with the other knife was tracing an involved design of circles linked together with spider-web lines. He did not pause until the pattern spread like a net from one side to the other. Then he pushed the door open, stood aside. Jane and Theresa moved forward and out into the darkness.

21
Dr. Ames Explains

When Jane awoke her room was bright with sun and Maria, like another sun, was beaming at her above a breakfast tray.

"It mos' one, minha senhora."

Minha senhora!

Jane lifted her left hand and gazed at the deeply etched red line curving about the cushion of the thumb. "It's true!" she exclaimed. "It really happened."

Maria nodded. "An' you is our senhora now, Miss Jane. Everybody here. Everybody stay—'cep' Inah."

Jane's words of relief died on her lips. "What about Inah?"

"She go away yestiddy. For marry, she say." Maria's tone was incomparable for the amount of distaste and doubt she packed into it. *"Não faz mal,* minha senhora. We no need her."

"But why did she go so suddenly, without a word?"

Maria shrugged and, to forestall further questions, announced, "Doctor Ames here. He say he talks while you eats."

The little gray doctor was smiling this morning, friendly and solicitous.

"You're just where you should be," he greeted her "and there you stay until tomorrow at least."

His altered manner disturbed Jane more than it reassured. Yesterday he had coolly ordered her to Buenos

165

Aires; today he was telling her to stay—at least in bed in
Rio. And there were other things she didn't understand
and some she thought she understood too well. As revela-
tions and suspicions of the day before returned, to revive
her horror and consciousness that even with the servants
she was still alone in Rio, she withdrew her hand quickly.

Apparently he did not notice. With his fingers on the
pulse of her left wrist he was scanning the palm sharply.

"What have you been doing?" he demanded. "That's an
odd place to cut yourself." Without waiting for an answer
he turned for his bag. "I'll dress it for you now, and you
keep it bandaged. You have enough on your hands without
risking infection."

When he had finished he drew a chair close beside her.
Leaning over, he cupped her hands and placed his own
within them. "Does that tell you that I'm at your service
hereafter? And that I regret many things I did and said
yesterday?"

"You mean—sending Vivian away?"

"No, I don't regret that. But I'm sorrier than I can say
that I wasn't here yesterday when you returned to tell you
about her going. When I left in the morning, as you know,
I intended to charter the plane for today. Then early in
the afternoon I learned of a special plane going to New
Orleans. And by luck my best nurse, Dora Martin, was
free. That was too good a chance to pass by. You weren't
here when I arrived, so with Theresa's and Maria's help we
got Vivian ready. Believe me, Jane, it was best for her, for
you, for all of us—"

"But when I found no one here, no message—and then
Noel—"

"Wait. When I couldn't be here myself I sent Noel. He
had agreed with me that you couldn't stay here alone, that
you should go home. In fact, he came both to tell you

about Vivian's departure and to turn over his own apartment to you until you sailed."

So Noel, too, wanted her to leave Rio as soon as possible. Her color rose. "I'm staying here, Doctor Ames, and
the servants are staying with me."

"Noel was rather highhanded, but don't be too hard on
him," the doctor urged apologetically. "He is Brazilian,
with something still of the old Brazilian point of view that
it is for the man to speak, the woman to obey. I'm sure it
never occurred to him that you would not accept his plan
for you. When he didn't find you home he went ahead,
ordered the servants to close the house and go home. Then
he sat down in the library to wait for you."

Dr. Ames paused to chuckle. "He met his match in Maria.
She agreed to go because she had to, but she didn't go
home and wouldn't let the others go either. They settled
down in the neighborhood somewhere, sending out a scout
occasionally. When the gate lights went on and stayed on
she shepherded them all back."

Jane tried to smile and failed. Memory of that faintly
clanging gate and all that followed was too vivid.

"And Noel? How is he?"

"He got a severe blow on the head, but he'll be all right
in a day or two. He's up walking around now."

"What happened?"

"He isn't very clear himself about that. All he knows is
that after the servants had gone he sat down in Jack's chair
to wait for you. He left the veranda doors slightly open,
probably fell asleep. He thinks he heard footsteps on the
veranda but isn't sure."

Dr. Ames spoke carefully, avoiding her eyes. "He thinks
he saw someone—man or woman—appear in the door, but
that is merely an impression. The next thing he knew, you
and I were beside him."

"There was someone, Doctor Ames," Jane began eagerly. "Arnaldo didn't close the gates after me, but someone
did. I heard—"

"Don't worry about that now."

"But I heard—"

She stopped. His face was noncommittal, his eyes
guarded. He didn't believe her! She drew a long, uncertain
breath. "So that's why you aren't urging me to go to Buenos
Aires."

"You can hardly leave now. The police are investigating
the death of that man you found in the gates. They believe
he was murdered."

"You think I killed Jack—for money, don't you?" she
flamed. "Do you think I killed that little man too? And
Noel—did I strike him—"

"Don't talk nonsense," he said sharply, then, returning
to his friendly tone, "Since you wouldn't and now can't
leave Rio, I have another suggestion—"

"Why didn't you answer me?" she cried. "Why didn't
you say, 'You couldn't have killed Jack, because he died
of heart failure'? Why didn't you? Because you know he
didn't—you've known all the time."

Dr. Ames appeared suddenly to be gray all over. "Yes,
I've known," he admitted. "Jack never had anything the
matter with his heart. That was an invention of his own,
made shortly after he was married, to help him escape too
much social life. Lately I've backed him up—on condition
that he'd leave here in June for a long rest. I've been trying
to get him away for more than a year."

"You signed that certificate—"

Theresa knocked at the door, entered to remove the
breakfast tray. The doctor rose and drew his chair back
against the desk where Jack's broken cigarette box was lying.

"These seeds take me back many years," he said idly,
sifting a few of the ovals through his fingers. "We youngsters

used to rub them on one another's arms. They have quite
a sting if you rub long enough."

"What kind of seeds are they? Is the flower as colorful?"

"Yes, a bell-shaped affair, as I remember it. We used to
call them Paternoster Peas."

"That's a help if any are missing when I mend the box.
Where can I get more?"

"Perhaps there's a bush or two on my fazenda. I haven't
seen any for years, but my foreman will know."

As the door closed behind Theresa he drew his chair
back and went on as if he had not been interrupted. "Yes,
I signed that certificate. I wish I had a dollar for every
time a physician in some foreign colony in the world has
diagnosed death by violence or suicide as everything from
measles to heart failure. Sometimes he does it for the prestige or safety of the colony; more often, I suspect, out of
friendship—"

"What was it?" Jane demanded. "What killed Jack?"

"Poison. I can't say what without an analysis."

Poison! Who could have given poison to Jack? When?
That impostor who called himself Garcia? The man he
had seen leaving the grounds—if there had been a man to
see? Never. Jack would not have been found sitting quietly
in his chair, the library undisturbed, if some stranger
had entered it. Someone at the golf club? Someone at the
Copacabana dinner?

Dr. Ames sat very still, watching her. At last he stirred
rose. "You might start your thinking by finding out what
Phil Monroe's up to," he suggested. "He did nothing Monday morning but file cables and make long-distance calls.
A brain's working behind that poker face. Noel hates him
and can't conceal it. Jack hated him but could. When and
if he returns—"

"Returns? Phil?"

Dr. Ames's eyes flickered. "He left his hotel yesterday afternoon in his car. No one has seen him since."

Jane's thoughts flew back to Excelsior, seeing Phil, hearing Phil, feeling his arms about her.

"Are you suggesting that Phil followed Noel here?" In spite of her own suspicions of Phil the night before, she grew hot with anger now. "He didn't. He couldn't—"

"Are you suggesting that you were here to know?" The doctor's smile was very bleak. "In any case it is just as well that Vivian's on her way to New Orleans, and it will be just as well if you will stay where you are."

He hesitated, then, taking up his little bag, turned to leave. "Noel is lying," he said brusquely as he went. "I think he knows who struck him."

22

Phil Takes a Decisive Step

Dr. Ames was no sooner gone than the house rocked with the tumult of activity and emotion South Americans can generate on a moment's notice. When Jane ordered that Arnaldo be ready to take her to Excelsior in twenty minutes Maria protested to high heaven, then insisted on knowing why, then on going along, equipped with food and brandy, blankets and a hot-water bottle.

Arnaldo added Ricardo to the expedition, and Ricardo, the huge and powerful Negro handy man, knowing only that he was going into the forests, added an old machete, a coil of rope and various other tools that seemed to him essential.

But twenty minutes later they were all in Phil's car, speeding out the gates. An hour later they were turning off the mountain highway, coasting down to Excelsior.

The clearing sparkled now in the high hot afternoon sun. Every leaf shone as the branches moved in the breeze. Mica sparkled in the sand and stones of the road, in the claybank. The air was alive with the hum of insects. But Jane saw only that the clearing was empty, her car gone.

She sat perplexed, doubtful. Had Dr. Ames's suspicions been right? Her own? She refused to believe it and turned angrily on Maria, who was viewing the scene with disapproving eyes and words.

"Mr. Phil no here," she declared. "Nobody here."

Arnaldo asked no questions. His sharp eyes scanned the road about the spot where Jane had said she parked her car. Then he walked over and studied the claybank carefully. A little further down, toward the railing, he stooped over a bank of silt washed down by rains.

"Look, Miss Jane." When she stood beside him he pointed to two small depressions in the clay. "One man in soft shoes come down here. Back there one man in hard shoes go up. You think one Mr. Phil?"

"The hard shoes," she told him quickly.

But he was listening to a hail from Ricardo, who already stood on the top of the bank, gesturing and mumbling in his thick Portuguese. "Wait. I look."

For a few minutes she could hear them breaking and slashing a way through the underbrush and vines, then the sounds died away. She was frightened now as she had not been before. Noel struck down in the dark in Jack's chair; had that blow really been meant for him or for her? Now Phil—had he sent her home and gone or been forced into the forest on his own account or hers?

She returned to Maria, sitting bolt upright in the car, and for a time they listened to the disturbed birdcalls that told of Arnaldo's progress. Shortly even those ceased.

The sunlight began to thin, deeper shadows to creep under the trees, before they heard sounds in the forest again. Minutes later Arnaldo appeared, behind him Ricardo with Phil slung across his shoulders.

It was a strange and haggard Phil they lowered laboriously down the bank and placed in the car. His face, drained of color, was swollen and splotched with bites and scratches. So, too, were his throat and hands. One eye was sealed. The other he half opened, gave Jane a long enigmatic glance, closed again.

"He all right, Miss Jane," Arnaldo assured her. "Give him brandy, food maybe. I go back. Something to find."

When he and Ricardo returned, their arms filled with branches of palm and fern, Phil was better. Deftly the chauffeur placed branches about the back seat so that Phil was concealed and Jane and Maria sat alone in a bower of green like any other raiders out for festal decorations.

"Hurry, Arnaldo," Jane urged, but Arnaldo did not hear or heed. He returned to the highway slowly, he and the big Negro watching the road as if they had never seen it before, might never see it again.

She slipped an arm about Phil to hold back the branches that fell about his head. His eyes were closed, his face blank and pallid, but as he slid down in the seat until his head rested on Jane's shoulder he appeared, to Maria's knowing eyes, vastly content.

Only when they reached the house and Arnaldo, as valet, was looking after Phil did Jane have time, as she changed herself, to think about Dr. Ames's references to Phil and cables, Phil and Noel, Phil and Vivian—and about the doctor himself.

He had sat at that Copacabana dinner table; he knew that Jack had been poisoned before anyone else. How much more did he know? If she had not entered the picture, Phil had said, the men closest to Jack might have suspected a link between Phil's public humiliation and Jack's death. Did Dr. Ames suspect Phil anyway?

The doctor knew she had found Pinto. Did he know about the money Jack had left for her? His anxiety to get her away from Rio, his return with another suggestion which she had prevented him from making—could he be the someone who might think she knew too much?

With a final glance in the mirror she hurried out to the living room. As she entered, the firelight, the soft lamps, fresh flowers within and the surge of the waves on the dark beach without caught her breath. This was the hour Jack had liked best of all the day.

"Jane, you're—" Phil's one good eye gazed at her with admiration for two. He tried to rise from a divan beside the fire. Shaved, clothed in a lounge suit of Jack's, he looked, save for a patch or two on the forehead and hands, but slightly the worse for his experience.

"Don't get up and don't talk," she said hurriedly. "I'll sit here and mend this box."

"But you're lovely!" he exclaimed, watching her arrange the loose seeds and paste on a little table beside her. "Do you know there is copper in your hair just the color of that dress you're wearing?"

"Of course, that's why I bought it." Her quick smile faded. "Oh, Phil, do you think we'll ever talk of silly things again? I never knew before how wise they were."

He studied more closely her shadowed eyes, her face pale and austere for all its youth. "One day we will," he assured her, then laughed shortly. "In the meantime this escapade of mine may turn out to be one of the silliest things in the world. Remember—I deliberately led you all the way to Excelsior so that we could talk freely? We did. Right into the ears of two expert listeners."

"But how could we? Where were they?"

"In the underbrush at the top of that claybank. Do you remember when some birds flew out of the trees and some pebbles fell to the road? They should have warned me," he said disgustedly. "But not until the second lot fell did it strike me as odd. Then I saw a branch move though there wasn't a breath of air stirring, then a face or part of one."

"Was that when—why you sent me home so quickly?"

"I wanted a look at that chap. He might simply have been a Brazilian brand of curiosity hound or he might not. He was not, and there were two of him. Naturally they didn't wait for me to reach them. One went one way, the other another. I crashed after the one who seemed familiar somehow. But he knew his way around. I didn't."

"How could you have gone into the forest like that alone! He might have had a gun or a knife."

"He didn't have a gun then," Phil said ruefully, "but I think he has one now—my revolver. That has me worried some. Of course it may have fallen further down the ravine he threw me into."

"And you say you're all right. You can't be."

"Just bruised and stiff, that's all. We didn't go far really, but I lost sight of him for a moment. The next he was behind me or, rather, on top of me. I'd give a good deal to know exactly what happened. I don't think it was his original idea to dispose of me so quickly. Something startled him and—well, I came to in a nest of vines and bushes as dark as a pocket, and my gun was gone."

He rubbed and scratched a bitten cheek thoughtfully. "I won't give you my lecture on the 'Night Life of the Flora and Fauna of Brazil,' but all I told you of ants and God knows what is true—except for snakes. Too cold up there, perhaps. Or perhaps they prefer more room to move around in."

"You haven't asked about Vivian," she said quickly, to change the subject.

"Should I have? I've been waiting for her to make one of her— That's not sounding as I meant it; her ability to make an impressive entrance is one of her charms."

"She won't make one here or in Rio for a long time," Jane told him gravely, then poured out the story of Dr. Ames's highhanded actions, Noel's too, and the attack on him.

But Phil was more concerned for her. "You heard someone shut the gates? You're sure of that?"

"Positive."

"Then for God's sake use your head!" he stormed. "Don't follow any more cars up mountain highways. Doctor Ames and Noel are right. You shouldn't be here. If that blow could knock Noel out, what would it have done to you?"

"Don't worry. Maria's taken command. She told me while I was dressing that Ricardo and José are going to sleep inside the grounds now and that Ricardo's a dangerous man if roused. That reminds me, what happened to my car?"

"Lord! I'd forgotten it. Let's have Arnaldo in. He'll find it."

"And he may know more than you about what happened in the forest."

As usual, Arnaldo was taciturn and noncommittal. It had been easy to follow Mr. Phil, he said, by the trail of broken underbrush—easy, with Ricardo's help, to get him out of the crevice.

"And the man with the soft shoes?" Jane prompted. "What did he do?"

Arnaldo corrected her. Two men had been on the mountain besides Mr. Phil. One with soft shoes, one with hard. Mr. Phil had followed the hard shoes, and that one had stepped aside, crouched down till Mr. Phil passed, then leaped. Broken ferns and bushes on the lip of the ravine showed where they had fallen together.

The chauffeur stopped, following some line of thought of his own; Jane felt his uneasiness about something.

"And soft shoes?" Phil prompted.

"He go other way, come back to bank, jump down where I show you, Miss Jane. He take our car, I think." Arnaldo's face showed satisfaction. "I think he dead now."

"Do you know that or wish it?" Phil demanded.

"He no drive good. Car marks on edge of road. He go off, I think, down, down. I telephone police just now."

"You what?"

"I no say my true name. I say maybe car go off road by Excelsior."

Arnaldo knew more than he was telling, Jane felt, but it was obvious that he did not intend to say more. As he departed she asked, "Did you find a revolver in the ravine?"

From the expression on his and Phil's faces she knew she had blundered. She turned hurriedly to her seeds, and Phil lit a cigarette.

"If Arnaldo's right," he said after a time, "and the police find your car, they'll trace it by the license. And if the chap who took it is with it, I may be able to get a look at him."

Jane's silence was so prolonged that he sat up, then rose stiffly and bent over the little table on which her gaze was fixed. He could see nothing except the lid of the cigarette box, each seed in place.

"Don't worry," he told her. "Arnaldo may be wrong."

"I— Look," she stammered, opening her hand. "I have one too many seeds!"

"You what? Good lord, is that any reason for turning into a ghost?"

His face changed as a nervous tremor shook her and the seed fell to the floor. "Tell me," he urged, "what does that extra seed mean to you?"

"I don't know. But there can't be an extra seed. I knocked this box off Jack's table myself Sunday morning. I picked up every seed myself. There couldn't possibly be any others. Yet—there is."

"Are you sure?" He stepped closer to take up the lid. "Perhaps you've missed a groove or—"

Something crunched, and he stepped back quickly. "Well, there's no extra seed now. I've just stepped on it."

Jane looked from him to the crushed oval, then, with a curious gasp, slipped to her knees on the floor, staring as if hypnotized.

In the light of the lamp above her the seed lay in powder, tiny flecks of red orange shining among yellowish-white grains.

"Phil," she whispered, "look! Powder like this lay on the floor beside Jack's chair Sunday morning—under his hand."

He seized her shoulder, drew her back as she put out a finger to touch it.

"Sorry, but you've got a bandage on your hand—I've been intending to ask about it—"

"It's nothing," she said impatiently. "Just a small cut. Doctor Ames—"

"—didn't bandage it for nothing," he finished for her. "Suppose you got some of that stuff in it?"

"What then?" She looked up at him oddly. "What then, Phil?"

"Perhaps nothing," he answered carelessly. "But a good many things in this country, innocent to look at, to touch even, if you're all right, can poison you if they get into the blood through a scratch or cut. Especially if your physical resistance is low, and you must be almost at the end of yours."

He was examining the powder as he spoke, didn't notice her start.

"Doctor Ames says Jack was poisoned," she murmured half to herself, "and Jack had a small cut on his hand."

"Jack!" Phil ripped a page from a magazine and was down beside her in one motion, it seemed. He wrapped his handkerchief about his own cut hand as he thrust the page under the powder. "I'll take this and some of the seeds to Don Grey, a chemist I know here. Perhaps he can find out what it is."

"I know what it is," she told him. "Doctor Ames told me. These are Paternoster Peas."

Phil frowned as he wrapped powder and seeds carefully and stowed them in a pocket. "Even if we find that this stuff is poisonous, I don't see how it's going to help us much. That powder can't be on the library floor now. We'd have to prove it had been."

Jane gazed at him desolately, then her face cleared. "Perhaps we can prove it," she said eagerly. "I have a pair of shoes."

23
Death on the Mountain

Phil rocked his head back and forth. "And I have a pair of Chinese sandals. Once I had some Indian moccasins. You've said too much, Jane, not to tell me more."

Her troubled gaze faltered before the steady scrutiny of his gray eyes. In spite of her doubts of him she felt reassurance in his quiet strength. From the first she had noticed that about him, noticed, too, that though he seldom exerted himself others deferred to him, hesitated to antagonize him. Even Jack had made no overt move—until that final incomprehensible outburst.

"You don't trust me, is that it?"

"I want to," she admitted. Her hand opened toward him in a small gesture of appeal, but he would not help her, waited gravely. "I don't understand how you know that Jack was murdered."

A smile touched his lips. "My answer to that will sound as irrational as yours about those shoes. I know it because of a knife, for one thing; Vivian's dreams Saturday night—Sunday morning, rather—for another; you, for a third. But what I know, he added earnestly, "isn't as important as what you know. Jane, all this mystery didn't begin last month or last year or last Saturday. It may go back to the time when you didn't marry Jack."

"That's impossible—all forgotten now."

"Is it? Would Jack have built those bank accounts for you over five years if he had forgotten? Would you stay here alone, risking your life to find his murderer, if you had forgotten? And Vivian—she might have had a very different life if she could have."

He leaned forward, his voice deepening. "You must tell me what you know. I have an idea—a mad one—but the first that makes any sense. We've come a long way already if Doctor Ames has admitted that Jack was poisoned, still further if we've discovered what poisoned him. And we haven't much time. Whoever killed Jack—well, he's still trying to find out something or stop something. That attack on Noel—"

"And on you." She drew a long breath. "Yes, I'll tell you now."

She was still talking, Phil questioning, when shortly after ten the telephone shrilled. "I'll go," he said. "Just as well to let whoever is calling know that you're not alone here."

Presently he called from the corridor, "It's Senhor Diego. Your car's gone over a precipice up near Excelsior."

As she hurried to join him he added, "Diego says your chauffeur is in it or near it—I'm not sure which. He's very excited about something, is going up himself. It's not a good road to travel at night, but shall I tell him we drive up too?"

"Should you?" She looked doubtfully at his patches and still half-closed eye.

"This may be the break we've been looking for, or I have—" He turned back and said into the phone, "Miss George and I will drive up, senhor. See you in an hour or so."

So for the second time that day Jane drove up the mountain highway with Arnaldo at the wheel. Phil, beside her in the rear seat, turned to look at her occasionally but otherwise seemed absorbed in his thoughts.

Two cars parked across the road a short distance before the turn for Excelsior stopped them finally. Their lights shone out over the inky gorge, and Arnaldo swung Phil's car round to add its lights to theirs. Together they made less than a pinprick in the enveloping blackness of mountains, trees and night. The half-dozen men grouped on the rim were black pygmylike figures. One of them moved forward as Jane and Phil descended.

"You came promptly," Senhor Diego greeted them, smiling. "I've been here but a few minutes myself. Ah, Mr. Monroe." His voice changed as Jane introduced Phil and his sharp eyes fixed on Phil's swollen eye and patches. "This is fortunate. I've been trying to find you for two days. What have you been doing to yourself?"

Phil laughed, grimaced painfully. "In the States the answer to that one is that I ran into a door. I don't know the Brazilian equivalent."

"That will serve—temporarily."

Phil's hand on Jane's arm tensed a moment, but his tone remained level. "And now that you've found me?"

"A few questions. But later. How does it happen, Miss George," he asked with one of his disconcerting transitions, "that your car is here?"

"I don't know. But you're wrong about the chauffeur. Arnaldo drove us up just now."

"Yes, I know that." He smiled at Arnaldo over Jane's shoulder. "My men assumed that the man they found near the car was your chauffeur. I'm sorry to have to ask you to look at him."

They followed him to the first police car, Arnaldo, curious, close behind them. The detective lifted a flashlight while one of the police turned back a blanket. Across the back seat lay a twisted and crushed body.

Jane shrank against Phil's arm as she looked at it. Even without the eyeshade she recognized the man she had first seen standing with his back to the light at the end of the long general office of H and H and heard saying, "I'm Garcia."

"He—he was an employee of Mr. Houghton's," she stammered. "An accountant. His name is Garcia."

"We know that," Senhor Diego said and turned his flash on the running board.

Spread out on it were letters and cards, a worn billfold, some loose change, a crumpled cigarette package. Only Phil's warning pressure stifled her exclamation when she saw among the letters the long white envelope she herself had placed in Garcia's hands the afternoon before.

"What could he be doing up here?" she asked. "I mean with my car."

"We hoped you would tell us that."

Senhor Diego drew the blanket over the body as he spoke, keeping his eyes on her. She shook her head, sick with horror at the sight she had seen and at the thought that she was, perhaps, the cause of this man's death.

"Strange that he should run off the road here," Phil said quickly. "There are many worse places on this highway."

"He didn't run off the road. He lost control of the car here because he was shot."

Jane, Phil, even Arnaldo, stood like statues, staring at him—Phil's revolver in all their minds.

The detective pointed to a spot above them on the mountain. "Someone up there caught him in the right shoulder as he rounded the curve from Excelsior. You can see in the loose gravel back there where he lost control."

He stooped, picked up the long white envelope and held it out to Jane, focusing the light on it without comment. On the back, printed in bold black letters, was her name. As she looked up, surprised, he passed the flash to a man behind him and slipped a finger under the flap. Some slender dark leaves thrust themselves up into the light!

Phil spoke promptly but not promptly enough to cover Jane's startled gasp of recognition. "It's late, senhor. It will be long after midnight when Miss George reaches home if she leaves now. I think we have proved our willingness to help by coming up here. Could you postpone your questions for both of us until morning?"

"*Pois não.* Why not? If I may have one little word with Miss George alone before you go."

In spite of Phil's protest he drew Jane aside. "Why does the sight of a few coffee leaves disturb you, Miss George? Is it because you remember that coffee leaves were found in the hand of that dead man in your gateway? Could they have been left there as a warning to Mr. Houghton, as these obviously were on their way to give a warning to you?"

She shook her head wordlessly, and he moved with her toward Phil's car. "I don't want to frighten you, but when I come in the morning I hope you will give me your confidence. Otherwise I cannot help you, and I think—I'm afraid—you are in very grave danger."

Jane remembered that warning when at seven o'clock the next morning Maria wakened her to say that Phil had arrived and wanted some shoes. Maria was the danger, she thought, looking at the black angry face and listening to the dark mutterings. The cook was taking her responsibility for Jane with unadulterated seriousness, and now, at sight of the heavy, clumsy shoes Jane extracted from their hiding place, her anger burned hotly.

"You goin' t'be awful sick, minha senhora, less you takes some sleep," she prophesied. "Mr. Phil no have need for such shoes. Why he come make me wake you up? You sleep some more, Miss Jane."

She carried the shoes away, threatening dire things for Phil, but Jane was too tired to sleep, and the thought of Senhor Diego's coming questions did not calm her.

The morning wore on endlessly, and the detective did not come. She wandered restlessly about the house, returning to the telephone every few minutes to call Noel's apartment, the H and H offices, Dr. Ames's office, for word of Noel. But he was not to be found, and finally, to escape Maria's concern, she sought the gardens.

The unreasonable conviction that she was responsible for Garcia's death would give neither her mind nor body rest—nor the conviction that there was some link between his death and Pinto's and Jack's and the attack on Noel, whether it was intended for him or her. If she had not given that envelope to Garcia . . . She had only wished to bargain with the false Garcia—

"Miss Jane."

She turned to find Arnaldo in the path, an Arnaldo as troubled as she.

"I no speak las' night," he said, "but I no understan'. Why you tell police that dead man is Garcia?"

"Because he is Garcia. But that other man, Arnaldo— why did you tell me *he* was Garcia?"

"He is—" Arnaldo stopped, corrected himself after a long moment. "Inah tell me he is Garcia."

He stopped again, his face, his whole body, stiffening with rage. "She lie," he burst out. "He no is husban' of sister of Inah. He is man Inah go to marry!"

Jane saw hope in that, if he didn't. "Could you find her?" she asked eagerly.

"I fin' her." Arnaldo took a furious step or two, as if to retrieve Inah at that moment from somewhere in the gardens, turned as furiously back. "I fin' him too. Miss Jane, you got his shoes?"

"No. No, not now. Why?"

"Wait. I show you."

In a minute or two he was back from the garage, carrying carefully a huge leaf but limp and pulpy now. He placed it on the garden seat beside her, drew from his pocket a small empty cartridge shell and held it out on the palm of his hand.

"That how I know man that take our car yestiddy is dead." He placed a finger violently on the leaf. "An' that how I know who shoot him."

"Be quiet!" Jane ordered, partly to restrain him, partly to give herself a chance to think.

She bent over the leaf, hiding her own rising excitement as she saw the impression of a footprint on it. Someone had stamped down on it, folding part of it under, grinding his toe, then his heel, back and forth, either through nervousness or to secure a firmer stance. And within the heel's outline were four broken impressions—that could have been made by nubs of rubber like those on the shoes of the false Garcia.

"Are you trying to tell me that the man who stepped on this leaf shot the man who took our car?" she asked finally. "You mustn't say anything as serious as that, Arnaldo, without more proof than a leaf and an empty shell."

"I say it. It true."

He stepped back to demonstrate. Graphically he portrayed the scene in the forest—Phil thrown down the ravine by the man who wore hard shoes, then his assailant's sudden flight.

"Why mus' he go way so fas'? Mr. Phil no can get him. I go back on mountain—an' Ricardo. We go where that man with hard shoes go. He come to tree that look down on road. He get down like this; he stan' up. An'"— Arnaldo stamped down imaginary underbrush about him—"he shoot."

His pantomime was so vivid that Jane's ears almost rang with the sound of the shot.

"We look, Miss Jane. Ricardo fin' this." Again Arnaldo held out the shell.

Jane turned it in her fingers with mingled feelings of relief and despair. The impostor Garcia could have been on the mountain. To replace the shoes she had taken from him he might have bought others with the same nubbed heels. But couldn't Phil have broken that trail Arnaldo followed to the tree, have fired that shot? At least, if the shell were fired from his gun, weren't there ways of tracing it back to him? Why had he wanted those shoes? And should she have sent them out to him?

She stood up impatiently. None of this explained the coffee leaves found in the envelope on Garcia. Or did it? The impostor Garcia could have taken out those printed pages, inserted the coffee leaves and given the envelope to the real Garcia to return to her as a defiance or warning as Senhor Diego had said. If so, he must know about the coffee leaves in Pinto's hand, the coffee leaves on Noel's car. He could be the one who placed them there!

Anger and fear rocked her. "Have the car at the door in two minutes," she ordered the silent Arnaldo. "We've got to find Mr. Noel at once."

24

"I Saw the Curtains Move"

Waiting in the foyer of the apartment house where Noel lived for the automatic elevator to descend, Jane was struck again with wonder at his choice of a home. Among hundreds of apartment houses in Rio, ranging in style from ultrabaroque to ultramodern, this was easily the most modern of all.

At night its foyer was brilliant, sophisticated, but in midmorning the gleaming mirrors, the stylized designs in silver on black walls, the implacably placed ferns, lacked all suggestion of warmth or hospitality. Had Noel chosen it to meet Vivian's taste?

But when she stood in his private foyer, tapping a knocker of contorted triangles against his door, she forgot the surroundings in a panicky search for words. Until the little grille beside her head was closing she was unaware that someone had opened it, surveyed her. Then Noel himself opened the door.

In her relief at finding him home she did not notice his surprise at seeing her there nor, in the dimness of a single wall lamp lighting the entrance cubicle, realize that something more than a blow on the head must account for his appearance and manner.

"You are good to come," he greeted her, "but what are you doing out? Doctor Ames told me he was trying to keep you in bed."

"I couldn't reach you by phone, so I started out to find you."

"Telephone?" he said hazily. "Oh, I told the switchboard operator not to call me this morning."

It was the lack of resonance in his voice, his heavy step as he led her into the characteristically small Brazilian living room which he alone seemed to fill to overflowing, that told her of some change in him. He almost stumbled over the round tables of metal and glass set, without relation to the other furnishings, about the floor. And when he reached the two deep chairs placed before closed glass doors leading out to a balcony he braced himself on one while motioning her to the other.

Before seating himself he turned to the drawn curtains behind him and drew them together so that they overlapped more securely. She was startled again to see the clumsiness of his hands. He always moved slowly but with great ease and surety for a man so large. Now, coming back to his chair, he literally dropped into it.

"Noel," she exclaimed in concern, her eyes on his bandaged head, "it's you that should not be up and moving about."

He was not listening, and her glance followed his to a letter crumpled beside the balcony doors. And beside his chair she saw a large envelope, stamped with the familiar blue and white air-mail stamps of the United States. The corner card had been torn in opening the letter, but one word—Laboratories—stood out in firm black letters.

When she looked at him again his face below the bandage, already drawn and worn, was fretted over with small lines and a ghastly color—like dried clay. Perhaps it was the lack of air. The room was close and hot with blazing sun. She longed to open the balcony doors, but when Noel, a fresh-air fiend, had not opened them she felt she could not.

"You do look tired, Jane, and thinner," he said, apparently unaware of what she had said to him. "I feel responsible, should have looked after you better. But I seem to make only motions since—these days."

"You're ill, Noel," she said again, leaning forward impulsively. "Let me call Doctor Ames."

"You're surprisingly like Vivian," was his answer. "I never realized that before."

"The candle and the sun. When she's gone you see me." Had he heard what she said, or was this his way of evading talk about his health?

"Doctor Ames thought—we both thought—" He roused himself, recovering something of his usual voice. "Jane, it was best to send Vivian away. I wish we could have sent you too. It isn't safe for you to stay alone in that house. This blow . . ." He lifted a hand to his bandage. "Suppose it had been you. It might have—"

"That's one reason why I'm here," she broke in quickly. "Noel, I don't think now—I did at first—that that attack was meant for me. Someone followed you to the house. I heard—"

"Jane!" His voice, stern now, silenced her. "I'm sorry," he apologized awkwardly. "You've been under a heavy strain. You're overwrought, nervous. I can understand that. But you mustn't let your imagination run away with you. Brazil isn't the musical-comedy country you foreigners like to think."

Color was returning to his face now. He sat erect, and the vague expression left his eyes.

Some part of her registered the change and wondered about it while she rushed on with what she had come to say. "I'm not imagining. Please listen."

She checked herself on the verge of revealing what Jack had said about Pinto's death, substituted, "Noel, a branch of coffee leaves was sent Jack last Saturday morning. Less than twenty-four hours later he was dead. Sunday night some coffee leaves were placed on your car. Monday evening you were attacked—"

"The prank of a boy in the street—the leaves on the car, I mean."

"And last night some leaves were discovered on their way to me!" When he raised his hand abruptly she added, "All right. Forget the coffee leaves. But I couldn't imagine this. Garcia, your accountant, was shot, killed, sometime yesterday in my car up on the Excelsior road. Do you know that? I know it, though the morning papers say nothing about it."

"Yes. I know that. I was told just a few minutes ago. I'm—I was about to leave for the office."

"Do you know who shot him?" Jane demanded and, when he shook his head, raced on recklessly. "I do. I've seen the man, talked with him twice. He came to the house Sunday morning, pretending to be Garcia. He was there again Sunday night. He's the one—I'm sure of it—who put those leaves on your car, tried to send them to me."

Noel sat with his head resting on a hand, his face half hidden. "And his name?" he asked without looking up.

"I don't know that, but I know how to find him."

Noel looked up, and for a moment, as the light from the balcony doors fell over him, Jane was touched again to see his grief, his bewilderment without Jack. Suddenly she knew, from the intentness that concentrated his eyes, the stiffening of his head, that he was alert, listening.

In the silence of the little room, with the hot sun reflected from every leather and glass surface, the feeling that came over her was fantastic. Danger in such a place at such an hour was incredible. Yet she felt it. Menace almost as visible as the dust motes in the sunbeams streaming between doors and rug lay on the close air.

Noel moved, lifted himself heavily to stand before her. "Perhaps I heard what you said correctly, though since I received that knock on the head I'm not sure I don't imagine things myself. You're hysterical, talking nonsense. I'm not in the slightest danger from anyone, if that's what you came to say."

Not in the slightest danger! Jane recalled those first few minutes with him but had to admit it was not fear or anger she had seen in his face. And it had not been illness either. His voice now was deep and vibrant, his color almost normal. But he had had some shock or some unexpected, overwhelming news. The death of Garcia? That seemed unlikely. News in that letter, crumpled and hurled to the floor?

She realized he was still standing before her, waiting apparently for an answer, and rose reluctantly. "I've expressed myself badly. I'm sorry. But what I say is true and much more. You are in danger—"

"And if I am, do you think I need the protection of a schoolgirl! Do you think me helpless?"

"That's what Jack said. And he is dead."

Noel stood like an image looking down at her. "Yes, he is dead," he said slowly. "I—I can't believe it. You loved him too, didn't you? You came to warn me because I was his friend."

As he put out a hand to touch her shoulder she stepped back, her eyes widening.

"Someone's here," she murmured, "in the next room—listening." When he stared at her, unmoving, she added urgently, "Behind you. I saw the curtains move."

He swung his huge frame round then and with one stride reached the curtains and ripped them apart. Her eyes traveled about a dining room crowded with massive furniture and cabinets from an old Brazilian home, all elaborately carved and gleaming with generations of polishing. But otherwise the room was empty.

"You see?" Noel drew the curtains together, looked down at her sternly. "Imagination. There is nothing here, no one. Sometimes," he added wearily, "I wish there were. Go back to the States, Jane, to your friends, before you learn what loneliness is."

Her eyes softened with pity for him, but she shook her head resolutely. "I'm not going back until I know who killed Jack. Noel, you must believe me. I did see those curtains move. And there isn't a breath of air in here to move them. I know someone was listening." She took his arm earnestly, forcing his glance to meet hers. "Don't treat me like a child. I know I'm in danger, but you are too."

Noel's jaw set grimly. "Doctor Ames is right. You mustn't stay in Rio a day longer. And you don't need to. I'll straighten out this Garcia business."

"I can't leave now, you must know that. The police are investigating the death of that man in the gates Saturday."

"I'll attend to that too. They have no right to hold you here."

Jane's round jaw set also. "Not until I know about Jack."

"Murder is a preposterous word to use about his death. He'd have hated it as I do, advised you as I am doing. Go home, Jane. Even Phil—"

"Phil agrees with me now."

"You mean you've discussed all this with Phil Monroe!"

His blue eyes, suddenly chilled, searched her face, read admission there. His great shoulders moved in a shrug.

"Run along now," he suggested like an adult tired of a child's nonsense. "I must get down to the office."

Somehow there was nothing more she could do or say. Though she stood beside him, she knew that a door had closed between them.

25

Phil Tries an Experiment

As she drove home she felt again her disloyalty to Jack. And Noel had felt it too, resented it. They both disliked— hated—Phil, Dr. Ames had said, and she had confided in him. She bit her lips as she remembered her glib advice to Vivian against doing the very same thing.

Did Noel suspect—in spite of his protests—that Jack had been murdered? Could he have realized that or learned something definite to prove it just before she arrived at his door? Certainly that would account for his shaken appearance and actions. She could think of nothing else that would rock a man like Noel so drastically.

Depressed with the flatness of her failure, feeling stupidly guilty, she reached the house with relief and hurried to her own room. But something made her turn back when she had passed the library. The door that always stood open was closed. She opened it quickly and remained quiet in amazement.

Phil, on his knees between Jack's table and his chair, was alternately moving the cigarette box a little further beyond the end of the table and shoving the chair away. As she watched he adjusted the box so far beyond the table that only the side of the chair supported it. Naturally when he moved the chair the box fell, cigarettes rolling from it, Paternoster Peas scattering from the lid as it struck the floor.

"Looks silly, doesn't it?" He rose and dusted his knees and smiled his awareness of her. "But I had to do it. I know now the reason for that extra seed. And you're right. It didn't come from the box, of course. Someone somehow managed to add it to the others—perhaps to add several—"

He still moved a bit stiffly but quickly to her. Gripped by his own strong interest, he shepherded her into a chair beside the jacarandá table and draped himself across a corner of it without noticing her intent face.

She sat in silence while her mind adjusted itself to this new development. Dr. Ames could have added that seed or seeds. The night she had found Noel he had helped Theresa carry her to her room. He might have seen the box on her desk then. And the next day he had played with those seeds while Theresa removed her tray.

"This," Phil was saying impressively, holding out one of the seeds, "is something more than a Paternoster Pea. Its scientific name is *jequirití.*"

She brought her attention back with difficulty. "You didn't know that last night."

"I didn't know several things last night. As you see, I'm still wearing Jack's suit; that means I haven't been home since I left you."

"After no sleep the night before!"

"I'll have time to sleep later. Do you realize what Garcia's death means? Whoever killed Jack never dreamed that his crime would be discovered. When you gave those printed pages to Garcia you announced that it had been. That you knew. Garcia took them to someone. Now that someone—the murderer or close to him—is as badly scared as I am."

"You're afraid?" she asked incredulously.

He nodded. "Scared to death. For you. For Noel. For a great many people who would be affected if anything happened to H and H. For fear of failing in what I'm down here to do. Incidentally, I don't want to die."

"I'm glad," she told him in a small voice. "I mean I'm glad you're afraid. I am too, frozen up inside, but I didn't think I should say so."

"You're rather adorable at times," he informed her, then went on briskly. "Now about these Paternoster Peas. We've found the poison. It's abrin. These seeds contain it." He took a notebook from a pocket and turned its pages rapidly. "Listen.

> *"The Paternoster Pea . . . blazes in the shadow of the bush like a fiery red eye with a black pupil. . . . These beautiful peas are threaded into rosaries or glued upon shell-covered boxes. Handling them is a dangerous occupation, for the peas contain a poison (abrin) of which a small dose is fatal if injected under the skin.*

"That's from a book, *A Naturalist in Brazil,* by Konrad Guenther, a German scientist brought into northern Brazil some years ago to eradicate some plant or pest. But wait. Listen to this. It's from *Pharmacopeia,* the Bible of the drug profession:

> *"Abrin: a yellowish-white powder, exceedingly toxic. Smallest particle of abrin in slightest wound may prove fatal."*

In the slightest wound! And Jack had had a cut in his hand made by that fragment of Venetian glass he had been holding.

Phil shut his notebook, misinterpreting her abstraction. "You don't have to listen to all this."

"But I want to know. Where did you learn about abrin?"

"From Don Grey, director of laboratories for Fabrica da Luz, one of the big American factories here. He's an industrial chemist really, but his hobby is poisons. When I left you last night I routed him out of bed and showed him those seeds and the powder. He recognized the Paternoster Peas but said they were rarely seen in the city now. He's right. I've spent the morning visiting chemists and doctors and old-timers generally around the town, and few even knew the name of the seeds."

"Doctor Ames knows them. He said he might have a bush or two on his fazenda. What does he grow up there?"

"Coffee, mostly—bananas, oranges. But to go back to last night. I got Don out to his laboratories where he has the books I've just quoted. They interested him and he made some rough tests. He's going to do them again more carefully, but he says Guenther is right, those seeds do contain poison."

"Was it for Don Grey you wanted those shoes?"

"Yes. And he found some grains in a nub of the right heel, enough anyway to prove them grains of the Paternoster Pea seed. So that fellow, whoever he was, did get into the library and did stand beside Jack—"

"But he couldn't have poisoned him!" Jane declared flatly.

"No. I have a hunch that his game was blackmail." Phil whistled, slipped off the table with an exclamation of disgust. "I do need sleep or something. Jane, my friend of the forest who tossed me into that crevice—he must have been the man with the nubbed heels!"

She nodded. "Arnaldo told me that this morning."

"Arnaldo told you! Would it be too much to ask how much and what else he knows?"

But she shook her head. She had said enough, too much, to Phil. After this she would keep still, learn what he knew and think things out for herself.

If he felt her distrust, he hid it well. With another exclamation he looked at the clock. "I must run. But I'll be back as soon as I can, this evening anyway. I want to make one more experiment. Then we'll know how Jack was murdered. Perhaps that will tell us also who did it."

26
Senhor Diego is Persistent

Until luncheon Jane sat in Jack's chair and through luncheon in the breakfast room, struggling to fit into an intelligible picture the facts heaped up in her mind like odd-shaped pieces of a puzzle. But none of them fitted together; many crucial pieces were missing.

Yet she must fit them together, see where they led. She had said so boldly that she would. And in almost a week she had learned so little, not even enough to remain silent, as Jack had warned her. Now Garcia was dead too; Noel withdrawn and angry; Phil deep in something about which he told her only as much as he wanted her to know; Vivian was gone, distrusting, perhaps hating her, and Dr. Ames was moving them all about like pawns on a chessboard.

True, she had the servants, and with Inah out of the house there was less tension and buzzing. But they were uneasy, watchful. Maria, for some reason, seemed always to have a candle lighted in the kitchen, and strange odors, as if feathers were burning, sifted through the house occasionally. Charms, perhaps; more *macumba*.

Just when she touched bottom in discouragement and uncertainty Senhor Diego arrived. A less suave and considerate Senhor Diego now. His eyes registered the purple shadows under her eyes and the droop of exhaustion in her shoulders as she entered the library, but he merely said after greeting her, "I'm sorry to have kept you waiting, Miss George. Your affairs, you see, have kept me busy."

He sat down again in Jack's chair and drew a fat folder of papers from his portfolio, tapped it significantly. "You don't read Portuguese? What a pity. You would find these illuminating."

He wasn't asking her questions or trying to win her confidence; he was telling her. What could he have discovered to give him such assurance?

"First, about this man Pinto. Sebastião Pinto. From São Paulo. The man you found in the gateway with the coffee branch in his hand," he added when she gave no sign that she knew the name.

"His picture appeared in the Rio papers Monday evening, in the São Paulo papers Tuesday morning. Tuesday afternoon a woman reported to the police there that the man was her husband, Sebastião Pinto."

Don't tell me this today, Jane thought, not today. To-morrow. I can't bear any more now. Wait till my head stops aching. . . . She hoped she had spoken aloud, but Senhor Diego was sorting papers, and evidently she had not.

"Here is her statement," he went on, taking up one set of clipped sheets. "Not very complete, because she hasn't known much of what her husband was doing during the past year. He spent most of it in the state of Parana, apparently as a laborer on a large coffee fazenda there, though by profession he is a civil engineer. She has his working clothes and some receipts like these which he received when he paid off his debts at the fazenda store. Their signature, José Sebastião, is his, though the name, of course, is incomplete."

He put down the sheets to take up an envelope. "And here," he said with slow emphasis, "are some canceled checks, made out to Sebastião Pinto, signed by John H. Houghton. Only two or three, for I imagine that whenever

possible Mr. Houghton paid for Pinto's services in cash.
These receipts of Pinto's and these checks of Mr. Houghton's are rather strong evidence, Miss George, that Pinto
was employed by Mr. Houghton as a spy to report developments on the Santa Maria and José fazenda and its coffee
company. Can you tell me why?"

The Santa Maria and José Coffee Company! That was
the name at the top of the report the false Garcia had
brought, the report in which she had found so little of
interest or importance.

"So far as I know," she answered carefully, "Mr. Houghton had no interest of any kind in coffee."

"So everyone has thought. And yet he was deeply interested in that Santa Maria and José fazenda The name
seems to startle you. Why?"

"It's—it's an odd name for a business, isn't it? If I
was startled, it was because you said—inferred—that Mr.
Houghton was interested in coffee. I can't believe it."

"He was and he wasn't." The detective picked up another
set of papers clipped together. "Yet here is proof that he
was willing to pay five hundred contos to prevent coffee
being grown or sold when at the same time he wouldn't
invest a milreis to grow or buy it himself. Not coffee in
general. The coffee he didn't want grown and sold was
Santa Maria and José coffee."

Of all his words only three meant anything to Jane.
Five hundred contos! Jack seemed to have been fond of
tossing such sums about.

"I don't understand Portuguese," she reminded him
when he offered her the papers, "and I don't think I understand just what you are saying in English either."

"I believe you. I don't understand all of this myself. But
somewhere Mr. Houghton had papers that should dupli-
cate some of these—unless you burned them last Saturday!
These mean little in themselves—they are merely notes

and most of them in code—but they corroborate, as I'll
prove to you later, these communications between John
H. Houghton and Senhor Adolpho Lourenço Gonçalves,
director of the National Coffee Department."

He paused impressively. "That means, Miss George," he
went on, speaking each word distinctly, "that on receipt of
five hundred contos from Mr. Houghton, Senhor Adolpho
would use his authority to forbid any coffee whatever from
the Santa Maria reaching a market."

"That's impossible!" The protest sprang involuntarily
to Jane's lips.

"Not at all. The NCD does not allow a kilo of coffee
from any part of the country to be shipped to any market or port without its permission. It's all part of Brazil's
price-maintaining policy."

His explanation gave Jane time to pull herself together.
"It's impossible, I mean, that Mr. Houghton would offer
a bribe—such a bribe," she corrected, remembering the
morning she had seen him slip notes into the policemen's
hands. "And surely it must be impossible too that a man in
Senhor Adolpho's position would accept one."

"You put it—baldly. We do not as a rule call such
arrangements bribery. The old word for it was 'eating.'
When a man first entered office—political or business—
he did not 'eat' at once. When he was ready, sure of his
ground, word went round quickly that he was 'eating' now.
It was an old custom, bestowed on us by the colonial Portuguese, I've heard. There's still too much money in the
country," he concluded, half bitterly, half as a statement
of fact.

"I don't understand that either."

"I mean that too much money is used too freely in such
'arrangements.' It won't always be so. Too many men still
enjoy 'eating,' and too many others—you foreigners among
them—are willing to feed them." He smiled wryly at her.

"Not that bribery is peculiar to Brazil; the practice is not unknown in your own country, I believe. Or in Europe."

Jane was silent, sunk in dismay. Bribery was bribery to her, no matter what its name or what the custom. That Jack should bribe a high official . . .

"But why would he do it?" she asked aloud.

"Why? The answer is obvious, isn't it? He wanted to ruin the man or men behind the Santa Maria and was willing to spend any amount to do it."

Slapping his hand down on the papers, he said firmly, "There's no doubt or question about it, Miss George. Mr. Houghton employed Pinto to find that fazenda and, when he found it, to furnish him with detailed information about it. With that information in his hands, he began negotiations with Senhor Adolpho. It took some time, but they seem to have approached agreement recently, as the dates of most of these memos fall within a period of little more than two weeks preceding Mr. Houghton's death."

"I don't believe it. I can't."

"No? Naturally such matters were not entrusted, except in minor and unrelated details, to paper or to the mails. They were transmitted through trusted intermediaries, and once, at least, Senhor Adolpho talked with Mr. Houghton here in Rio, perhaps in this house. It was these intermediaries who came and went by way of your rear gate after midnight."

As she continued stubbornly incredulous the detective's face became grim. He took up still another set of papers, turned to a page and showed her the signature of Adolpho Lourenço Goncalves. Beneath it were the signatures of two witnesses.

"This is Senhor Adolpho's own statement—confession, if you like—giving names, dates, places, amounts. These memos I've shown you are his. And in tonight's papers you will find a copy of this." He placed a single sheet before her. "That is his resignation as director of the National Coffee Department—due to failing health!"

Jane brushed a hand across her throbbing head. "Why do you tell me all this? I know nothing about it. I can't help you in any way."

"Pinto left São Paulo Friday morning for Rio, Miss George. Saturday morning you found him dead. He brought to Mr. Houghton Senhor Adolpho's final agreement to the terms of the 'arrangement.' He delivered his message to Mr. Houghton, was caught when he left the grounds—"

Jane suppressed an exclamation. Jack had said Pinto did not reach him! "You don't know that," she protested. "At least, you didn't know it Monday."

"I hadn't gone through these personal checkbooks of Mr. Houghton's on Monday," he reminded her. "If he hadn't received that final word, Miss George, would he have signed a check for five hundred contos Saturday morning?"

He drew from his portfolio two of Jack's checkbooks. "This one is on the North American; this on the Royal Bank of Canada. In both are keyed checks, written monthly, which we had no difficulty in tracing to accounts he held for you. But those accounts were added to each month by amounts ranging from eight to fifteen contos. Why—by what possible coincidence—would he write a check to you last Saturday morning for five hundred contos if he had not intended it to go to Senhor Adolpho?"

Wordless, cold now with understanding, Jane stared into his probing eyes. The amount of the bribe—five hundred contos; that incredible check Jack had slipped into her pocket—five hundred contos!

It had not been meant for her. In those papers stolen from the hidden drawer he must have told her how to get that money to São Paulo—how to place it in Senhor Adolpho's hands. Facing death himself, he tried to make sure of that!

And Jack had involved her—or intended to involve her—in the ruin of one man and in the bribing of another! He had taken advantage of her love for him to use her as a tool to carry out some personal vengeance in case, by that one chance in a hundred, he lost his own life.

Her mind was clear now, swept clean of all but that staggering, humiliating realization. Blindly her feeling for him tried to defend him. He had been desperate; he wouldn't have asked her if there had been any other way. Perhaps his reason—he always had a reason—justified the means and end.

Some other self wouldn't listen. He had taken her love once, then turned from it to Vivian. She had accepted that, understood, continued to build her life on his, to love him. And he had known it, used her love deliberately to further—

She was going round in circles, unconscious of the room once so filled with Jack, of the dark-faced man watching her, waiting patiently.

"Yes, he wrote that check," she heard herself murmuring. "He made it out to me."

"And you did not know until this moment why?" The detective spoke softly, careful not to make her too clearly aware of him.

"No. No, I didn't know."

"Just one more question, Miss George. Don't answer it now, but think about it. You may remember something you've seen or heard. Mr. Houghton was not interested in coffee. Neither is Mr. Hardwicke. That is, he believes in coffee's future, as we all do, but of course he would not have invested H and H funds in any coffee fazenda against Mr. Houghton's wishes. The Santa Maria is a huge fazenda—a million-tree property. That requires capital—a great deal of capital. Mr. Monroe represents a great American investment house, unlimited capital, Miss George. As we all know now, Mr. Houghton disliked him—disliked him so much that he struck Mr. Monroe in the face in one of the most public spots in all the city—"

Jane rose unsteadily as the room began to grow dim about her and her ears rang with the words Senhor Diego was yet to say.

"You are ill!" He rose at once. "I won't trouble you further now. But don't you think that a man like Mr. Monroe could be the man behind the Santa Maria?"

27

Liberty Palm

Far away, millions of miles away, Jane could hear Maria's anxious murmur and Dr. Ames's reply. "She's all right, Maria, but I'm glad you called me. Don't worry."

Another voice was speaking, and for a time she did not recognize it as her own. It went on and on, repeating senseless words about Jack, a Jack who had never really loved Jane George, had merely used her.

Daylight was dim in the room when the voice died away and Jane tried to sit up. Her head felt so light, her feet so heavy, that for them to be part of the same body was very curious indeed. She felt Dr. Ames's cool hand on her burning forehead, Maria's warm ones tucking a light cover about her shivering shoulders.

"Disillusionment comes hard, Jane," Dr. Ames was assuring her. "No one enjoys it. When one is young it's very painful."

He waited until her eyes showed that she recognized him, then smiled and, taking up her left hand, began gently to remove its bandage.

"That's better." He smiled. "You're on the way up now. And tomorrow we're going to take you away from this house where you've had so many difficult times. You're coming up to Liberty Palm to stay as long as you like."

"Liberty Palm?"

"My fazenda—up in the Organ Mountains beyond Petropolis." He paused to scan her hand carefully. "Fine; another day or two and you won't need any more dressings. Keep this one on until you reach Liberty Palm. Then we'll give the old tree another testimonial."

"Perhaps I'm still a bit dizzy," Jane suggested. "I can't understand what you're saying."

"No, you're not. I'm just a mile ahead of you. You're coming up to my fazenda tomorrow. It's name is Liberty Palm. And the royal palm from which it takes its name has had, since heaven knows when, miraculous powers. You'll see why when you see it—the palm, I mean. It's not only the only one in the valley for miles, but it stands on the highest ridge of the highest hill on my ranch. Been a landmark for generations, perhaps a century."

"But why Liberty Palm?" she persisted, hoping to gain time for her head to clear, so that logical reasons for refusing to leave the house could enter it.

Dr. Ames laughed. "It's a Liberty Palm for me, for one thing, though the name is probably as old as the fazenda. I took over the name when I bought it years ago and the legend that goes with it. The fazenda is in the Parahyba River Valley that, until the abolition of slavery in 1888, was the greatest coffeegrowing region in the world. When the slaves were freed they simply walked off the plantations and the coffeegrowers and their families were forced to abandon them too. The whole valley was practically deserted until a few years ago, when people like me began to buy up the old fazendas for a song."

He snipped the bandage roll free and made the dressing secure before he went on. "Well, the legend is that the slaves somehow got the idea that my royal palm—*Palmeira da Liberdade,* they call it—had magic powers. It stands on the brink of an almost straight fall to the Parahyba River hundreds of feet below. Not a very nice river, so don't

imagine yourself swimming or sailing on it—too many
rocks and rapids. But the slaves believed that if they could
reach that palm in the dark of the moon and step off into
space they would be free forever. They were, too," he said
a bit grimly. "Nobody that fell in that river was ever seen
again. . . .

"The slaves credited this phenomenon to the magic of
the palm. They thought it gave the man—or woman—who
reached it invisibility for three days. When he returned to
human sight he would be far away in some marvelous land,
a heaven on earth, where slavery and all the evils of this
world were unknown."

He stopped, added with a shy smile, "I kept the name
for a sentiment of my own. When I reach Palmeira da
Liberdade—the fazenda—I feel as if I'd reached freedom
too. My wife and two sons are there, everything I care for.
And when I told them about you they all insisted that I
bring you back with me."

"It sounds marvelous, but really—"

"Wait till you see it," he interrupted enthusiastically.
The view of the hills alone is worth all the adjectives you
can dig up. And there's a swimming pool, horses to ride,
wonderful trails, dogs. And wait till you see Pride—young
Tony's new horse. You have to see to believe. Shee's turning my gray hairs white for fear she'll kill the boy, but
she's a beauty."

"Was it Tony who was hurt last Sunday? Is he all right
now?"

The doctor laughed. "My wife was more upset than
Tony. Pride had just kicked him in the shin, he said; nothing at all. Just the same, I've forbidden him to ride her
until Noel tries her out. He's coming up tomorrow too."

Jane sighed. "I'd love to go, but I can't leave Rio—yet."

"You think you can't, but I know better. I have an idea
that what you're trying to discover will never be found

here now. We'll try a change of venue. And I need your help, yours and Noel's and Phil's. One of them will drive you up."

He refused to listen to further protests and called Maria. "See? Miss Jane's all right now and going to be hungry any minute. But don't let any more detectives or policemen into the house. Send them to me. And you, young lady, are to do nothing whatever but take care of that hand and get some rest. Well, almost nothing. Phil telephoned while you were sleeping. I told him he could come in for a few minutes around eight."

When Phil arrived Jane was dressed and in the library waiting for him. Some inner compulsion seemed to be driving her to learn all he knew before it was too late.

"Your hand again?" he asked when he saw the fresh dressing. "Doctor Ames had me worried when I called this afternoon. I promised I wouldn't stay long, but there are some things I must tell you. They may make something click in your mind."

As she remained silent in Jack's chair he bent forward, took her good hand impetuously. "Don't look so still, so far away. You make it difficult."

"I'm listening."

"First, then, it was I who broke that candlestick last Saturday afternoon."

So much had happened since that she had forgotten the candlestick. Now the memory of the sharp sound that had wakened her from sleep on the veranda chilled her afresh.

"You remember our talk in the garage and—my flat failure to persuade you to do the town with me? When I left you, came in here, I thought of another idea—that perhaps I could induce you to induce Vivian to go away for a time—a sort of sight-seeing jaunt for you both, to Montevideo or Buenos Aires. With both of you gone, I thought Jack and Noel might solve the situation."

Phil was speaking almost as awkwardly as Noel did sometimes. Her silence made him uncertain, Jane knew, but she made no effort to help him.

"I sat down to wait, thinking to talk with you when you came in from burning those papers. It was cool and quiet here, and I didn't notice the time. When I did you were asleep on the veranda and looked so unhappy and tired I couldn't—wouldn't wake you. I slipped back through the library to go home and on the way out knocked over that candlestick beside the door. It sounded like the crack of doom!"

"You didn't break the candlestick beside the library door," she said idly. "Not that it matters—"

"Matters?" He jumped up. "What do you mean?"

"That candlestick is standing there now, just as it always has since I came. You broke the other one, near the living room. I found—or Inah did—the pieces and candle behind the door."

Phil paced the room in agitation, went into the corridor and looked at the table, returned, exclaiming, "What a fool I've been! Inah, of course. That's the link that has driven me crazy. Inah and the man who said he was Garcia."

He began his pacing again, stopped abruptly before her. "Jane, Jane, we've got something now! Inah wasn't finding that candlestick when you walked out of the library Sunday morning. *She was putting it there!*"

Whirling round, he pulled open the table drawer. "She couldn't have found the pieces there. I picked them up myself and put them in here. I meant to tell Vivian later."

Jane was tracing an aimless design with her slipper toe on the rug. Phil, she remembered, had been in the library Saturday afternoon for an hour, at least, within arm's reach of that little hidden drawer. "What had upset you so much that you didn't see the candlestick?" she asked.

He came over to stand in front of her. "What makes you think anything had?"

"You know your way around this house as well as I do. You have perfect control of yourself every moment of your life."

He drew up his chair again before answering. "I'm a little afraid to tell you what had upset me. You may refuse to believe it. It doesn't fit in with your idea of Jack."

"Tell me. You can't change my feeling about Jack—now."

He looked at her quickly, his eyes wary, but all he could see was the top of her shining head, the soft coppery hair, loose now, falling in little curls.

"I found a knife," he said reluctantly. "It was pushed down between the cushion of Jack's chair and its right arm. A short knife—a saddle knife, I think—with a double-edged blade and a sharp triangular point. It was placed so that it could be grasped instantly, ready for action. Jack must have put it there himself, either for protection or—"

"Where is it now?" Still she did not raise her head.

"I wish to God I knew. I looked in that chair as soon as I could Sunday morning, but it was gone."

Her head rose then. "How could it be?" she demanded. "You and Doctor Ames were the first to touch Jack." As he flinched she said quickly, "It could have been gone, of course; it certainly wasn't there when I went over the room."

He made no comment on that but continued in matter-of-fact tones. "The other thing I want to tell you is that I think it was for me that Vivian opened the back gate Saturday night."

Her composure broke then, but before she could speak Phil hurried on, not looking at her.

"Vivian told me on Sunday that she had been afraid of Jack all day Saturday. And before that, of course, she had been worried for weeks about him. After the dinner party she didn't know what he might do and she didn't think I would take that slap in the face quietly. She didn't mention the gate, but she did say she had thought I would come to the house to have it out with Jack.'

"Why didn't you come?"

"Why?" Phil shook his head. "Jack didn't stage that show at the Copacabana for nothing. He knew all the lines, but I didn't—and I wasn't going to play any part blind. He never did anything in public if he could do it as well privately. If slapping my face was his object, he'd had plenty of opportunity to do it without witnesses. If he preferred to do it in public—that was his business, but from that moment his business wasn't mine. I went home and stayed there."

He waited a moment for that last sentence to sink in before he rose.

"Now for my final experiment. Here, take my watch. It's just thirty-two minutes past eight. Go into Vivian's room and close the door. Sit on her bed or near it and when you hear my voice look at the time, then come back."

28
Voices Through the Wall

Five or six minutes later Jane re-entered the library. Her pale face was flushed, her eyes dark and troubled. She looked nervously toward the curtains drawn across French doors and windows, started to speak, then stopped in astonishment.

Phil was standing close to the bookshelves that lined the wall between the library and Vivian's sitting room, reading aloud title after title in tones growing increasingly loud. As she watched he crouched down and started on a row of encyclopedias.

When he had reached EM to F she said quietly, "I heard you two or three minutes ago, but if you were reading those titles, I couldn't distinguish the words."

"Two or three minutes ago!" Phil rose and spun round. "But you haven't been standing there two or three minutes! And you let me go on—" His quick glance searched hers, then he smiled. "A fine laboratory assistant you'd make. Luckily. Look here."

When she stood beside him he pointed to shelves above her head. Dickens and Thackeray! Complete sets.

"Why would Jack have those, I wonder? And why do they interest you now?"

"You aren't looking. Take down a book," he told her.

Puzzled, she raised an arm and tipped a finger over a green-bound volume of Thackeray, drew it back. A false front ripped off an entire section of shelf, disclosing stacked paper-bound books and pamphlets.

As she gazed from them to the length of cardboard in her hand Phil laughed and lifted down a thick volume, then a handful of pamphlets.

"These are part of the secret of Jack's profound knowledge of coffee—government and National Coffee Department publications and privately issued reports. Incidentally, those printed pages you found in the little hidden drawer must have come from here. We'd better make sure."

From beneath the pad on which the typewriter stood Jane took the rest of the printed pages and the report of the Santa Maria and José Company. Phil's eyes brightened when he saw the report.

"I'd like to go over this carefully later," he said and thrust it in a pocket.

Only a few minutes were necessary to verify the source of the torn pages. They came from reports and pamphlets on top of the various piles.

"Whoever was thoughtful enough to put them in that little drawer for you to find," Phil commented as he returned the unneeded books to the shelf, "must have enjoyed thinking of you as he read through Jack's instructions."

"Whoever it was," she pointed out, "must have known more about this room than I did. How did you discover that shelf?"

"That extra minute or two you gave me for some reason of your own. I was afraid to shout too loud for fear of rousing the servants. I walked close to the wall instead and threw my voice at different levels."

As he turned from her toward a window Jane said hastily, "If you were trying to prove by all this that Vivian heard anything Saturday night, you're wrong. I'm sure she didn't."

"She thinks she didn't," he corrected, turning back. "But remember, after she came in from unlocking that back gate for me she took three sleeping powders and went off in a drugged but not deep sleep. She told me Sunday of the frightful dreams she had had. She thought a moving belt was carrying her into roaring machinery; above the noise she could hear Jack's angry voice shouting orders."

"Yes, I know. She told me too."

"What she actually heard, I think, was the sound of loud, angry voices in here. Her mind simply translated the fears she already had and the sounds she was hearing into other terms."

"Maybe," Jane agreed doubtfully, then added, "Phil, if she did hear some voice—besides Jack's, I mean—I know whose it was. The owner of the Santa Maria and José fazenda!"

The expectancy in her eyes faded as Phil smiled at her, almost laughed.

"So Senhor Diego has been talking to you. I heard about that fazenda today also. But no one knows who owns it. The man who poses as its owner is merely a figurehead. The police believe some foreigner is behind it."

"Who?" Her gaze returned quickly from the window.

"Oh, it might be any one of a dozen heads of big European or American companies here. Usually such companies forbid their foreign executives from engaging in outside businesses of their own. How long, for example, do you think Tom Hughes would remain head of the North American if it were known that he owned a million-tree fazenda?"

Phil renewed his aimless pacing. "Let's call Jack's unknown visitor X, shall we? We know Jack was poisoned, and we think—or I do—that we know why. Certainly X had good reason to come here. He had learned that Jack knew about his ownership of the Santa Maria and intended to make capital out of his knowledge or because he had learned that Jack was going to prevent him from selling his coffee."

"Make capital out of it? What do you mean?"

"Well, Jack was apt to use anything—anyone—to the best advantage for Jack. Suppose X came here to deny his ownership of the Santa Maria or to deride Jack's threat to ruin him? You know Jack; he'd have had all the proof necessary before he acted. And hating X anyway, for some reason, he'd be furious with the man for trying to lie or bluff him, wouldn't he?"

"Yes, furious. He'd have flung the proofs in his face."

Phil smiled with satisfaction. "That's just what I think he did do. And where were those proofs? In that little hidden drawer with that letter of instruction to you!"

Again he began his pacing, and Jane's troubled eyes watched.

"They were both angry, remember," he was saying. "Jack's voice rising above X's, if Vivian's dreams mean anything." He stopped beside a window, turned to face her. "I can almost see Jack thrusting those proofs on X, watching him as he read—yes, and pulling down those pamphlets and private reports from that shelf to convince him of something about coffee from the government's own figures—"

"But if Jack wanted to ruin X through coffee," Jane interrupted, "why didn't he encourage him to go on with the fazenda, plant more trees? He used to say that the gamble had been taken out of coffee, that there was no chance to win."

"I don't know, but look here. If all this war talk means anything—and it certainly looks as if it does—Germany's going to move in on France and Holland, Denmark, heaven

knows where. And Brazil's going to lose more of her markets. Millions of pounds of coffee will be dammed up here
as they were during the last war. X will be rubbed out
as neatly as a chalk mark on a slate. Lord! when I think
of those two men facing one another here, X after five
years of work at least—it takes that long for coffee trees
to mature—seeing his work, his investment, his reputation
threatened with ruin—" He stopped, his face grim.

"That's a big if," Jane said. "Perhaps the war has nothing to do with this. Perhaps Jack merely wanted X to agree
to something. He may have offered to destroy those proofs
of ownership of the Santa Maria if X would agree to what
he wanted—"

"Blackmail?" Phil looked at her curiously, went on
quickly as her face flushed. "No, it was too late for that.
Jack may have offered X such a chance once and X refused
it. He'd already gone through with that bribe, remember.
He'd even written the check." He stopped significantly.
"Or don't you know yet what that five hundred-contos
check of yours was intended for?

"I know."

Phil turned away from her, muttering savagely under
his breath. "We don't know what Jack's purpose was yet,"
he went on more calmly after a moment. "We don't know
who made the first move here last Saturday night, Jack
or X. I'm sure of this though—that they struggled for
that knife and that Jack's hand was nipped by it before X
knocked him out."

"How can you be sure?" Jane's voice was oddly on edge,
yet she had to ask, to know all he thought.

"Those Paternoster Peas. X must have had a minute or
two to realize that if he used his hands or the knife that
murder would be known immediately. Everything Jack
owned would be searched for clues, and perhaps other
copies of those proofs might be found and X's identity

revealed. But everyone knew about Jack's heart. If he could appear to have died of heart failure, X would be safe. Doesn't that sound reasonable?"

"Yes, assuming that X knew those seeds are poisonous when no one else does apparently."

"When we understand everything I don't think X's knowing is going to prove a coincidence. X did know those seeds are poisonous. Jack's hand was already cut a little— or even if it weren't, the knife was here. And the box might have been on the table as usual or might already have been brushed off and a seed or two crushed. It wouldn't have taken more than a second or so to use that powder or to crush some—"

Phil's tense voice, his restless pacing, halted suddenly. Jane, on edge herself, shrank a little in her chair as she sensed rather than saw that he was steeled with anger. His eyes went round the room from her to the clock, and he stood a moment, his lips tight.

"I've stayed much too long," he said, regaining his level tone with an effort. "I'll go now, but may I borrow Arnaldo for half an hour? If I'm to drive you up to the Ames' fazenda tomorrow, I'd like to have him test my brakes."

"Of course, but why not have him do it in the morning?

"I'll need the car then. There's still a lot to be done."

He hurried away with the briefest of good nights. Jane stood a moment thoughtfully in the corridor door. Then she walked across the library to the veranda doors and opened them.

"Won't you come in now, Noel?" she asked quietly.

29
"Leave Jack's Death to Me"

Blinking a little in the light, Noel stepped into the library from the darkness of the side veranda. Tonight he looked more like a Viking than ever, huge and blond and fundamentally untamed. Or perhaps it was his riding clothes and the feeling of outdoors and freedom that gave her that impression.

"I saw you on the veranda some time ago from Vivian's room," she told him, reserve in her tone and manner.

He nodded. "I've been thinking over what you came to tell me this morning—also some news I received just before you arrived that I wish I had told you about then. So on my way home from riding I stopped in to see if you were alone. When I saw Phil's car I walked round the veranda to see if he might be ready to leave. What I heard—made me decide to stay."

"News?" she asked cautiously, remembering the many-stamped air mail from the States and his ghastly color of the morning. "Oh, Noel, not more trouble for you, I hope."

"No, not bad news," he assured her, and a hint of his slow smile touched his lips. It vanished as that look of dull, bewildered pain she recognized now as a sign he was thinking of Jack crept into his eyes. "God! If it had come

223

three weeks ago, one week ago, Jack and I would have welcomed it with bonfires."

He opened his hands in a hopeless gesture. "It—everything comes too late!"

Her resentment at his manner of arrival vanished in concern for his unhappiness and despair. And in alarm, too, that he should be out alone. Someone had followed him to this house once!

"Sit down," she invited, "and tell me, Noel. If it was good news a week ago, it should still be good news now. Wait, I'll get you a drink."

He shook his head. "It's late, and the news can wait. I just want to say one thing, then I'll go."

When she chose Jack's chair he drew up another to face her, sat a moment looking at her gravely. "You have a good clear head, Jane. That's why I was surprised at some of the things you said this morning. I wondered where you could have acquired such ideas. Now I know."

"From Phil, you mean?"

He nodded slowly. "Your conversation tonight sounded like some of the romantic novels I read as a boy. What Phil thinks is of no interest or importance to me, but I—I am sorry to find you absorbing his dramatizations of the—the experiences you and I have known lately. Jack would have hated it. Doesn't that mean anything to you?"

"If you mean," she said unsteadily, "do I still love Jack as—as I used to, no—no, I don't, Noel. I don't think I ever really loved him, or I couldn't feel as I do now. And I don't believe he ever loved me or even Vivian. I think now that Jack never gave real friendship, real love, to anyone but you."

Flushed, shaken by the outburst that had poured so spontaneously from her lips, she shrank back in her chair, abashed for herself and for the chord of emotion she had touched in Noel. He sat forward, his head in his hands, his face half concealed from her.

He looked up presently, but his voice could not hide his feeling. "You are right—about Jack, about me too. For fifteen years we worked and lived and struggled together to get H and H on its feet. We didn't have anyone else. Finally, I suppose, we didn't really need anyone else. That is why I ask you to go back to the States, Jane. Leave Jack's death to me."

"Then you know," she said almost inaudibly, "you know Jack did not die of heart failure?"

"Yes, I know."

They were silent, each absorbed in his own thoughts. Jane was the first to stir. "Then you must know that you too are in danger—"

He thrust the subject away impatiently. "It's Phil—you, rather—that I want to talk about. I hate to see you led into something—"

"Led?" She picked up the word quickly.

"Think over this evening," he advised. "Perhaps other evenings. Did you contribute anything to Phil's preposterous theory? Not a word. Yet little by little he is building an idea in your mind, and little by little you are making it your own." His deep slow voice was not emphatic, merely tired.

She moved uncomfortably under his grave eyes.

"I'm not expert at theorizing," he went on, "but if I were to guess—as Phil seems fond of doing—I'd say that his next step will be to urge you to take some definite action, do something to discredit your judgment, make you unfit for any large responsibility—" He fumbled, lost in his long sentence, stopped.

"I have no large responsibilities," she protested.

"You will have soon. Three months ago Jack made a new will. He appointed you trustee of his estate and provided for a fixed monthly income to be paid Vivian."

"Three months ago? That's when he and Vivian cabled me to come to Rio."

"When Jack cabled."

Her color drained away. "What are you saying?"

"That Phil is a clever young man and an ambitious one. He did a brilliant job on this railway electrification program. That's done—months ago. Yet he stays on in Rio. Perhaps Jack and I talked with him too freely when he first came down. His father is head of Monroe Brothers in New York, one of our best clients. Recently we learned that Phil has been buying up our stock wherever he could get it. He's our largest stockholder now."

"But what has that to do with me?"

"Jack didn't want Phil to get control. That's why"— his voice was suddenly bitter, his eyes like cold blue marbles—"he didn't leave his interest in H and H to Vivian. Next Monday our board of directors meets. Phil has a right to be present. But he does not ask. This afternoon he informed me by letter that he would be present and that he wished time in which to present a resolution in behalf of what he calls a majority of our stockholders."

As his anger blazed openly, sending dull color to the roots of his hair, Noel rose abruptly, towering over her.

"In addition to filling your head with his theories, Phil has had time to acquire, by cable, authority to speak for this 'majority' of stockholders and clients. He intends to submit a proposal for the reorganization of H and H—the company Jack and I built up over twenty years. From what I heard here tonight, it is obvious that he is either trying to discredit your judgment as a trustee or—by some method—to win your support for his plan."

Stung by his implication that she was permitting Phil to make a puppet of her, Jane leaped up too, her eyes blazing. "That's neither true nor fair, Noel. Phil has said nothing of this to me. I would have told you what I've told him—if you had—would have listened."

She took a step forward to stand directly in front of him to add, "And this isn't fair either, Noel, but it's meant a lot to me. Phil is the only one of you who hasn't suspected me of murdering Jack—of killing him for money that I didn't know about. The Hugheses and Barassas, Mercer, Doctor Ames, even you—you all tried to drive me away. You sent Vivian away, tried to send the servants. If it hadn't been for Phil and Maria—"

Her voice broke on a sob and she turned blindly. Somehow she was in his arms and he held her tightly while she poured out her story of fears and uncertainty and loneliness.

"I didn't know, I didn't know," he said helplessly over and over. She could feel and hear his heart pounding in his breast, feel the intensity of an emotion he could not express.

She lifted her head, tried to smile at him. "I know you didn't, Noel, and I didn't know you knew—about how Jack died. If I had only known—"

"Yes?"

"I—I wouldn't have turned to Phil."

She felt him start, then he released her gently. "You must get some sleep now. And don't worry any more. Doctor Ames means all right, and you're going to enjoy his fazenda. It's one of the finest in Brazil." He smiled at her shyly. "And I'm going to drive you up there."

Jane locked the doors after him thoughtfully, smiling a little to herself. This was a new Noel. Perhaps the sun and the candle simile applied to him and Jack too. Certainly with Jack gone one began to see Noel.

30

Wisdom Comes at Midnight

While one hour slipped into another Jane lay in darkness, thinking of Noel, of Noel and Phil, Noel and Vivian, of Dr. Ames who had sent Vivian away—or said he had.

No, she wouldn't think that. Anything else. About Noel again, then, and his deep voice tonight, saying so little, meaning so much. Of the Noel beginning to emerge as a personality himself. Unconsciously she began to weigh him against Phil. Both were mature and controlled emotionally—though Phil's smooth poise now showed signs of wear, and some deep burning anger in Noel seemed to threaten his impassivity. Noel had loved Vivian, and Vivian—had she really been in love with Phil and he with her? Somehow Vivian always rose in her mind when she thought of either man; everything seemed to trace back to Vivian.

She sat up suddenly, reaching for the lamp cord. Outside rapid footsteps crunched on gravel, echoed lightly on the rear veranda. Then Phil's voice was calling her name softly. As she pulled on her robe she glanced at her clock. After one! What could have brought him back to the house at this hour?

"Lord, you're well protected," he greeted her when she opened the rear door to him and led the way up the corridor to the living room. "Do you know that Ricardo is sleeping outside your French doors, José across that back one? If Arnaldo hadn't been with me, I'd never have reached the house. Mind if I light a fire? It's a dark and chilly night."

"And what are you doing out in it? You can't have been testing brakes all this time."

"Primarily I've been controlling my rage," he informed her, smiling up from the hearth where he was touching a match to the laid fire. "Would you mind telling me why Noel Hardwicke was stationed on the veranda listening to our conversation?"

"How do you know he was there?" She pulled a low chair closer to the fire and looked down at him coolly.

"It took you two minutes or more to return from Vivian's room to the library, and for the rest of the evening you were on tenterhooks. When I found Arnaldo he told me Noel had arrived shortly after I did by taxi and hadn't left the grounds."

He shrugged and swung round to look up at her. "But I didn't come back to talk about Noel. As a matter of fact, I think it is all to the good that he heard what we said. We'll go into that later. Arnaldo and I have done a great deal more than test brakes. We've been to see Garcia's widow. And now we have all the threads in our hands, Jane—except one."

"What did she tell you?"

"Plenty. In the first place, the true and the false Garcias are brothers; to be specific, her husband was the bona fide Garcia and your unpleasant friend is Domingos. And their family name is Silva. And Garcia's wife is Inah's sister—so that's all clear."

"Did she tell you where Inah and Domingos are now?"

"Gone—vanished—since Monday evening. It's a long story. Domingos arrived in Rio about two weeks ago, and from the first he and Inah became close friends—meeting frequently out on the beach here, I gathered, during

Inah's free hours at the house. Domingos had almost nothing when he arrived, but last Sunday he flourished several
contos and he and Inah were both excited, said wild things
about marriage and traveling round the world—"

"Don't go so fast," Jane interrupted. "Does Garcia's
wife know that Domingos shot her husband?"

"If she does, she isn't saying so. All she was willing to
say was that Domingos has been in trouble in various parts
of the country. When he came to Rio she didn't want to
take him in, but family ties are strong in Brazil and her
husband insisted."

"The poor thing!" Jane exclaimed. "I'll send Maria in
the morning to see what she needs."

"In the morning she'll be gone. Noel has been very
good to her, she says. He sent someone from the office to
take care of everything for her, and he's giving her a small
pension and sending her back to her home."

"I should have known he would. That's like him."

Phil poked up the fire. "Of course if Domingos has
suddenly acquired a lot of money, that means we're on the
right track. Blackmail is his game. He either saw or heard
what happened in the library Saturday night. And that
means . . ." He paused significantly. "That means that he
knows who X is."

"You think he has been getting money from X!"

"Looks like it, doesn't it? No money Saturday, contos
of it Sunday. And that, I think, explains the candlestick."

"Candlestick!"

"I broke it, picked up the pieces and put them in the
drawer of the library table Saturday afternoon. Sunday
morning they come to light behind the door to the corridor. Where were they between times? My guess is that
when Jack opened that drawer to get out the proofs in the
hidden one the pieces were still there. He and X both saw
them."

"And Jack picked up that piece I found in his hand? He wouldn't have held it all the time—"

Phil shook his head. "Now you're going too fast. I doubt if Jack touched the glass. I think that when Jack was dead—or dying—X worried about that knife cut in his hand. Someone might be curious about it. So he put that broken bit over the cut and left the rest in the drawer. That way anyone could reason that Jack himself had broken the thing or cut himself handling the pieces—"

"You're just guessing," Jane challenged, Noel's words loud in her ears.

"Of course I'm guessing. But it's all beginning to make sense, isn't it? We're on the right track. Suppose Domingos, having seen or heard all or part of what took place here, had gone to X with empty hands? X could have denied everything, perhaps have put him out of the way. No, Domingos had to have something to make X listen to him and profitably for him. But the library was in order. He saw nothing but that broken candlestick and candle in the drawer. So he took them and hurried after X to prove he had been in the library and to demand as much as his imagination could conceive."

Phil thrust at the fire viciously. "The idea haunts me that Jack may not have been dead. The only satisfaction I have," he substituted quickly, "is in thinking of X's emotions when Domingos arrived on his doorstep. X had worked everything out so carefully, left nothing to chance. He'd stuffed the little drawer with those printed pages to confuse whoever found them, arranged that cigarette box to fall at the slightest touch and so account for any missing seeds. He'd even put that piece of glass in Jack's hand. Unless a miracle occurred, no question about Jack's death would ever be raised. And then that little piece of glass threatens to destroy him unless he can get the candlestick back in the drawer!"

"Two little pieces of glass," Jane reminded him. "It was the second one that convinced me Jack had not died of heart failure."

Phil shook his head again. "X has still to learn about that second one. But can't you see what he would do when Domingos began making demands? He gave the fellow a few contos on condition that he get that candlestick back, probably promised him a fabulous amount later. Why not? X could promise anything, for he would have no intention of paying it. The candlestick back, he was clear. But Domingos was an old hand at blackmail—or, at least, at trickery. He couldn't get that candlestick back himself, so he gave it to Inah, and you almost walked into her with the pieces in her hands—"

"I wonder if I hadn't been sitting on the veranda if he would have tried to replace it himself. It would have taken only a moment."

"Perhaps," Phil agreed doubtfully, "but he still would have had to find you or someone to take that report away from him. It probably was the thing he hoped to sell Jack in the first place. It certainly must have been the whip on which he counted to keep X under control."

"You think too fast for me," Jane protested.

"If X laughed when Domingos returned to tell him that the candlestick was safely back in the house, he didn't laugh when he heard where that report was. He probably put the fear of God into Domingos to get it back within a few hours."

"That's why Domingos was so terrified when I said I'd give it to its owner myself!" Phil's theories did begin to make sense now.

"And that's why you were going to receive some coffee leaves. You set off a string of fireworks when you gave those printed pages to Garcia. He must have gone straight to Domingos."

"And Domingos was hiding in the forest at Excelsior! He must have gone directly there from here."

"Where would he get coffee leaves up there? And shoes? Perhaps he went there later to lie low for a time or—"

"Or followed us."

"No, I'm sure they must have been there when we arrived and that until then Garcia was just a simple accountant who didn't know what it was all about. When he heard what we were saying he must have realized what Domingos had led him into. And when he saw me coming up that bank, go crashing after Domingos—well, I think he took your car either to get away or to go for help. Anyway, Domingos couldn't let him get away—he knew too much. And my gun provided a means of stopping him," Phil concluded regretfully.

He fell silent, staring into the fire. Jane, silent in the chair above him, watched the firelight on his face pick out lines and shadows that had not been there a week ago.

Phil appeared much older as well as very different from the man who had gone about so gaily with Vivian. And, incredibly, her antagonism for him was gone! In spite of her own suspicions, in spite of Dr. Ames, of Senhor Diego and now Noel, she found herself longing to believe in him and trust him.

Yet Noel was right. Little by little Phil had built up a theory for Jack's death in her mind. For each suggestion she had offered just now he had substituted another or pulled hers around to fit his own ideas. With a sinking heart she knew then how gullibly throughout the week she had accepted his interpretations as her own. More, she had incorporated into her theory events of which she knew nothing.

The analysis of the Paternoster Peas—he had made that with Don Grey. She did not know Don Grey, had not been in his laboratories when the tests were made. It was Phil who had found the knife in Jack's chair, Phil who had found those government reports and coffee statistics, Phil who had read a meaning into Vivian's dreams, quoted her when she was not there to agree or deny. It was Phil who had shown her that check Vivian had found—and who had led her up to Excelsior while Dr. Ames spirited Vivian away! Phil had broken the candlestick—or said he had; Phil had spent Saturday afternoon in the library!

Her heart pounded as she thought of the use he could have made of his hour or two there. And she had told him in detail all she knew, had turned over to him her bits of glass, Domingos' shoes, the report of the Santa Maria and José, all her evidence! Yet he had told her only what he wanted her to know when he wanted her to know it.

Unconscious of her, Phil faced the fire. What was he thinking that his gaze should be so concentrated, so intent? Of the board of directors' meeting on Monday? Did he see his ambition to head up H and H within his grasp now? Was it part of his plan to lead her further and further from the truth about Jack's death, defeat the purpose for which she had remained in Rio?

Why? What could he gain by it? Unless he was, as Senhor Diego had hinted, the man behind the Santa Maria!

Phil raised his head but did not turn. "Jane," he said thoughtfully, breaking startlingly into her questions, "I've gone over everything. Only one thing remains to learn—a single name. We may learn it tomorrow, perhaps not for a month or a year—*quem sabe,* who knows?"

The night wind rushing about the house deepened the silence within. Jane sat hushed in it, enclosed with him in a situation she had neither courage nor will nor—the racing of her heart told her now—the desire to face.

"*¿Quem sabe?* I do. I know the name," she thought and was glad her lips refused to serve her.

31
Noel Takes the Wheel

Phil did not drive Jane up to the Palmeira da Liberdade fazenda Friday afternoon. Instead he sat in the rear seat of Noel's powerful roadster, playing guide to Mercer as a breathless tourist. Jane, beside Noel, alternately marveled at his driving and at the skill with which Mercer managed them all. Or was it Mercer? At least on the surface it had been her fear of traveling the mountain roads in any car but Noel's and her insistence that they all go up together that accounted for the arrangement.

"How is your hand, Jane?" Noel asked after a long silence during which Phil droned on, guide-fashion, about a prim little church perched high on a rock. It was irritation at the sound of Phil's voice, not solicitude, Jane suspected, that moved Noel to speak. On previous occasions when she had seen him he had noticed the bandage but said nothing.

"Quite all right, I think. Doctor Ames has promise to take the bandage off tonight. Oh!" She broke off to point inelegantly toward a blackened field on the right. "What a fire they've had out here!"

"Ugh!" Mercer cried. "Don't mention it. That's where they burned the coffee. I can smell it yet."

"Not *yet*," Phil slipped in quietly. "But *soon*. Any day now millions of little coffee beans will be sending up their incense to the two-faced god of supply and demand."

"Again!" Jane turned. "Why, Phil?"

"Simple enough. There's a war on in Europe. Brazilian warehouses are already full to bursting with coffee that can't go to market. And the National Coffee Department is preparing for another 'sacrifice quota' of twenty-five per cent of all coffee grown. Only this time they are going to call it the 'quota of equilibrium,' I believe."

"How dreadful! Oh, there must be some other way—"

Jane stopped at sight of Mercer's startled eyes, followed their gaze to Noel. Angry color burned beneath his tan from throat to hair, and his lips were compressed in a straight line as if to bar equally hot words from being said. As she looked at him the lips parted to say flatly, "Brazil will never burn another bean of coffee." They pressed close again, and he sent the car forward savagely.

"All I know, of course, is what I read in the papers," Phil commented, a flick in his voice.

"Stop it," Mercer commanded, then laughed and yawned. "If you can't talk about something more interesting on a glorious day like this, I'm going to sleep."

Noel ignored Phil but said quietly to Jane, "More nonsense is talked about coffee than any other subject in the world. Brazil has always held the leadership, always will."

Again he seemed to check some urgent words on is lips, added lamely, "This war isn't going to last forever. The National Coffee Department and the São Paulo Institute aren't asleep."

"Does Doctor Ames grow much coffee?" she asked.

"He can't yet. A law passed in 1935 prohibits the planting of new trees. One day he will."

Jane was impressed with the confidence and surety of Noel's speech. When Jack was alive Noel had always deferred to him. "Don't stop," she urged, more interested in Noel than in the subject.

Again that strange hesitation, but in the blue glance he turned on her she saw that he was pleased—perhaps with her interest, something certainly. The expression was gone in a breath, and the old dull look of pain replaced it. Jane looked away. "I'm a constant reminder to him of Jack or Vivian—or both," she thought ruefully.

As if he caught her thought, Noel went on about coffee, though reluctantly; he might have been reading aloud from a book.

"Other countries do produce coffee, but the basis of all coffees sold on the market anywhere is Brazilian coffee. Our bourbons and hard coffees are blended with the soft grades of other countries to give them body, taste, what you call up north—the kick. Mild coffees supply only the aroma, so that when you buy Arabian coffee you are paying for the aroma of Arabian coffee. What you taste is Brazilian. No matter what happens to other coffees, there will always be a market for ours. And that isn't all . . ."

A slow smile of genuine pleasure and pride touched his lips, then he lifted a hand to indicate the view of the mountains on the left. She had been too absorbed to watch the road, but now she forgot coffee and everything else, caught her breath with pleasure too. They were mounting steadily, the road hairpinning back and forth, higher and higher, disclosing at every turn vistas of range after range, until mountains entirely enclosed them, shutting away the lowlands and Rio.

As she peered down sheer abysses, deep in a thousand variety of trees, and up rock-gouged slopes Phil's amused voice asked, "Looking for boa constrictors and jaguars, Jane?"

"It is a jungle, isn't it?" She turned defensively. "Everything is buried in trees."

"Not a jungle, a tropical forest," Noel corrected.

"But Rio is below the tropics."

"Rio, yes. Here the mountains shut in the heat, and with the heavy rains you get tropical conditions. You won't see any animals, however—that is, to recognize them. There's a butterfly."

"Where?"

"That withered leaf on the bush we just passed. Those red berries may be berries or beetles. Even if we saw a puma, you wouldn't—"

"It's a deceptive country, Jane." Mercer laughed. "Don't believe anything or anyone. That's the best way."

Noel stopped the car abruptly. "You can believe this," he said when a startled moment had fled away. "There— more than forty miles away—is Rio, and beyond it the bay."

Above them circled the rugged patterns of cone-shaped peaks, some vivid green against the clear blue sky, some deep blue, others silver gray, rich brown or plum. Between two virile shoulders they could see, far below, the lowlands and in the distance the pale design of the city, enclosing a shimmer of water hardly distinguishable from the pale mother-of-pearl horizon sky.

"Thank you for stopping, Noel," Jane said softly. "No wonder you love Brazil."

Only then was she aware of the tension in the car. It stood just at a turn of the highway, facing over a valley a thousand feet or more below. Behind her Mercer and Phil sat in rigid silence. Beside her Noel, rigid too, stared out over space. For a moment, as she looked at his grim face, Jane was reminded of something; then the thought fled, and the tension of the others gripped her too.

Her words reached Noel after a long time. Slowly he turned, and she met in his eyes that same driven look she had seen in Jack's. It was gone in a moment. In the next the car was mounting.

Mercer released a long sigh. "Next stop, Petropolis," she tried to say gaily, but her voice was thin and tremulous. "And do stop, Noel, I'm choking for tea."

Noel didn't stop, however, and no one protested as he sped through the pretty tree-lined summer capital of Brazil and out to stark, treeless hills and narrow valleys lying in the shallow light of the sinking sun. No one protested either when he failed to slacken speed on the rough, twisting highway. Mercer even tried to be bright about it.

"This was the old stagecoach route once," she began, but her words were lost in a lusty bump that threw them all high in the air. Thrown round, Jane saw, as Phil's coat flew open, the holster of a revolver under his left arm.

He smiled at her coolly and buttoned his coat but spoke to Noel. "H and H are responsible for a lot of the development around here, aren't they? Didn't you tell me once you owned a fazenda up here?"

"Near here," Noel told him briefly. "I haven't had time to develop it, even see it, for years."

Mercer and Jane exchanged glances. What would a week end be like with these two men fighting some battle with every word they said? Mercer shrugged.

A few miles further a side road ran down to meet the highway, and with a word of warning Noel turned into it. Darkness deepened round them as the hills grew higher and wilder on all sides. At last the car began to climb, then glided down a comparatively smooth road to the cobbled court of the Ameses' fazenda.

"Well, we've crossed the great divide, I take it," Phil said. "We're in the Parahyba Valley now."

Jane was busy peering through the darkness to long low buildings topping an embankment on the left, hills black now behind them. More buildings, stables, storehouses and a colony of small cabins of the employees of the fourteen-thousand-acre fazenda disappeared on the right, a lantern or candle gleaming here and there. Before and a little below them loomed the house, an enormous affair, with lighted windows in two large wings and the tower of a little chapel rising beyond the far one.

Lusty young voices called, and the two broad-shouldered sons of Dr. Ames swung into sight with a lantern.

"Welcome to Liberty Palm," one said. "I'm Tony." His smile passed quickly to Noel. "Did Dad tell you about Pride, sir? I can't wait for you to see her."

The older young man laughed and turned to the others. "I'm Juan—if Tony can stop talking about his horse. Will you come down to the house? Mother's waiting there for you." He led the way with the lantern, and Noel, with Tony, followed slowly in the rear. Jane smiled as she listened to Noel's questions about Pride. His voice was as vibrant as Tony's; he seemed scarcely older than twenty-year-old Tony in his eagerness to see the horse.

"You'll have to wait till morning, no matter what Tony says," Juan called back. "Dad wants to see your face when you see her. We're all a little mad about the beast," he added under his breath to Jane. "Even Mother. And here she is."

At the top of wide steps leading up to a high veranda little Mrs. Ames was waiting. "You are very welcome," she said in precise English. "And very tired, I know. The road, it is not good. But you will have time to rest. Dinner is at nine."

She led Jane and Mercer up a curving stairway to adjoining rooms overlooking sweeping lawns. In their center a long swimming pool shimmered in the starlight. Far beyond, on all sides, dark hills of mountainous outlines rolled up in silhouette against the sky. And on the highest ridge of the highest hill, directly at the head of the little valley, soared a royal palm, its restless fronds alternately concealing and revealing a bright low star.

With a word about tea Mrs. Ames left them, and Jane
stood at the window silent, awed by the beauty of the
scene and the night.

"I'm glad we're together, Jane," Mercer said behind her.
"I feel uneasy, don't you?"

"This place is too beautiful for trouble," Jane murmured, though with more assurance than she felt.

"I hope Noel and Phil are as susceptible to scenery.
Why do they hate one another so? Or do they? Perhaps
it's hunger that makes me suspect the worst." She moved
closer and put an arm through Jane's. "I was serious this
afternoon—though never say I admitted it—when I told
you not to believe anyone. *Anyone,* Jane. You're beginning
to, aren't you?"

Jane kept her startled eyes on the palm. Whom did
Mercer mean? Phil? Or Noel? Voices and laughter—hilar-
ious laughter, excited voices—saved her from answering.

Mercer looked down. "Just a quiet week end, Doctor
Ames said! And here he is with two or three carloads of
guests!"

She leaned out, answering gaily greetings from below,
but when she straightened her laughter stilled abruptly.
"Jane, look! Is that odd or isn't it? The doctor's brought
up the same people Jack had at that awful Copacabana
dinner!"

32

Death Reaches the Fazenda

"I don't know how it happens myself," Dr. Ames assured Jane as she sat beside him at dinner. "One person leads to another in Brazil. Probably others will drift along tomorrow. The full dinner table is an old Brazilian custom."

"But where have they all come from? Yesterday you spoke only of Noel and Phil and me. Now"—she looked about the long table, counting noses in the candlelight—"now there are twenty-two."

"Well, those four young giants are friends of my boys, Tony and Juan. Aren't they amazing? You must see them ride. One day they will be as good as Noel. The two Brazilian men with their wives and assorted youngsters are all relatives of my wife—third or thirteenth cousins; it's all one in Brazil. The Hugheses and Barassas you know, and Mercer—well, try to have Noel, and you get Mercer. I think she does it with mirrors."

"Is it an old Brazilian custom for the Hugheses an Barassas to be here?" she persisted. "You know you brought them up yourself and for some reason."

He twinkled at her. "So inquisition is my reward for taking that bandage off your hand. I brought them up because I have an idea. I'm a great believer in letting things work out their own way. That is, after I've brought them together so they can."

His smile changed to concern. "Did I send a cable up to your room, or did I only think I did in the excitement?"

"Cable! From Vivian?"

"No, from Miss Martin. Just a short one to say that they had reached New Orleans safely. We'll probably get one from Vivian herself tomorrow or Monday."

As someone down the table claimed his attention Jane had to be satisfied. Her brown eyes, deeper somehow in expression and warmer after the week she had been through, went round the table. If the members of Jack's dinner party thought it strange that they should all be brought together again just a week later, they concealed their thoughts well.

In fact, she felt, studying them, they hid them less well than some other emotion that consumed them. They appeared excited, pleased about something. Their eyes met one another's now, but not blankly, and once or twice she saw Angelo and Tom Hughes lift their glasses in secret toasts. And they all paid special deference to Noel. Even Varta, who considered him hopelessly dull, sparkled in his direction.

Portuguese, French and English flashed across and around the table. Noel, under the undisguised hero worship of the young men, was smiling, telling tall tales of riding days on the pampas. But more and more, as the dinner progressed and the unrestricted merriment of the Brazilians progressed with it, Jane felt the force of some countercurrent. She felt curiously alien there and suddenly tired, weak, as if she had been through a long and terrible sickness.

"Don't be a hussy," Dr. Ames hissed in her ear. "Can't you see these youngsters are tearing themselves apart to make you smile?"

And then she was swept into the merriment herself as shouts of laughter applauded the antics of the six young Brazilian men. If everyone else in the room had been dumb, they would have been an entertainment in themselves. Now they were matching couplets, flinging impromptu verses in Portuguese from one to another with amazing speed. One had scarcely uttered the last word of his rhyme when another caught it up and flung a new couplet in another direction. When at last Tony hesitated for a word, went down to defeat in a howl of laughter, Jane was laughing too, applauding with the rest.

Before she knew it dinner was over and everyone sipping coffee and liqueurs in an immense salon. A moment later and it was midnight when, to her amazement, Jane found herself diving breathlessly into the long, deep and cold pool.

Everyone was as at home in it as a fish, diving and racing, then splashing out to dance on the tiles to the music of an accordion that Juan played with abandon. Even Tom Hughes threw off his dignity and reserve and, seizing Jane, whirled her round and round, finally danced her off into the pool.

She came up gasping, to find Mercer beside her.

"Jane, Noel's gone," she whispered anxiously. "Phil too, I think. They must have slipped away while we were all changing. Should we say something to Doctor Ames?"

"Not a word," the doctor's voice said beside them. "Help me get these ducks to bed, will you?"

As Jane returned to the house Phil appeared beside her. "Enjoying it?"

"I love it," she said impulsively, and noticing as they came within range of the porch lights that though he wore trunks and robe he had not been near water, she added, "And you?"

"Make that question mark a period and I'll tell you," he smiled.

While he spoke the call of an owl drifted through the night. Jane stopped short, shivering with the foreboding an owl's call would always mean to her now. As two long notes came faintly in answer Phil laughed.

"All's well. Those must be real owls, Jane. The trees are probably full of them."

Sleep claimed her the moment her head touched her pillow. When a pebble struck her arm, waking her, her windows were pale with approaching dawn. As she sat up another and another came flying through the window. Five minutes to four, her watch said. Reaching for her robe, she went to the window to investigate.

On the ground stood Phil, also in dressing gown and pajamas. He kept one hand in a pocket while with the other he indicated graphically that she should come down and let him in. Cautiously she slipped down the stairs and opened the door.

"Leave it open and come out," Phil greeted her. "It's a glorious morning, and I want to show you something."

"What?"

"Eight pups—Dalmatians—beauties."

"You woke me up to look at pups!"

"You'll be sorry if you don't see them now," he said lightly, but his eyes said something else.

She stepped out into the cool, fresh morning. Phil gave her no time to look about, however, but hurried her away, up the lane to the court and across it to some spiral stone steps in the embankment and up it to a worn path. It led through feathery bamboo to a clearing where a wire fence enclosed a kennel with eight fat white pups, dotted and splashed with black, sprawled and tumbled before it.

Phil paused, but not to look at them. "Remember where they are in case we need an alibi," he said while he maneuvered his hand from the pocket. Her eyes widened when a broad knife with a double-edged blade and triangular point came with it.

"Don't say anything else has happened!

"Plenty," he assured her grimly and, without further explanation, plunged again into the path, slashing away occasionally a branch or vine.

The path led them to the rim of a broad ravine whose slope was evidently, from the mound of still-green vines and branches in its center, in the process of being cleared.

"This isn't going to be easy to take," he told her, leading her straight to the mound. "Keep your chin up."

With the knife he tossed aside a tangle of vines. Jane gasped as the head and shoulders of a man, face down on the ground, came into view. Between the shoulders rose the hilt of a knife that duplicated in shape and design the hilt of the knife in Phil's hand.

She didn't need to see the heavy cheeks that sloped to a narrow forehead to know what man lay there. The vari-colored hair, shading from dark brown to light to yellow, was sufficient.

"That—that's the wrong Garcia," she said with chattering teeth. "It's Domingos, I mean."

Phil nodded. "I thought so, but I had to be sure."

"I'm sure." Shudders, though not from cold, shook her as he tossed the vines back into place. "But, Phil, that knife—and your knife—are they like the one you found in Jack's chair?"

"One of them is *the* knife, I imagine."

Where had he secured his? Why had he brought her out at such an hour? And why was he acting with such cold precision, as if this were just the prelude to something more dreadful? A dozen questions rose to her tremulous lips, but before this remote, relentless man she had no courage to ask them.

"There's a trail, but a bad one, through those trees," he said, looking from the dense woods, that ran down to the

gully and up the other side of the ravine, to her wool robe
and Mexican sandals. "Think you could make it? It can't
be more than a mile or so."

"To where?"

"To wherever Domingos came from."

"But he's here," she protested.

"Have you forgotten Inah? If she came with him, she's still
where he left her. She's the last link we have now—with X."

Jane drew a deep breath. "Yes, I can make it," she heard
herself say coolly.

"Good girl." He led the way down the slippery, twisting path where signs of Domingos' stumbling passage were
clear and into the woods. They might have been moving
through a tunnel, so interlaced were branches, vines, lia-
nas, bushes, ferns, so deep the shadow and so deathly still.
Except for the occasional slash of Phil's knife, the rustle of
a leaf or distant birdcall were the only sounds.

When she could lift them from the path Jane's eyes
fixed in fascination on that knife. And when she was not
looking at it questions tortured her. It drew her like a
magnet to whatever end there was in Phil's mind.

Not until they reached the bottom of the gully, where
another trail paralleled a little stream, did Phil pause.
"Want to rest a minute?" he asked and swept a space clear
on a fallen tree with the knife.

She sank down on it breathlessly. "I—I want to know
a few things before we go any further. Where did you get
that knife? And how could you have found Domingos in
that out-of-the-way place?"

"I'd like to know whose knife this is myself. It came to
me—and took me to Domingos."

His steely gaze softened before the incongruously
youthful figure she made in that wild gully, her face rosy
as a child's with exertion, her soft hair disheveled and with

bits of green clinging to the curls. Though her eyes were dark with apprehension, she was making such an effort to appear calm and resourceful that he turned away with a curious sound between a laugh and a groan.

"You might as well know," he told her after a moment and seated himself beside her. "Someone tried to give me this knife personally two hours or so ago."

"Like—like Domingos?"

He nodded. "Fortunately I wasn't unprepared. It seemed odd that I had no bed lamp, odder still that when I switched my lights off I couldn't switch them on again, so I didn't indulge in any sleeping. My room is on the ground floor, connected by double doors with the next one. Those doors were locked when I went in, are probably locked now—"

"Who opened them?"

"I didn't wait to find out. As soon as I saw the outline of a window not in my room widening and a darker blur in the darkness—either a small man or a large one bent down—I made a flying leap for the window. It was further to the ground than I thought, and while I was trying to pick myself up I got this." He held up a corner of his robe and thrust the knife through a jagged hole there. "I had dropped into an angle of the house, dark as a pocket; who-ever threw this couldn't see too well."

"If it was a small man, it could only have been Doctor Ames," she tried to say but couldn't. "How did that take you to Domingos?" she asked instead.

Phil hesitated. "Luck, perhaps. I didn't want to try to get back into the house till daylight, and it was too cold to do nothing. Bumping around, I found that path and, following it, stumbled over Domingos. At least, I thought it could be no one else. I covered him up and went back for you— What's the matter?"

Jane was listening intently, but not to him. He rose, listening too.

"What is it?" she asked uneasily. "A bird?"

He pulled her swiftly to her feet. "Can you run? It's a woman—screaming."

33
"We'll Know Tonight"

The screams had ceased when they emerged at last on the plateau across the ravine from the Ameses' fazenda to face a round hot sun swinging clear of the horizon—and nothing else but the ruins of what had once been a fine old mansion surrounded by gardens and orchards.

Panting with exhaustion, Jane would have dropped with relief on the coarse, matted grass, the tumbled stones of a crumbling wall, anywhere, but Phil pressed forward.

"Call Inah, Jane," he urged. "She must be here and might be afraid to answer me."

Jane followed him, calling Inah's name and her own, over and over again. At length nearby rose a long, hysterical wail. Phil sped toward the sound, stopped short and pointed. Before him was the low roof of a root cellar, its broken doors covered with tarpaulin and weighted with heavy stones.

The woman they found beneath it, hair matted about a swollen and discolored face, clothing torn and stained, bore little resemblance to the once pretty and provocative mulatto maid. She lay on tumbled blankets spread over two worn car seats. Beside her was a clay water jar and tins of food on a crate stamped with the trade-mark of the Palmeira da Liberdade fazenda.

At sight of Jane she began to laugh and cry shrilly. "He say he come back," they made out. "He lie. He take the money and leave me to die."

"Who?"

Inah looked fearfully about before anger overcame prudence. "Domingos. Domingos Silva. Oh, Miss Jane, take me home."

"Why should Miss Jane take you home?" Phil demanded. "You left her without a word when she needed you. You helped Domingos cheat and frighten her."

"He say he marry me. He say he will be mos' rich man in the world." Torn between grief at her plight and the future she had lost, Inah moaned and wept and in incoherent words poured out the tragic story of Domingos' dreams of grandeur and her own eagerness to share that grandeur with him.

Domingos, it appeared, had been a very important man on the Santa Maria and José fazenda, but when Pinto paid him sixty milreis for only a few lines of handwriting that proved the ownership of the fazenda he had realized he was wasting his time there. So he had taken a paper that contained much more information about it and trailed Pinto to São Paulo, Rio and finally to the Houghton's rear gate.

Having discovered where Pinto's patron lived, he arrived at his brother Garcia's home to plan his next move and, learning that Inah lived most of the week within the Houghton grounds, had offered her a share of the wealth soon to be his in return for detailed information about all she saw and heard in the Houghton home.

On the previous Saturday Inah had carried him details of the death of the man in the Houghton gates and of the conversation between Jack and Jane about the secret drawer. Domingos had become inspired with the value of papers hidden so carefully and of the still greater riches to be theirs through stealing and selling them. But all she had done to help him, Inah assured Jane naively, was to persuade Arnaldo to let Domingos use his room on Saturday night.

Domingos hadn't stolen the papers; someone else had, and that had pleased him very much. He had talked of contos and contos to be theirs as a result, providing that Inah would restore the pieces of broken candlestick to the library table and return to him the paper he had given Jane Sunday morning. Inah had not been able to find the paper but she had done everything else he wished, and on Monday afternoon he had come for her, promising marriage, travel, great wealth, if she could leave with him at once. Not until he had her securely isolated in the root cellar had he revealed that the money would not arrive until Saturday night.

It must have come, she raged again, and Domingos had taken it all for himself and left her to die.

"What about Pinto?" Jane asked hastily, more to divert her attention than for any information she expected to receive. "Did Domingos ever see him again?"

Inah's wet eyes became secretive, then blazed with vengeful hatred.

Domingos had not only seen Pinto again, she cried, but had killed him when Pinto refused to help him sell his paper to Jack.

A strangled sound burst from Phil's throat. "You're lying, Inah," he accused hoarsely. "Domingos didn't kill Pinto."

Terrified by his steely eyes fixed in incredulity and horror upon her, by his face now tinged with a curious pallor, Inah grew voluble in her assurances that she spoke the truth.

Domingos had killed Pinto. When Inah could not help him to talk with Jack and Garcia would not, Domingos had watched and waited until Pinto came again to the rear gate. But Pinto had called like an owl twice, and the gate had opened for him before Domingos could reach him. He had waited then till Pinto came out, tried to win his confidence and help.

Sick at heart, Jane listened while Inah described Domingos' pride in his cleverness at placing a spray of coffee in Pinto's dead hand, to show Jack that if he wanted information about the coffee fazenda Pinto was not the man to give it to him, and Domingos' boasts that he could never be accused of Pinto's death because he held some rich and powerful protector in the palm of *his* hand.

Phil sat as if paralyzed. Finally, with an effort, he rose, his expression so strange that Jane, alarmed, sprang up between him and Inah. He paid no attention to either of them. Slowly he mounted the few steps cut in the earthen wall and disappeared through the opening overhead.

What had Inah told him that she had not heard? Jane wondered frantically. Was he horrified about Pinto's cruel death—or was he X himself, enraged at learning how Domingos had betrayed him. Hastily assuring Inah that Domingos was dead and that someone would come for her shortly, she sped up the steps.

Phil stood motionless near the cellar door, staring into the distance. Until she touched his arm and for the second time demanded, "What did Inah tell you?" he was unaware of her.

"Jack!" he said in a dry voice. "Jack didn't know about Domingos. He thought that X killed Pinto, that X was threatening him."

Jane shrank away from him. "Phil," she cried after a time, her own voice dry and tight too, "I don't believe Jack was dead when Domingos entered the library. His eyes—something about him—when Vivian and I found him—looked just as you do now. Jack must have learned before he died that it *was* Domingos who killed Pinto."

"And he had prepared to fight it out with X!" Phil spoke as if talking in his sleep. "And to let me take the consequences."

"You? Phil, you're mad. Inah said nothing—"

"Mad? Far from it! I'm understanding that Copacabana dinner for the first time. Why did Jack infuriate every man at that table, strike me? To bring me to the house blazing with anger! And what would I find? A dead man! And what would Jack find when he walked in? Me!"

"You are mad."

"Am I? Every man at that table would know his own anger. Who would believe that I, with greater provocation, hadn't forced my way into Jack's house, struck down an innocent man, believing him to be Jack? Tom Hughes was right in calling that dinner a show. It was. Jack asked me to arrive at eleven. I did. He wanted that dinner to end then. It did. He was expecting X to arrive at the house. And he was expecting me!"

"I tell you it's impossible!" Jane cried. "How could you have come in? It wasn't Jack—it was Vivian who unlocked that gate for you."

"Vivian!" He whirled round. "Vivian must have known whom he was expecting, who was in the library. She couldn't have unlocked that gate, Jane. Jack unlocked it himself to let X in and left it unlocked for me. *Vivian locked the gate!*"

"It was Domingos who said she unlocked it," Jane admitted. "He either lied or didn't know. And we believed him! She *must* have locked it. She must have known or guessed what was in Jack's— No, that's too horrible. But she must have been afraid you would come. Oh, what shall we do? How can we get to her?"

"'We'll go back to Doctor Ames' now," Phil said grimly. "He sent Vivian away—to make sure of her silence. Those car seats mean that there's a car here," he added swiftly.

"Can you fix that door again while I find it?"

Jane did not move. "Phil, I'm afraid. Let's go back to Rio. Now. This minute."

"No. It's too late." He paused, aware of the anger in his voice. "We must go back," he urged more gently. "And we must appear as though we knew nothing about Domingos, Inah, any of this. Perhaps we can get in without being seen; if not, then we're just a couple of fools returning from a silly escapade. You can do it; you've kept that head of yours up for a week. Trust me a little longer."

His quick glance caught her fleeting expression. "Or do you trust me?"

"I—I'm afraid for you too. And I don't think I trust anyone now—not even myself. You haven't been telling me the truth."

"Not all of it," he confessed, his eyes searching hers again. "But what's this about your trusting no one, not even yourself?"

"Oh, why ask me that now?" She turned from him miserably.

"Why?" He was in front of her, his hands on her shoulders, forcing her to look up at him. "Don't you know that what you feel about me, about you and me, means all there is in the world?"

Under his clear eyes her own fell, and her hand went out to a stunted branch beside her for support. "You have no right to ask me such a question now. I—I can't answer it."

"I didn't intend to ask it now. I had to. And you must answer. Because I love you."

Quiet, deeper than the stillness of the abandoned fazenda, enclosed them.

"I don't trust you." Her voice was so tiny it was hardly audible. "I don't know really who you are or what you've done, but—"

"But?"

"It doesn't make any difference."

For a moment he stood uncomprehending, then his hand tightened over hers. "Look at me, Jane. You mean you love me? That you can care—like that!"

Her hand turned under his, clasped round it. He lifted hers swiftly to his lips, stopped, his eyes fixed on the short line that still shone faintly red in its palm. His expression veiled, hardened.

Startled, Jane tried unsuccessfully to free her hand, to draw away from him. His eyes came back to hers, softening a little, but his mouth remained set.

"Forget what I said just now—rather, wait until to-night. I love you, Jane; that can't change, ever. But I've got to hurt you, use you—"

"You can't hurt me—now."

"I can. And I will. It's the only way left that stands a chance."

He lifted her hand again, looked at the line, dropped a kiss on it and folded her fingers over it.

"We'll know tonight who murdered Jack. After that—well, after that you may feel differently."

34

The Dimple in the Mountain

Only Mercer's smile questioned Jane when she appeared in riding clothes on the veranda. All the rest were there, including Phil, and breakfast was being served to them and a half-dozen newcomers. Among them were three spruce young men, and among the spruce young men she recognized, with dismay, Senhor Diego.

In every sort of riding costume, they sat where they liked, most of them on the broad steps where sunshine fell over them from a sun high now in a turquoise sky. Jane answered lightly their greetings and comments on her laziness, but her thoughts were heavy with knowledge of that unbidden guest lying in a field with a knife in his back.

Dr. Ames, plate in hand, wandered beaming from group to group. "Phil's just reminded me that you want some of those seeds," he said, pausing beside Jane on the top step. "My foreman tells me there is a bush up in that dimple on Palm Mountain. He'll send a boy up for them if you like."

"Don't spoil the child," Phil interposed from his perch on the rail above Jane. "She's perfectly capable—"

"He's taking words right out of my mouth, Doctor Ames." Jane smiled. "I'd love to get them. Right now, if it won't delay the riding."

"Nonsense. No one can ride immediately after the breakfast this crowd is eating. You'll have plenty of time."

Noel looked up from the step below Jane. "If Jane wants something on the mountain, I will help her to get it."

"Let's all go!" Mercer cried, jumping up. "The climb will be good for my figure. I hope the bush is just beneath that royal palm."

"You hope nothing of the sort, Mercer, and you know it," the doctor told her sharply. "You're free to go anywhere on the fazenda except up there."

"I suppose that means," Phil groaned, "that I must go along to watch Mercer. What are man-made laws to a lady when her figure is involved!"

Senhor Diego stood up alertly. "Let me go for you. Both ladies and laws are my duty to protect."

Some sound or movement from Phil caused Jane to pivot on her left hand and smile up at him. "Come now, then," she invited, ignoring the detective.

Phil did not smile in return. Instead, deliberately, holding her eyes with his own, he stepped on her hand as he swung down. Heedless of her gasp of amazement and pain, he seized Mercer's arm and started her briskly down the lawns. Jane followed slowly between Noel and Senhor Diego. No one else had energy or desire to go.

"What is the matter with your hand?" the detective asked as Jane tried, surreptitiously, to wind her handkerchief about it.

"Nothing, really," she said, annoyed. "Just a small cut that's opened a little. It's all right."

"Not if it's reopened," Noel declared. "Let me see it."

As he looked a tiny blot of blood welled, formed a drop.

"If you'd been in Brazil long enough," he told her, his slow smile appearing, "I'd say you had been fooling with *macumba*. Blood drawn from that line about the left thumb had some special significance, insures against death or treachery—" He released her hand abruptly and moved ahead. "Jack knew more about such things than I ever did. You'd better have that bandaged again when we return."

From some bushes on the other side of a shallow gully that separated the lawns from the hill a small Negro, evidently sent out by Dr. Ames, rose to guide them to a vague trail that corkscrewed upward through tawny grass. They climbed slowly, Mercer protesting and panting at the heat, the dust, the possibility of snakes. Finally she rebelled.

"Let me die here," she begged and shook her head to all encouragement. "No, under that tree down there. Will you stay with me, senhor?" she invited, smiling at the detective.

He hesitated but, after a moment, gallantly turned back with her. Her chatter, rising to the three climbing, sounded anything but fatigued, and though she looked like a doll, Jane knew now, she was as wiry as a terrier. As they reached the ledge, where shrubs and vines vividly green about a small spring gave the appearance of a dimple in the tawny slope, she forgot Mercer. The youngster was pointing to a shrub a few steps above them where bright flecks of color appeared here and there.

"I'll get them." Phil tossed a coin to the boy, who scampered happily away, then swung himself up. For a moment he was busy among the leaves, then, turning, smiled down at Jane and held out his hands. "Catch!"

She dropped her handkerchief to the ground, cupped her hands and raised them high. But before Phil could drop the seeds Noel, reaching up, struck Phil's hands away.

"Sorry," he said stiffly. "Jane has an open cut in her hand."

Surprised, startled, first by Noel's swift action, then by some alert, intent expression on Phil's face, Jane remained motionless, her hands still held up before her.

"That cut's all right, Noel," Phil said carelessly. "I saw it this morning."

Again he held out his hands.

"You fool!" Noel shouted, striking them away again and thrusting Jane back. "Those seeds are poisonous." He stepped back himself, glaring up at Phil, and added, dropping one word at a time, "And you know it."

Phil jumped down to face him. "Yes, I know it," he admitted. "You and I are two of the few people in this part of the world who do know it, Noel."

Angry, determined, they eyed each other, battling as visibly as if with their fists. Without taking his gaze from Noel, Phil moved one hand toward an inner pocket of his coat.

"Keep your hands down!" Noel shouted.

A smile touched Phil's lips. "I have a report in my pocket which Jane once said she would return to its owner himself. A report of the Santa Maria and José Coffee Company, Noel. Perhaps you will let her take it from my pocket, give it to you."

"To Noel!" Jane turned on him angrily.

"Why not?" Phil's eyes remained warily on Noel. "Noel built the Santa Maria and José fazenda, established his coffee company, with H and H funds. When he could not replace the money he killed Jack to conceal the loss."

Straight and silent as the royal palm, Noel for a moment seemed to increase in stature, to tower above them. The next, color drained from his face, his arms hung limp, his knees sagged slowly, letting him down on the bank behind him.

"Yes, I killed Jack," he said bitterly, "and you stand there and tell me why I did it! How can you know, when I don't know myself? Do you have blood that runs hot with the south, cold with the north? Did I kill Jack because he was a success or because I was a failure? Tell me!"

Noel! Jane, motionless as Phil, struggled to credit what her ears had heard. And Noel talked on, half to them, half to himself, each word welling to his lips slowly to fall through silence.

"Jack had the ideas, he could get the financing. He was the famous Jack Houghton from Brazil to Chile. And I was proud of him, proud, I tell you. But my name was a name only because it was linked with his; I wanted him to have the same pride in me, my judgment and my word to be accepted as his were . . .

"Seven or eight years ago, while Brazil was burning coffee, I wanted to invest in coffee lands on a large scale. Jack wouldn't listen, and everything seemed to prove him right. He ridiculed the waste in the burning; I couldn't bear to see it, to hear him. We quarreled bitterly, and finally he left me—went back to the States—until I would cable him that I was wrong.

"I never cabled; I knew I was right. And I thought night and day of some way to prove it and to stop the burning. It seemed there must be other uses for coffee, and to find out I gave every conto I could raise for laboratories and chemists in São Paulo to experiment. They did find other uses for coffee—medicinal, industrial—but we haven't facilities or men in Brazil—yet—for such large-scale experimentation."

Noel raised his head, his face impassive but his eyes glowing now with pride.

"I didn't tell Jack—there was nothing to tell him—but from their experiments I knew I could prove my judgment was right. Two years ago I went to New York, to one of the largest industrial laboratories you have. They've been working with coffee ever since. Thursday I received a letter—"

Jane leaned forward, her eyes bright. "The news! The news you told me didn't matter! Oh, Noel!"

"The news," he agreed. "They've found that coffee can be used in a plastic—for airplane wings, walls, floors, furniture, scores of things, perhaps. One day its industrial

Vera Kelsey

importance for Brazil may equal its agricultural. We've already applied for patents; it's to be known as Cafelastic."

He stopped, gray creeping under his tan, his eyes dulling. "I was waiting for that letter—to tell Jack. It came too late."

Excited words of praise and congratulation froze on Jane's lips. Noel had done this incredible thing alone, against such odds. Now it was too late—for him too.

"Noel, Noel," she murmured, "why did you wait? Jack have been so proud—"

"He had found out about the Santa Maria and José fazenda. I started that, too, while he was in the States, when there was opportunity to secure new, rich land in Paraná. Not for myself—for both of us, for H and H. I bought it, developed it for the day when the market was steady again and my experiments—"

His tired eyes sought Jane's. "Perhaps if you had come back as Jack's wife—I would have told him about the fazenda and the laboratories."

She sank down beside him, pity and understanding in her eyes. "But Jack didn't consider you a failure," she assured him tremulously. "Vivian didn't. Just a week ago she told me that without you H and H couldn't—"

"Vivian! A woman like Vivian could love Jack. I wanted her love too, not to have it, just to prove to myself I could have it." He knotted his great hands between his knees, shook them despairingly. "You can't understand. It wasn't for myself I wanted to do—to be—"

"Don't, Noel, don't try to tell us," she urged. "We do understand."

"How can you," he cried angrily, "when Jack didn't? He found out about Vivian too, that I loved her. And about the men who helped finance the Santa Maria when—when I could not get financing in New York. He—he gave that dinner to humiliate her and me and the men who stood behind me. And he danced with Vivian like that—to prove that she loved him!

"I went to the house afterward—he knew I would; he was waiting for me—to make him understand. He wouldn't listen—he taunted me with my failures, taunted me to madness. And he had a knife—a knife against me, Noel, his friend!"

Noel's head drooped forward and he buried it in his hands. Helpless for words, Jane could only stare at Phil's motionless shadow falling darkly over him.

"I understand more than you think about you and Jack," Phil said then. "But last night, Noel, you killed another man, tried to kill me."

"Domingos!" Noel's head thrust up in anger and contempt. "I killed him as I would a scorpion. He's bled me all his useless life for a mistake I tried to hide when I was too young to know better."

Ignoring Phil, he turned to Jane. "I was riding cattle for his father years ago, before you were born. Domingos and another gaucho were with me. Domingos had some of those Paternoster Peas and knew they could sting if rubbed on the skin. One night, fooling with the gaucho, I rubbed a seed on his wrist. He had a cut there, was dead before morning. I should have admitted what I had done, but I was scared to death. I gave Domingos my horse to keep him quiet and persuaded my father to let me go to the States. That's where I met Jack. And that's how," he concluded, angry again, "Domingos got the idea that blackmailing was more profitable than work."

"Why was he on the Santa Maria?" Phil asked.

"I put him there to keep him out of my affairs and away from Garcia, who was weak but a good man. But Pinto found the fazenda—for Jack—and Domingos sold what he knew for a few milreis. He came to Rio to get more money from Jack. He—he was outside the library windows when

I—talked with Jack after that dinner. He tried to use his knowledge to wring thousands of contos out of me—and when I couldn't satisfy him he placed those leaves on my car to show that he had access to you, Jane—could tell you what he knew or injure you."

Noel glanced at Phil, his eyes icy blue. "I planned to get rid of him then—at Excelsior. I thought he was the only one who could ever prove Jack's death. Then Jane took some pages to Garcia—"

"We know about them," Phil said briefly.

"Garcia should have brought them to me, but he was furious when he learned from Jane that Domingos had used his name. He—he got to Excelsior first, but"—Noel threw out his hands—"you know what happened."

"Then it was Domingos who tried to send me coffee leaves," Jane exclaimed, and when Noel nodded she added, "and it was Domingos who followed you to the house, Noel, struck you—"

A groan burst from Noel's lips, and in the stillness that followed Jane could hear the breathing, almost the thoughts, of the two men.

"No. No, I closed those gates," Noel admitted heavily. "I intended— I couldn't do it, Jane. You looked so young, so frightened. I struck myself. I was out of my mind," he shouted as she shrank from him, "about Jack's death. And you—you wouldn't give up, go home. It seemed the only way to stop this—this horror—"

Jane could no longer look at his tortured face, did not dare look at Phil though she could feel him standing over them, silent, inexorable. When Noel spoke again it was to Phil alone, as if a world now rolled between him and Jane.

"Domingos was in my apartment the day Jane told me he had shot Garcia. I was afraid for her, too, then. I sent him and that wench Inah up to my fazenda—it's just across the ravine here—promised to bring him all the money he wanted last night. I met him in the ravine while everyone was swimming and did then what I should have done years ago. I do not regret it."

Noel shook his head as if coming out of a heavy sleep and rose to his feet to face Phil. For a long minute they faced each other, their faces expressionless, their eyes steady. Then Phil stepped back, waved a hand toward the trail.

"Perhaps you will go down first, Noel," he suggested. "Join Mercer."

Noel hesitated. His eyes, avoiding theirs, moved slowly about the dimple and over the mountain slope. For an instant he seemed about to speak but, with a courteous gesture, turned and left them.

35

The Royal Palm Stands Alone

When Noel's slow, heavy footsteps grew faint Phil dropped down beside Jane. She sat as if stunned, her hands gripped tightly in her lap. "Noel! Noel!" she was whispering. "Noel killed Jack. How he is suffering!"

Freeing her hands, Phil held them in his own, smoothing a finger over one thoughtfully. "Suffering for a great crime or a great wrong may have its own compensations," he suggested. "I wonder if we could bear it if we knew we had been merely stupid."

"Stupid?"

"Wasn't Noel stupid to value himself in terms of Jack's values, when in many ways he was superior to Jack? I'd say he was stupid about Vivian too, when all the time a woman almost as lovely and far more clever was right at his elbow."

He nodded toward the valley where Mercer had risen as Noel approached. Senhor Diego was already far on his way toward the house.

"She knew? That's why she took Senhor Diego away?"

"I asked her to. If she suspects, she isn't saying so."

"Jack!" Jane cried bitterly. "You can't say he was stupid, Phil. He seems like Machiavelli himself now."

"If he wasn't stupid, why didn't he take a rest a year ago, when Doctor Ames advised him to? Because he thought

271

H and H couldn't get along without him! Worn out and nervous from overwork, he burst into a flame of suspicion against Noel when he found out about the Santa Maria. And instead of understanding Noel's feeling about Vivian, he used it as another form of torture. . . .

"Why didn't he go to Noel, fight things out with him as they've done over one matter and another for twenty years? God! When I think of Noel— Coffee as an industrial product! As a plastic! Why, Jane, he's accomplished a miracle. And he did it—the big, stumbling, humble fool— to make Jack proud of him!"

Phil shredded a leaf savagely. "What right have I to criticize either of them? How much of this am I responsible for?"

"You!"

"Why not? When Noel came to New York he moved carefully, but not carefully enough to prevent men like my father from learning he was there on some sort of coffee project. They knew Jack, knew his views on coffee. Yet there was his partner avoiding them, going elsewhere to secure financing—as they thought. Naturally they were disturbed. They felt that someone should come down here, keep an eye out."

"You?"

He nodded. "Application for a loan for the electrification of the São Joaquim came along about that time. I was sent down to investigate the loan and at the same time to keep in touch with H and H. Perhaps it was because I came so soon after Noel's return from the States, perhaps because I've stayed on—anyway, something roused Jack's suspicions, set him—or Pinto for him—on Noel's trail."

"They were suspicious of you too," Jane said. "They thought you wanted to get control of H and H someway. You did buy their stock."

"Why not? It's an excellent investment." He smiled at her shrewdly. "And you thought I owned the Santa Maria, didn't you? That I might be X?"

He touched a hand gently to her scarlet cheek before he added generously, "That's all right. I thought for a time you were one of the cleverest little gold diggers in history. I'd heard from Vivian of the accounts she knew Jack was building for you. She didn't know how large they were, but that five-hundred-contos check she found confirmed her idea that they were fabulous."

At her choked protest he turned and gathered her fiercely in his arms, held her close, his lips hard on hers. She clung to him, returning his kiss with all the ardor of a heart free at last of doubt and danger. When she drew away her eyes were aglow, but she shook her head with a guilty sense that their happiness now was unfair.

"Not yet, not now," she murmured.

"Not yet? Not now?" he repeated, refusing to release her and sending his clear gray gaze deep into her eyes. "You told me this morning that you loved me. And I've been telling you for days, in every way I know, that I love you, have loved you since the first moment I saw you—"

"The first moment!"

"Haven't you gained a few years in experience since last Saturday in the garage? Didn't you have an inkling of my real reason for trying to get you out of that house—and why I've been hurling myself right and left all week?"

"Women are supposed to be the first to know, aren't they? But," she added honestly, "I didn't."

He held her away from him for a moment, shook her gently. "God! woman—wasn't it to my interest as well as everyone else's to accept Doctor Ames' diagnosis of Jack's death?" He shook her again, then pulled her close. "Stop detecting, my darling idiot. You're a complete failure if you don't know that when I saw you were going to walk right into murder I—I came too."

He kissed her cheek shakily, murmured into her hair, "It's all over now, dearest. And we're together. Don't be stupid. Say you'll marry me—tonight—tomorrow—the first—"

"You're the stupid one," she whispered, shakily too, into his shoulder. "Stop talking—"

A long halloo, then another and another, from the house recalled them. Reluctantly they began the descent to the tree below, where Noel sat in earnest talk with Mercer.

"Poor Noel," Jane said softly. "Did you know all the time?"

"I suspected him on Sunday, but those coffee leaves on his car and that attack in the library put me off."

Jane shivered, remembering that terror-ridden hour again. "And I tried to believe it was Doctor Ames. He seemed always to be around so patly—"

"Doctor Ames began to suspect Noel when he found him faking. That blow with Jack's riding whip wasn't enough to make him unconscious." Phil hesitated, went on. "That's why we're all here. Doctor Ames knew, as I did, that Noel had killed Jack; but unless he would admit to knowing that those seeds were poisonous, we had no way of proving it. We had a number of ideas to try out, then that cut in your hand suggested a better one. I—I had to use you. I hated it. But it's all over now."

"It's not over here," she told him uneasily, looking up at the green patch with its glint of bright seeds. "Oh, if I hadn't wanted those stupid seeds, we might never have known!"

"Why not say that if Domingos hadn't stolen that report we might never have known?" Phil substituted. "That was the greatest stupidity of all. It gave no clue or proof of ownership of the Santa Maria and could have been read by

anyone. Jack would have laughed at him for the simpleton
he was."

Jane gripped his hand wordlessly, and they continued
the descent in silence. Mercer and Noel, at sight of them,
had risen and were moving toward the house.

Before the veranda was great activity. Saddle horses
waited at one side, Negro boys among them. Other boys
were bringing more mounts down the cobbled lane.

Juan's and Antony's friends were showing off horse after
horse and, incidentally, their own riding. From the steps
the guests applauded, and Dr. Ames beamed on everyone.
As Noel approached he shouted, "Here comes the real rider!
Tony, where's Pride?"

"Coming now, sir!" Tony cried proudly.

Two stableboys with a flash of black lightning between
them—or, rather, a black flash with a stableboy dangling
at either side—appeared around the corner of the house.

Pride danced and curvetted forward, shaking her shining black mane. From ears to withers, and on to the silken
tip of her tail, light shimmered over her like quicksilver
on ebony. Sensitive ears pricked back and forth.

As Noel gazed at her his gray face changed subtly. And
when he put up a hand to her head Pride, as if she had
at last found someone who understood her, nuzzled his
shoulder. Trembling but quiet, she allowed his hand to
move down her neck. And when he walked round her she
turned her head to watch him.

Jane watched him too, something tight in her throat,
her eyes misted. Here he was at home. With hills behind
him, the horse beside him, he was master of himself and
the situation. Suddenly, with one movement, he was in the
saddle.

Horse and man raced away around the oval. Pride
changed pace, walked and danced on her hind legs, tossing
her head as if she would fall backward, bearing her rider

with her. She whirled and twisted, stopped within inches, flashed away. Noel remained light and firm in the saddle.

At last she yielded, stopped under a wide-spreading tree, her head moving up and down as Noel talked to her. Finally she moved smoothly forward to the veranda. Comments and applause greeted them but died quickly as Noel did not dismount or speak.

His eyes moved slowly from one face to another, lingered on Jane's, passed on to Phil beside her, and Jane winced at the pressure of Phil's hand on her arm. Noel signed to Pride, and while guests and servants gasped in amazement they sped away, this time straight across the lawns. In moments they had reached the gully. Pride skimmed it like a bird. Then horse and rider were mounting the trail to the Liberty Palm.

"Noel!" Dr. Ames cried out then. "Juan, go after him."

Juan forced two words through dry lips. "What with?"

Uneasy movement ran round the veranda, but no one moved or took his eyes from that black pattern weaving back and forth, higher and higher, smaller and smaller . . . On a final turn it moved straight for the royal palm.

For the space of a breath horse, rider and tree were silhouetted against a clear turquoise sky. In the next the royal palm stood alone.

About the Author

Vera Kelsey (1892-1961) was the daughter of an American couple, born in Winnipeg, Ontario. She grew up in Grand Forks, North Dakota. She was a reporter for the *Fargo Forum,* and graduated from the University of North Dakota. Her early writing career included working for the *North China Daily News,* which allowed her to travel extensively in Asia, and then she spent almost five years in South America, particularly Brazil, before making her home in New York. She wrote mystery novels, travel books, and historical and regional nonfiction. She spent her last years in Minneapolis, and owned a cottage on Lake Minnetonka.

SATAN
HAS SIX
FINGERS

VERA KELSEY

Coachwhip
Publications

THE BRIDE
DINED
ALONE

VERA KELSEY

CoachwhipBooks.com

CRIME IN
CORN-WEATHER

MARY MEIGS ATWATER

Coachwhip
Publications

POISON CASE | MURDER CASE
NUMBER 10 | NUMBER 33

FROM THE FILES OF
THE MICHAEL JOYCE AGENCY

LOUIS CORNELL

CoachwhipBooks.com

LOUIS F. BOOTH
THE BANK VAULT MYSTERY
BROKERS' END

Coachwhip
Publications

MURDER IN THE
FAMILY

NICE
PEOPLE
MURDER

Mary Hastings Bradley

CoachwhipBooks.com

Coachwhip
Publications

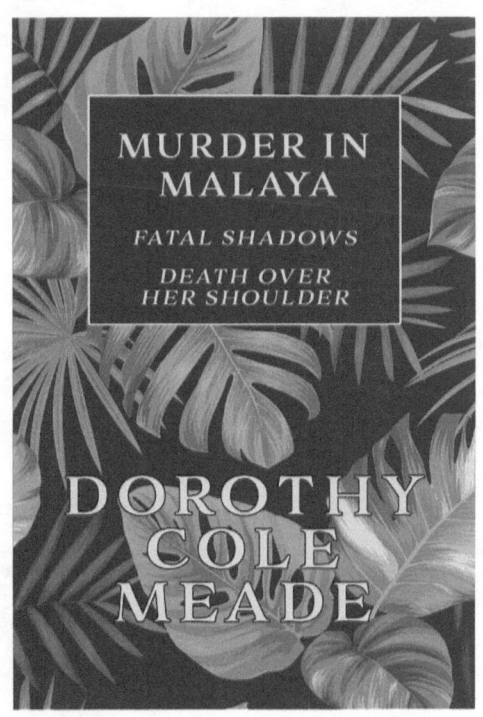

CoachwhipBooks.com

Coachwhip
Publications

CoachwhipBooks.com

Coachwhip
Publications

CoachwhipBooks.com

Coachwhip
Publications

CoachwhipBooks.com

www.ingramcontent.com/pod-product-compliance
Lightning Source LLC
Chambersburg PA
CBHW031003260626
47169CB00002B/671